THE QUEEN'S SECRET

Also by Melissa de la Cruz

The Queen's Assassin

The Alex & Eliza Trilogy

Book One: Alex & Eliza

Book Two: Love & War

Book Three: All for One

Heart of Dread Series (with Michael Johnston)

Book One: Frozen

Book Two: Stolen

Book Three: Golden

Witches of East End Series

Blue Bloods Series

Beach Lane Series

The Ashley Project Series

The Descendants Series

The Ring and the Crown

Surviving High School (with Lele Pons)

Something in Between

Someone to Love

29 Dates

Because I Was a Girl: True Stories for Girls of All Ages
(edited by Melissa de la Cruz)

Pride and Prejudice and Mistletoe

Jo & Laurie (with Margaret Stohl)

THE QUEEN'S SECRET

SEQUEL TO *THE QUEEN'S ASSASSIN*

MELISSA DE LA CRUZ

G. P. PUTNAM'S SONS

G. P. PUTNAM'S SONS
An imprint of Penguin Random House LLC, New York

G. P. Putnam's Sons is a registered trademark of Penguin Random House LLC.

Visit us online at penguinrandomhouse.com

Library of Congress Cataloging-in-Publication Data
Names: De la Cruz, Melissa, 1971– author.
Title: The queen's secret: sequel to The queen's assassin / Melissa de la Cruz.
Description: New York: G. P. Putnam's Sons, [2021] | Summary: "When Cal and Lilac are forced to face dark forces apart, the strength of their love—and their kingdom—are put to the ultimate test"—Provided by publisher.
Identifiers: LCCN 2020052623 (print) | LCCN 2020052624 (ebook) | ISBN 9780525515944 (hardcover) | ISBN 9780525515951 (ebook)
Subjects: CYAC: Assassins—Fiction. | Kings, queens, rulers, etc.—Fiction. | Apprentices—Fiction. | Fantasy.
Classification: LCC PZ7.D36967 Quk 2021 (print) | LCC PZ7.D36967 (ebook) | DDC [Fic]—dc23
LC record available at https://lccn.loc.gov/2020052623
LC ebook record available at https://lccn.loc.gov/2020052624

Printed in the United States of America
ISBN 9780525515944
1 3 5 7 9 10 8 6 4 2

Design by Kristie Radwilowicz and Suki Boynton
Text set in Adobe Caslon Pro

For Mike and Mattie, always

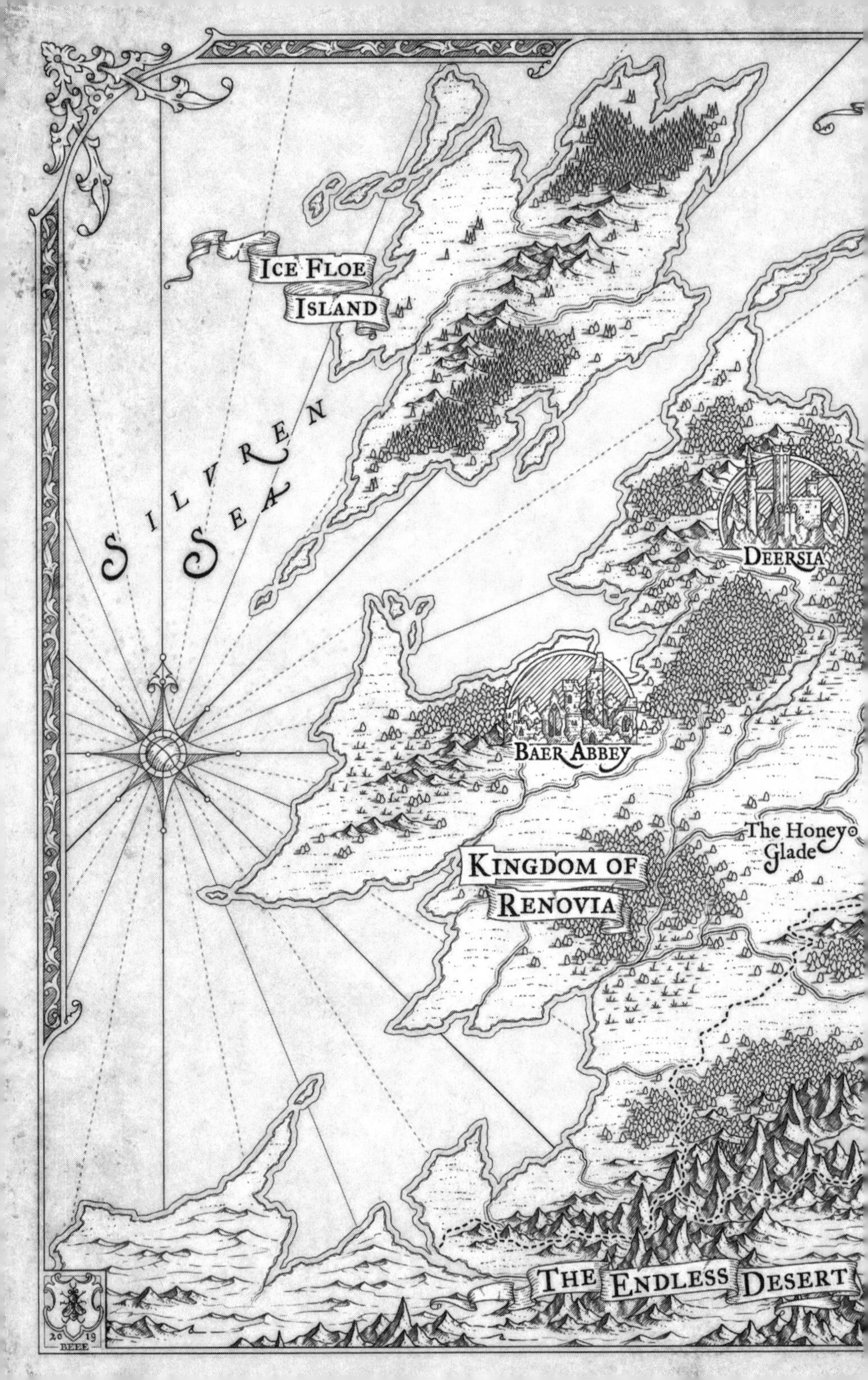
Ice Floe Island
Silvren Sea
Deersia
Baer Abbey
The Honey Glade
Kingdom of Renovia
The Endless Desert
2019
BEEE

World of Avantine

Duchy of Stavin

Kingdom of Montrice

Mont

Violla Ruza

Serrone

Argonia

The Story So Far . . .

A DEMON STALKS THE FOUR kingdoms of Avantine—Renovia, Argonia, Montrice, and Stavin. He is the tyrant King Phras, a monster of legend and a stain on Avantine's history.

Mortal death many centuries ago did not free Avantine of the tyrant. The ashes in his urn mean nothing. When his human form was first cremated, the fire of Deia failed to purify his spirit. Phras's violent sect of followers, the Aphrasian monks, made sure of that. Their incantations and enchantments around his funeral pyre ensured that the king lived on.

For hundreds of years the shapeshifter Phras has possessed many bodies, many faces, and consumed countless lives and souls. If a possessed body dies but is not in the fire of Deia before sunrise, Phras's spirit lives on.

With the disguised king hidden in their midst, the Aphrasians grew in strength and audacity, having taken possession of the Deian Scrolls, the repository of Avantine's magical knowledge. Centuries passed and the brave King Esban of Renovia stood against the

Aphrasians, dismantled their monasteries, and demanded the return of the scrolls and the sharing of their knowledge with all his people. The Aphrasians responded with a bloody rebellion, launched from their stronghold, Baer Abbey. The Chief Assassin, Cordyn Holt, led the strike against the Aphrasians. Alas, King Esban was killed on the battlefield.

Cordyn Holt swore a blood oath to the newly widowed Queen Lilianna to restore the sacred scrolls of Deia to the kingdom. He pledged his own life, and those of his heirs, to the service of the queen, to defend the crown, and to return the mystical texts. Yet now, a whole generation later, the scrolls remain in Aphrasian hands.

When the Tyrant King ruled, he ruined or murdered many of his subjects. One he even cursed to a life of perpetual service to him: a stable boy named Jander, who spoke so rarely that he was thought mute. He escaped from slavery but remains doomed to immortality until the king himself is killed.

Cordyn Holt had one son, Caledon, who took his father's place as Chief Assassin. Queen Lilianna had one daughter, Lilac, who assumed the guise of a girl named Shadow of the Honey Glade and longed to be an assassin of the Hearthstone Guild. Together Cal and Shadow journeyed to Montrice to uncover a plot against Renovia, and with Jander's help, they unmasked the Duke of Girt as the shapeshifting, soul-stealing King Phras.

Regrettably, they were unable to burn the king's spirit, and so the demon lives on to plague the kingdom. And only when the king is truly dead can Jander be free of his curse and rest in peace.

Complicating matters, Cal and Shadow fell in love, and when

Cal was found guilty of the duke's death, he was sentenced to death himself. Shadow revealed her true identity as Princess Lilac to save his life, and married the King of Montrice to unite the two kingdoms, forsaking their love forever.

But Queen Lilac has a secret . . .

The Ducal Palace

- Duchy of Stavin -

Your Majesties,

Felicitations to you, King Hansen and Queen Lilac, and to the Kingdoms of Renovia and Montrice. I salute you in the name of our great goddess Deia, who once united the four kingdoms of Avantine, and pray that one day we may know her blessed peace once more.

Your blessed wedding last month, at the time of our annual harvest celebrations, promised a golden autumn and a new era of abundance, harmony, and fruitfulness.

But now, the abundance of autumn has passed. We have learned of new and terrible activities along the southern border of Stavin. It appears that the Aphrasian order is on the rise again. Their monks have been sighted crossing from Montrice into Stavin. Lately there have been a number of border skirmishes and incursions into Stavinish territories, including horrific raids on Stavinish villages and farms. We believe the Aphrasians are responsible for these. Stavin will not stand by while our citizens are in peril. If dark magic is at work, it requires action without delay.

I am also in the possession of some unfortunate intelligence from Argonia. It is said that Renovia not only harbors the Aphrasian order, but may be deploying the Aphrasian attackers on a campaign designed to invade and annex Stavin. It has been suggested to me that this is why Your Majesties, and your combined kingdoms, have made so little progress in uprooting the Aphrasian order. The presence of a Dellafiore queen on the throne of both

Renovia and Montrice spurs these speculations. There is fear within the High Council and among my generals that a renewed Dellafiore dynasty may have territorial ambitions that extend to Stavin and Argonia.

This is why I write now, to urge you both to take public action. If members of the Aphrasian order retain a hidden stronghold in the swamps and forests of Renovia, they have a base from which these incursions and attacks may take place. Their ongoing presence can only fuel these unhappy rumors that Renovia—and, by implication, Montrice—not only tolerates, but encourages their violence and terror.

Personally I do not suggest for one moment that Your Majesties do not desire the obliteration of this relentless scourge. Still, it is vital that you turn your attention at once to its immediate eradication.

If you are unwilling or unable to suppress the Aphrasian order and cannot secure the ancient scrolls and keep them away from evildoers, then the Duchy of Stavin must take action. Our military forces will be forced to enter Montrice to protect our own lands and people. We will not be annexed by another kingdom, and we will not permit ourselves to be attacked by terrorist forces based in another kingdom, however unwelcome and covert a presence they may be there.

This is an unprecedented act in peacetime, but let me be clear—Stavin, too, is a sovereign nation, and I am its ruler. With every week that passes, more and more of my subjects believe that Your Majesties are unwilling to take action, and the burden of suspicion falls on Renovia and Your Most Serene Majesty, the queen Lilac Dellafiore.

I await your reply with much interest and, as always, the deepest respect.

Goranic R.
Grand Duke of Stavin

PROLOGUE

IN THE FAR NORTH OF the Kingdom of Montrice, winter arrives early once more. The mellow days of autumn are over, the fruits of the harvest hastily packed into granaries and cellars, and cured meat dangles from oak rafters. The fields are empty apart from golden bales of hay ready to be transported to stables and stacked high in barns. This far north, they are accustomed to snow.

So when a blizzard swirls in before the trees have shed their last leaves, no one gives it much thought at first. For three days the wind howls and snow falls in frigid ropes. In the village of Stur, snow piles so high that tunnels must be dug to allow doors to open, and every family wakes to darkness, their houses packed in snow-drifts. At last, when the blizzard passes, they climb out to find snow heaped on rooftops, clogging chimneys, and encrusting wells.

The village elders say that Stur has never seen so much snow, not in living memory. It makes them uneasy about the winter that lies ahead. But the snow has transformed the muddy streets and plowed fields into a sparkling white wonderland. After the children of Stur finish their morning's work, they gather to play on snowy banks, creating makeshift sleds by lashing branches together. The village rings with the happy shouts of children tumbling down hillsides and jumping into drifts.

The pond is covered by thick white ice; its surface is the face of the moon. A dog skids across the ice, barking with surprise, and some of the children decide to try skating, something they've heard about but never experienced. They hurry to strip bark from the birch trees around the pond and strap it to their boots with ribbons of leather. The bravest go out first, soaring across the ice, laughing when they lose their balance and sprawl across its hard, slippery sheen. Soon the village children play on the frozen pond.

A crash of thunder sounds, splintering the calm of the afternoon. A dark cloud moves across the wintry blue sky so the snow no longer glints in the sun. Some of the children look up, hoping for more snow.

But no more snow falls. Not one crystal snowflake. Thunder crashes again, so loud the nearby houses shake. Lightning cracks open the sky, and ink-black fingers shoot across the pond's surface, staining the ice with veins of ebony. The same black ripples from the hillsides to the banks surrounding the pond, and outward to the snowbound streets of the village.

Along these ominous fault lines, ice begins to crack. Snow melts as suddenly as it fell. Torrents of freezing water pour down the hills, and Stur's main street is transformed into an icy river, sweeping people and animals into its freezing surge. With a thunderous crack, the frozen pond splinters and the children sink into the frigid water, screaming and thrashing. As the hills above churn with cold water, the pond becomes a drain, drawing everything—and everyone—into its icy whirlpool.

When the dark cloud passes, all evidence of snow has disappeared. All that remains are soggy fields, bare hillsides, and streets thick with sludge. The village pond is still, its bright moon face gone. The villagers who survived the deluge rush to its banks, and there, through a thin layer of frost, delicate as a spider's web, lie the frozen bodies of the children, their faces distorted with terror.

By the time the messenger rides out to the capital of Mont, he is reminded to report that of all the day's strange and horrifying events, there is one detail that is so curious that it must not be overlooked.

The layer of frost across the pond was not gray, or even dirty white, the usual color. It was the color of fresh spring lilacs.

I

Chapter One

Caledon

He can't take his eyes off her. The royal procession—newlywed king and queen on horseback, trailed by courtiers on their own steeds, marching guards, and a tootling band squeezed into a decorated wagon—is out for another jaunt into the countryside surrounding the capital of Mont.

Cal has positioned his assassins throughout the procession, to stay alert to any threats from within as well as among the gaggles of farmers and villagers thronging the road. He's sent Jander to ride at the front, along with the scouts and the royal crier. Cal will never get used to the lilting sound of the Montrice accent. Better the flat tones of Renovia, where everything—people and geography both—lacks pretension. There's an ostentation to Montrice, and its court, that he doesn't like. Even this procession is ostentatious—thirty courtiers and twice as many guards.

The distant mountains are capped with snow above the tree line, but here in the lowlands it's still autumn. Since their marriage several months ago, King Hansen and Queen Lilac have ridden out like this at least twice a week, to visit hamlets and villages, and to preside over harvest celebrations.

Queen Lilac. His friend Shadow's true identity, revealed to the world. It has taken some getting used to, even if he has accepted it, accepted her, for who she is. He watches her up ahead, a slim and graceful figure on her horse, cloak thrown over her shoulder because the day is so fine. Hansen, her husband, leans toward her and says something; Lilac laughs. She lifts her face to the light, but Cal's behind her and can't read her expression. A spark of jealousy shoots through him, painful and sharp. The king is handsome in the bland, expected way of titled monarchs, but handsome nonetheless, sitting regally on his majestic steed, waving to the crowd.

The Kingdoms of Montrice and Renovia are united: Look at the happy young king and queen—so beautiful, so well dressed—delighted to be meeting grubby country folk in their muddy villages. It's all designed to dispel rumors that the marriage is one of mere political expedience.

Lilac might be Hansen's queen in public, but at night, in private, thanks to the secret room and passageway adjacent to her own, she is still his Shadow. Just this morning they were entwined in each other's arms. But now she rides next to the king while Cal remains on the fringes, watching for danger.

The fact that Cal shares the queen's bed, while the king sleeps with his own rotating array of favorites, is nobody's business but their respective royal Majesties. Hansen and Lilac are cordial, distant. If the king is unnerved about his wife's curiously close friendship with the royal assassin, he has made no indication of it.

"Long live the king!" people shout from their perches on hedgerows, or from stations along stone walls and tumbling wooden fences. A few cheer for the queen as well, the local maidens and lasses the loudest in their admiration. Lilac is young, energetic, and vibrant—an equal to their handsome king—and her blood hails from the old and storied line of Avantine's ancient rulers. Not only that: Everyone knows that she's brought Renovian bounty to the Montrician coffers.

There aren't as many people out today, Cal observes, reining in his horse and falling farther back. It's later in autumn now, and most of the harvest festivals and rituals are over. Lilac will miss the outings, Cal suspects, though she always complains afterward about being forced to ride alongside Hansen and pretend his conversation is sparkling. She finds him exceedingly dull, and Hansen has been chafing about having to visit villages rather than riding to hound out in the forest. Every cold day reminds the king that hunting season is underway, and he wants to get back to his usual pursuits.

A village looms, one of several the procession will pass this morning on its way to the town of Sancton. Cal gallops to the front, whipping a glance at Lilac as he passes. She's smiling, but it looks strained. At least the village visit will cheer her up. During these autumn processions, in every hamlet and village, every tiny settlement and every town, Cal has seen lilac-colored ribbons tied to window latches and branches of trees. The people of Montrice are welcoming Lilac as their queen. In the towns, small girls present her with bouquets of autumn leaves and flowers. Hansen is asked to drink a symbolic draft from a horn of plenty, and he makes the same joke every time about wishing for ale rather than well water. Everyone laughs, he plants an awkward kiss on Lilac's cheek, and then the entire royal procession moves on.

Today should be no different, but Cal feels uneasy. He rides up alongside Jander and nods at his slight, frowning apprentice. Some people are surprised that the Chief Assassin trusts and relies on a skinny boy, but they don't know that Jander is more than just a humble stable hand, and older than everyone in the entire kingdom.

"It's quiet on the road," Jander observes in his low, rasping voice.

"Too quiet?"

He gives the slightest of shrugs. But Cal trusts Jander's instincts, and his own. Something *isn't* right today. Perhaps the news from Stur has already reached this village. He had urged the king not to make this trip, but Hansen insisted. Behind Cal, a few people are cheering for the king, but with less gusto than usual. The country folk lined up to watch are craning to get a glimpse of Lilac, but they're not smiling or cheering. The village that lies ahead looks the same as so many others in this part of Montrice—while the capital city, Mont, is rich and dazzling, the countryside is full of thatched roofs, daub-and-wattle walls, penned goats and sheep, water troughs, a makeshift shelter over the well where chickens peck around in the dirt, and a donkey or two tied to a post. Cal has seen dozens of these over the past few weeks. The only difference among them is the general dirtiness of the populace, and whether the tree of life grows in the middle of the road or in an overgrown village green.

"Long live the king!" bellows the crier from Castle Mont, in his green-and-white livery, his beard as rusty as the leaves drifting from trees. "Long live the queen!"

"Long live the children of Stur," a voice in the crowd says. So they do know about Stur. The speaker is a young man, maybe, but when Cal tries to single him out, it's impossible. There's a sour look to the people assembled here; they seem discontent, which is understandable.

In a moment the villagers have all taken up the cry. "Long live the children of Stur! Deia bless the children of Stur! May we never forget the children of Stur!"

Cal looks around. There are no lilac ribbons tied anywhere, not a single one.

"Pray for the souls of the children of Stur!" shouts one old woman, her voice high-pitched and cracking. "Deia damn the evil magic that killed them!"

Cal trots back toward Lilac and Hansen, scrutinizing their expressions. Both have heard the shouts of the villagers. Hansen looks ill at ease, as though he's ready to turn his horse and gallop home. Lilac appears serene and untroubled: That's her aunts' assassin training at work, Cal thinks. Give nothing away with your face or your body language. Make no rushed gestures. Let no enemy perceive you as nervous, startled, unprepared. Afraid.

"Deia damn the witch who killed them!" a man shouts, and Hansen's horse rears a little, unnerved by the noise. Cal doesn't like this. The witch—who do they mean? He glances around. They all seem to be looking in one place. At one person, anyway. The queen.

The lilac-frosted ice.

"Boo! Boo!" The sound is all around them, men's and women's voices, sour and angry.

That's it. Cal has to stop this, right now.

"Your Majesty," he says, drawing his horse close to Hansen's. "I believe we must return to the capital."

"What's going on?" Hansen asks, bewildered. "They're upsetting my horse."

“The terrible news from Stur has upset our people,” Lilac says in a loud, clear voice, no doubt aware that her words will carry. “That’s to be expected. We should have canceled this visit today as I suggested. It is . . . unseemly at such a sad time.”

“I don’t know why they’re angry with *us*,” Hansen complains, frowning at Lilac. “Hang this. We’re in the dark like everyone else, and news of Stur arrived just this morning. I saw no reason to change course. This is still my kingdom.”

“Quite,” says Cal, keen to end the conversation. The booing intensifies, the crowd growing more brazen. He holds up an arm to summon the assassins, and they gallop up, circling the monarchs.

“Rally to the king and queen,” he mutters. “Follow me.”

“What on earth is going on here?”

It’s the Duke of Auvigne, his face even ruddier than usual. “What is all this to-do? These subjects need a good thrashing, if you ask me. I’ve never heard such disrespectful nonsense.”

“We’re returning to the castle, Your Grace,” Cal tells him. “At once.”

“Very well, but the guards should arrest some of these louts and make an example of them.”

“That won’t be necessary.” Once again, Lilac sounds calm and firm, though Cal knows that she must be in turmoil. When he looks into her dark eyes, there’s no sparkle. “We should make haste.”

At a nod from Cal, Jander takes off toward the back of the procession, to spread the word of an about-face. In an instant, they’re on their way, retracing their progress along the road to Mont. The city is visible on its hilltop in the distance, and Cal wants to set a quicker pace than their journey out.

The countryside isn't a happy place anymore, and it's not a safe place. *Deia damn the witch who killed them.*

In the minds of the people of Montrice—so adoring last week—has everything changed so utterly? Is Lilac the "witch" they fear? Cal is troubled, but for now he needs to get Lilac back behind the city wall and into the castle, where she will be safe from her people.

Chapter Two

Lilac

It's been three days since our last attempted journey, and for the time being no one is allowed out of the royal castle. People here in Mont call it a palace, but it's more like a fortress, the moat a weed-infested gully strewn with iron spikes to deter invaders. At nightfall the heavy portcullis clangs shut and the drawbridge rises. We're all trapped in here, for our own safety. These are dangerous times, and I fear the danger will only grow.

Aside from an emergency meeting of the Small Council, I haven't seen Hansen. He has always had the love of his people, and I don't think he's taken our recent reception well. Maybe he thinks it's my fault. In fact, I'm sure he thinks it's my fault.

The weather has turned chilly and wintry, and it's been decided that we should suspend further excursions around Montrice until . . . until what? Until spring? No. Until the rumors die down, and the anger.

The day drags, and then at last, night falls. I sink into my vast bed, its brocade curtains drawn around me before my ladies depart, fussing with their candles and competing to be the last to wish me good night.

"Sleep well, Your Majesty," they say, though their faces are anxious, and I doubt any of us are sleeping well right now. All the talk is of the terrible news from Stur and the people who died there. The *children* who died there. My ladies are careful not to say anything directly to me, but the men in the Small Council are less circumspect. Anyway, I knew—as soon as I saw their faces and heard their displeasure when Hansen and I rode out the other day. They hate me. They blame me.

The lilac-colored frost over the pond. A curse from the Renovian witch. It is easier to blame the devil they know—the foreign queen—than the one they don't, the demons who walk among us once more. The King of Stavin is convinced the Aphrasians have returned, and who am I to dispute this? Stavin is right: We *have* been slow to act. The problem is that the king does not even know where to start looking for perpetrators. The Aphrasians seem to have disappeared into thin air. I have pushed Hansen to send soldiers to Baer Abbey, but the king does not listen to me. And my mother is still, for all intents and purposes, the leader of Renovia.

I lie in my vast bed, propped up on my pillows, listening to the soft night sounds of the castle, waiting.

Hansen, in his own apartments at the far end of the hall keep, may be hosting his usual revelries—drinking, gambling—games that might be raucous or debauched. All with his favorites and his dogs. I actually have no idea. He could be brushing up on the scrolls and drinking tea, but I doubt it.

He's kept his distance from me since our marriage, which is a great relief.

He hasn't insisted on my presence at any of his evening entertainments or once tried to join me in my bed, or summon me to his.

This is a marriage of political expedience for both of us, after all. A political disaster right now, especially since the people blame or suspect me for the terrible things that have happened lately.

The guards call to one another across the battlements, and an owl hoots from a distant perch. Sometimes, if there's no wind, I think I can hear whinnying from the stables, when the horses board for the night, though maybe this is my imagination. I'm longing for the castle to settle, and for the business of the day to be over.

Because that is when Cal will come to me, through the door in the hall's cellars, all the way up the narrow stone staircase, to the tiny antechamber we call the Queen's Secret. I'm waiting for his knock on the door. Waiting, waiting, waiting.

It has been three days since the ill-fated trip to the village, three days since he has visited. I can never acknowledge our friendship in public, but I saw the alarm in his eyes when the crowd turned ugly. I want to tell him I'm all right, that I can take care of myself, that he doesn't need to worry so. But I also, selfishly, just want to be with him.

The fire in the grate is low now, no longer spitting and hissing. The taper by my bed is still lit, but it throws little light, and I can't see into the recesses of the large room. I just need to wait, and to listen.

Tap-tap-tap.

I fling myself out of bed and snatch the key from its hiding place, inside the bound edition of Renovian legends that I keep on a high table, within arm's reach of my pillow. Then I scamper into the room's darkest corner, not bothering to fetch the taper. I know the path by heart, know every chair and footstool to avoid. Cal will have made his way up the stairs in darkness as well, slipping through the recesses of the cellars in stealth to make his way here. To reveal the door, I must pull aside the tapestry and trace the oak panel down to the lock.

With a click it's open, and just knowing he's there is intoxicating. I can sense his tall, broad form before me, even before he says a word. All I have to do is reach out a hand and touch his chest, so firm and broad, and I am weak at the knees, swooning.

"Lilac," he says, his voice low and soft, loving, and he steps into the room, swallowing me in an embrace before we close the door. I don't want to let him go. I burrow into his neck, breathing in his particular scent that's impossible to describe. There's a musk to it, and the subtle hawthorn aroma of the soap we make in Renovia. Cal smells like home to me, in every way.

"I missed you." I hadn't realized the strain of keeping up a false front all day. "Where have you been?"

"Interrogating the messenger from Stur, and sending our own people down there to ask more questions," Cal says, and he draws my head back and kisses me gently. "I need to know what's true and what is just fear and rumor."

"And did the messenger tell you anything we didn't know?" I ask. Cal shakes his head, and I see how tired he looks—the dark rims under his eyes, his hollow cheeks, rough with stubble. It's no surprise that he's exhausted: Since the parade, the capital has swarmed with spies from Argonia and Stavin, their embassies merely public fronts, the ambassadors entertaining the rich and mighty of Montrice while their spies sneak and snoop behind our backs.

"Too many stories," he says. "Half of it from legends and old crones' tales."

I put my hands on his temples and massage. If I could take his burden, I would. He is more husband to me than my own.

He leans back, his olive skin against the crisp white linen sheets, his eyes glinting in the flickering light of the taper. "The villagers swear the pond went black with dark magic, and then lilac. And news has leaked of the letter from Stavin—"

"Which no one cared about until now," I interrupt. "Even Hansen thought Goran was merely a warmonger looking for an excuse to invade us. But now it's different. People are scared."

Cal sighs, tracing a hand over my hair. His touch is pure comfort and I have to resist the urge to close my eyes. "Fear is contagious," he says, "especially where the Aphrasians are concerned. But we need to know more. It's possible the story is exaggerated."

"Tell that to the people booing me in the countryside. Maybe Hansen is right for a change, and we can't trust Goran. Stavin has never been one to shy from a conflict or a chance to expand its borders."

"Part of the issue," Cal says in a deliberate way, choosing his words carefully, "is that this happened in Montrice, not Renovia. It reminds everyone that you're Renovian."

I lean against him, trying to draw on his strength. "But why would I do something so cruel, and then leave a sign that blatant?"

"No one who knew you would ever believe it," says Cal.

"But they don't know me at all," I say in despair. It suddenly dawns on me that my position here is as flimsy as my marriage.

"I will never let anything happen to you," says Cal, his gaze steady. He puts his arms around me and I feel my heartbeat slowing.

"The Montricians associate the Aphrasians and their dark magic with Renovia," I say. "It's only fair, I suppose. The Aphrasian king ruled Renovia, and since that time our kingdom has failed to defeat or contain his followers. And now here I am, married to the King of Montrice."

Cal winces, as he often does at the mention of my marriage and my husband. He would rather we had run away than see me as another man's wife. The life we have eked for ourselves in secret, in shadow, wears on him. I begged him to make this sacrifice, but it does not come without heartache.

For now, however, we both must push our feelings aside. I clear my throat. "So I'm the evil queen," I say, my voice low. "They believe I'm in league with the Aphrasians. But why?"

"With Aphrasian magic at your disposal," Cal reasons, "you plague Stavin until it's weak enough to annex. Then you undermine Montrice in a campaign of magical terror. Next target is Argonia, I suppose. Everywhere would be subject to the Kingdom of Renovia and its Dellafiore queen. The Avantine Empire intact once more."

"All hail Avantine," I say, unable to suppress my bitterness.

"All hail the queen," Cal says, with a raised eyebrow. I know he's teasing, trying to make me feel better about this absurd theory. This plan I would never want. I never wanted to be a princess, let alone a queen. That is my mother's plan, my mother's wish, but it is not mine.

"Just last week they loved us," I tell him, pulling away from his embrace. "Hansen and me, I mean. They all wanted us to visit their manor houses and villages and harvest festivals. The groveling, the declarations of fealty. How quickly things change."

"The kingdoms may be united in name," Cal says, "but suspicion persists toward Renovia. Everything about this situation is new for the people here. Montrician queens are meant to be consorts, not joint rulers."

"I may as well be a consort," I say, unable to shake my dark mood. "No one listens to me in court. And my mother doesn't seem to need my help back at home."

"You'll never be a consort." Cal's face softens and he smiles at me. "You're a born leader. And a wild Renovian. That's why they're scared of you."

He's right. When they think that I can't hear, Hansen's courtiers speak of Renovia as a haven for animals, criminals, and the very darkest magic. They probably consider me half savage myself.

"They have long memories when it comes to old gossip about Renovian royals poisoning one another," I tell Cal. "But short ones when it comes to how much my father—and *your* father—sacrificed while trying to break the Aphrasians."

"The worst rumors have a way of lingering," he says. "If people believe that your father poisoned his own brother, they're ready to believe the worst of his daughter as well."

"Especially with a lilac-colored pond full of dead children," I say, shuddering. All the village's children were taken in one fell swoop. Of course they would hate me. I hate myself right now, for being helpless against such violence. I should have protected them. I should have done more about the stories from the borders, warned them, shielded them. They are my people too. Perhaps it *is* my fault that they were so vulnerable.

Cal reaches over and lays a warm hand on my back. "It's a message, isn't it?"

"Not from me, it isn't."

"Not *from* you. But to you, and about you."

I see what he is saying. "They want people to blame me. Hansen already blames me, I think, though he hasn't said it out loud."

"What do you care what Hansen thinks?" Cal's tone is impatient.

"Well, he is my husband, and the King of Montrice."

"In name only, according to you, at least." Cal pulls away from me, frowning.

"Cal, we need him on our side."

"Our side?" Now it's Cal's turn to sound bitter. "Earlier you talked about him as 'we.'"

"No, I didn't."

"Last week the people 'loved us,' you said. Whose side are you on, Shadow? I mean, Lilac. Her Majesty Queen Lilac."

I turn to him, alarmed at this shift in tone. "I *have* to be on Hansen's side," I tell him. "He could be a powerful ally if we let him."

"*We* again?"

"You and me. *Us*."

"Is there an us?" Cal growls.

"I know this isn't ideal."

"The furthest thing from it," he says, so sharp he's almost spitting his words.

"But it's the only way for us to be together," I remind him. "If you no longer want to . . ."

Cal sighs and gazes at the wall.

"I want you," he says softly. "I've always wanted you."

I reach for his hand and take it in mine. "You have me. Here. Right now. It's just us."

He pulls his hand away. "I wish that were true." Cal lies back onto the bed, exhausted, staring at the red canopy above. I lie next to him. We're together, but something is separating us. A nagging mistrust that won't go away, no matter what I say.

"We can't go back to the way things were," I say softly, almost a whisper. "But we can make this new life work."

Cal says nothing. I kiss his cheek and then roll toward him so I can kiss him some more. At first he just lies there, unmoving. But I am persistent, and at last he turns toward me, and when his mouth meets mine, strong and urgent, there are no more arguments between us.

CHAPTER THREE

Lilac

IN THE MORNING WHEN I wake, Cal is gone. When my ladies flutter in to pull back the canopy curtains around my bed and open the shutters across the windows, it looks as though I spent another night alone in my big bed. The key to the Queen's Secret is back in its hiding place, and there's no trace of Cal. It is as if he were never here. It is both a relief and a sadness.

I drink a little ginger tea from the jug my ladies carry in, and nibble on a piece of toasted bread. Every day it seems to take longer and longer to brush back my hair and pick out the day's wig. They help me dress as well, because it takes at least two ladies to lift an embroidered gown over my head—wool at this time of year, trimmed with mink—and arrange it over my linen shift. I miss the days when I could wear my hair loose. I miss the days when getting dressed meant slithering into a simple gown, eager to bound out the door. Or dressing like the assassin I was trained to be, ready to clamber onto a horse or fight any opponent.

I miss Cal already. I never know when I will see him next. I wish that one day I could wake up with someone I love by my side, rather than have him slip away at dawn to avoid detection.

"Perhaps Your Majesty would prefer some honey with your tea?"

"Or perhaps some elderberry jam for your bread?"

"Or perhaps—"

"Nothing." I wave them away.

Down in the courtyard, far below my window, I can hear bustle and shouting. When I peer out, I'm surprised to see all the ranks of soldiers, most of whom look incredibly young, marching up and down in new boots.

"What's going on?" I ask Lady Marguerite. She's slight and fair, with a face that's always worried—certainly not the prettiest of the ladies-in-waiting. But although she's the youngest of the group, she's the most astute, the most political. She always seems to know more than the others about what's going on in other parts of the castle.

"Your Majesty," she says, "I believe the men are training to march north. To the border with Stavin, and also to our own northern lands where . . ."

She trails off, and I nod. Around me, nobody likes to talk about what happened in Stur.

"They seem so young," I say. Most of the recruits look like farm lads, pulled from working the harvest. They have ruddy faces and broad shoulders, but they're sure to be more adept at handling a pitchfork than a sword.

"Many soldiers are required for the two missions," Lady Marguerite says. "And we must maintain a strong guard here, of course, to protect Your Majesties."

"It's a fine day for marching about," one of the other ladies says. "Isn't it?"

The speaker may be a dull woman who only ever trots out platitudes, but on this occasion, she's quite right. I can't spend another day sitting indoors. It's fine outside, despite the chill of late autumn. Who knows how soon the snows of winter will fall?

"Ladies," I say, standing up. "I've decided that I need some fresh air."

"You wish to promenade around the courtyard?" Lady Marguerite sounds alarmed.

"Tell the Guild master I wish to train this morning. Outside," I correct her. "Please convey my request to the assassins' quarters and tell them I will be ready soon."

"But the courtyard is so crowded," one of the other ladies protests. "All these country oafs! You don't wish to be on display, Your Majesty."

Actually, I do. But I'm not telling them that. It's not a bad thing for the people of Mont—the people inside the castle, at least—to see me in fighting mode, and remember that I'm more than some ornamental prize Hansen has won from Renovia. I'm a trained Guild member, and anyone who seeks to harm me will find a fighter, not a spoiled pet. In the Guild we learn how to fight, track, and live by our wits, as well as to understand the natural world—its rhythms, its hidden messages. Being a member of the Guild means staying active in mind and body. I'm not going to rot in this castle while dark magic swirls through the kingdom, implicating me in its evil.

While one lady hurries away to find me a Guild trainer for an impromptu session, the others deal with peeling back the layers of my clothing and fetching more suitable garments from the heavy oak chest under the window. It's a relief to replace the flowing yards of embroidered wool with hide leggings and a tunic. My ladies wrap leather protectors around my forearms and help me lace my favorite deerskin boots. I feel a crackle of pleasure, a happy anticipation about being outside again and moving freely.

"Are you sure?" my ladies keep asking me. What they mean is, are you sure about appearing this way in public, dressed as a fighter rather than the queen? I ignore such concerns. How can I explain to them that the only time I feel alive is when I'm *not* acting like the queen?

There's so much I can't say to them. They're not my friends, or even my allies. At least one of them, I suspect, is paid by the Duke of Auvigne to relay information.

"If His Majesty should visit?" Lady Marguerite says, lifting my jerkin from the chest. It's not really a question. She's formulating a plan about what Hansen should be told.

"The king knows full well that I train every afternoon with a Guild member. He will be pleased that I am getting fresh air, instead of cowering up here like a ninny."

Firstly, I don't think for a moment that Hansen will visit me. He's too busy cowering in his own chambers. And the longer I sit here, the more my fevered imagination will start conjuring unhelpful scenarios. What is Hansen being told—and by whom? Does he believe this story of the lilac frost in Stur? Does he think I might actually be involved in the black magic there? What if he's persuaded to renounce me and annul our marriage? This could throw our countries into war. But what if he feels he has no choice, because Stavin threatens to invade unless these alleged dark forces are dispatched, along with me? Montrice could be facing down another war, even if he stands by me and this sham marriage of ours.

A breathless lady of the bedchamber returns, wheezing that a Guild member awaits me downstairs. I wave away the loden-green cloak someone is trying to fasten around my neck.

"It is true," Lady Marguerite says to the others, "that His Majesty wants our queen to be happy and fit. If she is to bear royal children, she must not be weak or in ill health."

Royal children. If I'm honest—with myself and no one else—that is the thing that has scared me most since my engagement to Hansen. And I can't discuss it with Cal, although he is well aware that the throne demands an heir. What if Hansen insists that we consummate our marriage? I cannot refuse him, as much as I would want to.

I am married to the king, and yet I have chosen to follow my heart. Oh, Cal. The path has never been a straightforward one for us, and time makes everything more complicated. I need to get outside. Training will do me good.

Down in the courtyard, it's noisy in an invigorating way, with the trainees on drill, the stable boys leading horses in and out of the blacksmith's yard, and fencing practice for the best men of the guard at the eastern end. This is more like it. Even with the queen's guard around me, there's still enough room for my work. And in this gear I don't draw much attention. I don't look like the queen. I don't look that different, in fact, from my trainer today, a Guild member I've never met before. She's a young woman, slight and tense as a wild cat. She bounds up and gives a deep, awkward bow rather than a curtsy.

"Your name?" I ask her. She can't be any older than seventeen, with thick auburn hair tied back from a heart-shaped face.

"Rhema, Your Majesty," she replies. Her eyes are dark and there's a glint in them that appeals to me. She's come ready to fight, and she's not intimidated by working with the queen.

"You're new here?"

"It's my third week, ma'am. I'm an apprentice assassin. From the mountains."

"I'm rusty," I tell her, twirling a spear to warm up my hands. Strange that Cal has never mentioned that one of the new assassins is a young woman. He's told me all about training them, and about sending several of the less able back home. Nothing about a red-headed girl from the mountains.

"Do you want me to go easy on you, ma'am?" Her voice is neutral, but I can see the disdain in her expression. She reminds me of the old me, of Shadow. I would have seen a grand lady like Queen Lilac as an amateur, too coddled to be a real fighter.

"No," I say, trying not to snap. I'm only two years older than her! I'm still twirling the spear when she leaps at me, feet high in the air. So impressed am I with the height she reaches that I'm a moment late with the spear block, and end up flat on my backside on the cold cobbles.

"Sorry," I hear her say, and she grips one of my hands to haul me back onto my feet. With my other hand I clasp the spear, and in a flash take out her legs; now she's on her back.

I clamber up, dusting grit and straw off my hands. Rhema grins.

"Well played," she says, and we face off again, both prepared this time. I have to admit, she has impressive agility and an admirable range of fighting skills. She's even better than my last Guild trainer, and he was excellent. She's more nimble than I was in my prime, but I've always had sharp instincts that allow me to anticipate my opponent. *These are acts of imagination rather than violence*—that's what my aunts used to tell me. A good fighter lives on her instincts, and fights on her nerves.

In the background, I'm conscious of a familiar voice. Cal is with the new soldiers in the courtyard now, barking commands at them. When I first hear him, I lose my concentration and end up with one arm twisted behind my back, Rhema breathing down my neck.

Hearing his voice gives me a twinge that's half pleasure, half panic. It's always strange to encounter him in a public place, where we have to be circumspect, and I have to remind myself not to smile or even look at him for a moment longer than necessary.

"Again, ma'am?" Rhema seems to burst with energy. She assumes a crouching pose, ready to pounce, and I hold up my hand.

"Just give me a moment," I say, pretending to be winded. Really, I just want to listen to Cal as he puts the lumbering recruits through their paces. He's shouting at them to drop to the ground and then spring back up, and I'm guessing that the dropping is taking too long, and the springing back is more like a slow climb.

"Will you hurry up!" he bellows, and I struggle to suppress a smile. "If this was a real battle, you'd be dead by now, lying facedown in a ditch with a spear through your guts and an arrow in your eye!"

Crows caw and swoop overhead, and the men under Cal's ferocious watch grumble. I wish I could find a way to speak to him at the end of my training, but I can't just wander over. I'm the queen, and I have my circle of guards who must shuffle everywhere with me. All I can do here is fight, getting out some of my frustration at being cooped up inside for too long.

"Right—again, please," I tell Rhema, and she swings at me before I have my staff in position. But I react in time, whacking at her own weapon so hard she spins away and almost falls onto a bale of hay. It's not just frustration that I need to get out of my system: It's pent-up aggression. A swipe with a fighting stick is a smack for the Small Council; a kick to the chest is a blow against the rumormongers spreading despicable stories about me and my supposed dark magic. I wish some of them were here in the courtyard so I could practice on them. I wouldn't be rusty or out of breath anymore.

By the end of my session, my face burns with the heat of strenuous activity, and I know my arms and legs will be stiff tomorrow. This is what I've missed—the brisk fresh air, the breeze on my face, the freedom to jump and run. My new Guild trainer bows and thanks me for a good session.

"Impressive, ma'am," Rhema says, and it doesn't feel like flattery when she follows up with criticism. "With more work, your reaction times will improve, and your arm reach will be more extended."

"Well, let's fight again in a day or two," I say before she can come up with any more helpful advice. Rhema nods. She's red-cheeked as well, I'm pleased to see. She may be fit, and a little younger than me, but I can still hold my own.

The new soldiers have been dismissed and are loitering in the courtyard, some bent double or crouching on the cobblestones. Cal is conferring with one of the officers, pointing to the unfortunate recruits.

One of my own guards hands me a flagon so I can take a drink, and I pretend to be standing around because of exhaustion. It's such a long time until I'll see Cal again tonight. Sometimes I long to speak to him during the day or share a meal with him. Just be in his presence rather than waiting until my ladies have gone to bed and I'm half asleep.

Rhema wanders away toward the stables, unlacing the leather guards wrapped around her forearms. But she stops for a moment and glances over at Cal. She grins at him and he notices: He smiles right back. The sight of this small exchange, nothing more than a moment, unsettles me. Cal's smile is broad and true. He must respect Rhema. He must like her.

So why has he never mentioned her to me?

Rhema strolls over to Cal and slaps him on the shoulder. Now they are smiling *and* leaning toward each other to exchange a few words like the colleagues they are. But my heart is speeding; I have to swallow back bile in my throat. She can touch Cal in public; I can't. Jealousy wrenches at my stomach. She is so young and so pretty and surely reminds him of me when we first met. When we first fell in love.

"Return!" I bark at my guards, and march back toward the main door of the hall keep. Their smiles are like red clouds blotting out the brightness of the day.

⚜

Chapter Four

Caledon

LILAC WAS OUT THERE IN the courtyard, Cal knew, but he couldn't see her. He was alerted to her presence by the stomping of her personal royal guards, ringing their queen to protect her from the eyes of common soldiers. Such was the racket in the yard, he couldn't even hear the clacking of staffs when Lilac took on one of the Guild fighters. All he could hear was the grunting and huffing of this sad band of new recruits, country lads who resent being dragged away from the harvest. Most are terrified at the prospect of marching north. The stories from Stur grow wilder by the day.

Just this morning Cal overheard one youth telling another that when lightning flashed there, it revealed a picture of the queen's face—her mouth twisted as though she were cackling like a witch. He dragged the stupid oaf out of the line himself, shoving him toward the captain of the guard for punishment. Gossip was one thing. Sedition was another.

Rhema, one of his latest recruits, was Lilac's trainer today. Cal only realized this when he saw Rhema walking away from the queen's guards, red-faced and looking pleased with herself. She's a smart young woman, Rhema, and never happier than when she's in action. Cal likes her work ethic as well as her skills as a fighter, and he also likes that she's always respectful and attentive to Jander. Some of the apprentice assassins have too much swagger and see meek, quiet Jander as nothing more than a boy and a stable hand. They have no idea of his history and his knowledge. They have no idea what he has witnessed and survived.

They have no idea of the curse on his head, placed by King Phras so many centuries ago, condemning Jander to an eternal life, trapped in a boy's body.

The ranks in the courtyard clear for a moment, and Cal glimpses Lilac disappearing into the royal apartments, flanked by her personal guard. Maybe she hasn't seen him out here. It's chaos—marching, shouting, training. Recruits are leaping from the battlements onto bales of hay, practicing the best ways to fall and roll. Some dolt has managed to shoot an arrow into a commanding officer's shoulder, and the braying and bellowing from that part of the courtyard is as loud as cattle stampeding across a field.

Wandering in an oblivious way through all this dirt and racket is the Chief Scribe, a plump and pale elderly man, scattering linseeds for the crows. The birds waddle and leap toward him, eager for the food. More swoop down from their perches on the walls, or from the narrow ledge of the chapel's small window. The scribe's blue robe scrapes the dirty stones of the yard, and a bag of seed embroidered with a pattern of delicate feathers swings from his girdle. Why he's feeding the birds now rather than at a quieter time in the courtyard, Cal doesn't know.

The scribe's name is Daffran, and he's lived in the castle all his life. Cal sees him at Small Council meetings, writing down proceedings in a looping hand, or in the courtyard, feeding the birds. The rest of Daffran's days are spent in his small, high-ceilinged library in the tower, working on his chronicle of Montrice.

Daffran shuffles in Cal's direction, giving him an uncertain smile.

"Morning." Cal nods at him.

"Good morning, Holt," the Chief Scribe says in a wavering voice, then clears his throat. "I wonder if I might trouble you, if you have a moment?"

"Is something wrong, sir?" Cal asks. Daffran rarely addresses him directly. He's always suspected that the scribe is a little afraid of assassins.

"Perhaps—in private?"

"I'll walk with you." Cal's glad for the opportunity to leave the recruits to their own pathetic devices for a few moments. He accompanies Daffran, at a frustratingly slow pace, back to the tall stone tower linked to the hall keep by a covered passage. On the lowest floor is the chapel, which Lilac visits every few days, and the vestry where her priest, Father Juniper, studies. The scribes' library is two floors up. The young assassins jokingly call the tower Old Man's Leap, because only elderly men live and work there. Even the junior scribes have white hair, or no hair at all.

Outside the main door Daffran pauses, as though he'd changed his mind about entering. Cal stands with him in the portico, puzzled. What is so important that the scribe sought him out? Is all this training of troops interfering with the bird feeding?

"I wonder," says the scribe in a low voice, "if it's better to speak out here, where none are too close to us, and the noise of this place will help keep our words secret."

"Fine," Cal replies, even more mystified. "Not inside the tower?"

Daffran shakes his head, his watery blue eyes darting from the tower to the courtyard and back.

"I trust no place," he whispers, standing so close to Cal that his scent of beeswax and linseed oil is overpowering. "And no man but you, Chief Assassin."

"If this is about the stories of what happened in Stur . . . ," Cal begins, but Daffran shakes his head again.

"It's about what is happening here, in Mont, within these very walls." His whisper is barely audible. Cal has to bend down to hear him. "I have seen things."

"What things?"

"The shape of a man."

"One man?" Cal hopes this isn't like the story of Lilac's face in the sky. He's bored with people reading things into cloud formations and lightning bolts.

"A hooded man in dark gray robes. I saw him on the stairs outside my library, when I had left the door open. Last night. I was waiting for my supper, you see, which I always take alone. Just a little wine, because I find it helps to relax me after long hours writing."

"The man you saw?" Cal prompts.

"Just a flash, as he passed my door. I could not see his face, so I can't be sure if he wore the black mask of the Aphrasians. But he looked to me to be one of the dark monks. There and gone, in an instant."

"A dark monk?" Cal is whispering too now. "But you didn't see his face. Are you sure it wasn't simply another inhabitant of the tower? Father Juniper, say."

"Father Juniper wears white," Daffran replies. "My junior scribes wear the same blue robes as mine. None of us are in possession of dark cloaks or robes."

"Perhaps a servant delivering food?"

"Gray robes are not permitted in the castle," Daffran hisses. "They are associated with the Aphrasians. Apologies, Holt, for my tone. You are new here, and do not know our ways. No servant of the King of Montrice may wear a gray or black cloak. Some ladies of the court may dress themselves in black, if that is their wont. I understand it is the fashion, perhaps, of our times, though I don't care for it myself. But I am not one to criticize any member of the king's retinue—please, do not think that for a moment."

He blusters on, and Cal realizes that he's talking about the king's current favorite, Lady Cecilia, who likes to wear black gowns and has been known to wear a black-feathered eye mask to balls and other revelries. Cal has to interrupt to get Daffran back to the point.

"What did you do when you saw this—figure?"

Daffran doesn't reply at once. Cal wonders if he just sat trembling in his chair, too afraid to move.

"The page arrived with my supper, and I asked him if anyone had passed him on the stairs. He said no. After he left, I bolted the door."

"You said to me earlier that you saw 'things,' not just one thing. Have you had any other sightings of this kind?"

"Early this morning, at first light, I rose to feed the birds." Daffran's voice is trembling. He seems genuinely afraid. "But when I descended the stairs, I saw the dark figure again, slipping out this very door."

Daffran points to the iron-studded door to the tower.

"You followed him?" Cal asks, knowing the answer. Daffran hangs his head.

"I had not the courage, Chief Assassin. All my life I have lived in fear of the gray monks, and I doubt I would emerge the victor from any confrontation with one. I wondered, too, at the testimony of my own eyes. I am old. Perhaps I see things that are not there. I don't know. But if anyone should be told of this, it's you. I know you have fought the Aphrasians and lived to tell the tale."

"Thank you, Chief Scribe," Cal says, patting Daffran's rounded back. The old man is evidently rattled by what he's seen—or thinks he's seen. "I will station guards at the tower's door, and they will conduct a thorough search of the building at sundown and sunup every day."

"I would appreciate that. Thank you. And please, Holt?"

"Yes?" Cal bends even lower to hear Daffran's whisper.

"Rest assured that I will not share this story with anyone unless you tell me to do so. There is enough conjecture and fear in the city as it is. We can say the guards are there to protect our ink and vellum from a thief, perhaps. They are costly items, you know."

Cal agrees with this plan and says farewell to the Chief Scribe; the old man wobbles back into the tower, barely strong enough to pull the door open.

The Small Council is scheduled to meet tomorrow, and Cal will raise the issue there. Lord Burley alarms easily and may want more guards at every door, not to mention all-night vigils on every floor of the tower. The Duke of Auvigne will scoff, no doubt, and cast aspersions on the elderly scribe's sanity. He's been rude before about the languid pace of Daffran's writing, and has suggested more than once that one of the younger junior scribes—one who still has his hearing and doesn't wheeze when he climbs the stairs—should take Daffran's role at the Small Council.

If the Small Council agrees, Cal will confide in the captain of the guard, and a thorough search of the castle can begin. This place is a small city, with many underground stories, cellars, and tunnels, not to mention the catacombs. If the Aphrasians have infiltrated Castle Mont, there are many, many places to hide. But why would they seek out the tower, which has no underground access, and a portico leading to its only door? It's the easiest place to be seen and unmasked, not to mention trapped.

On the far side of the courtyard, the captain of the guard is waving. He needs Cal to resume his duties. The first contingent sets off for the north in two days, and not a man among them is ready to fight.

Chapter Five

Lilac

In my chamber I hurl my jerkin and arm guards to the floor and dismiss all my attendants, apart from Lady Marguerite. She drops to her knees to unlace my boots, but I practically kick her away.

"That Guild fighter," I say. "The one training me today. Who is she? Can you find out?"

Marguerite stares up at me, eyes wide. "The girl from the mountains?" she asks. "I believe she is called Rhema."

"I know *that*," I say, a surge of irritation pushing out my words. "I mean, why has she been taken on as an assassin? She could be anyone. She could be here to murder me."

"Oh no, Your Majesty!" Lady Marguerite looks horrified. "She is highly regarded. I'm told that she was personally selected by Caledon Holt to join his elite group."

I say nothing. I just stand with my back to the window while Lady Marguerite unlaces my boots and eases out my stockinged feet, one by one. Really, I don't trust myself to say a word.

"Also, ma'am," Lady Marguerite adds, her voice hesitant, "there was a rider at sunup with some missives taken straight to His Majesty the King."

"Missives? From where?" It's ridiculous that I have to rely on my ladies for such intelligence.

"Stavin, I believe, ma'am. And another report from the northern region where the terrible . . . terrible . . ."

"Yes, yes," I say. "Very well. Please leave me. I wish to write a letter."

Lady Marguerite bows and leaves the room.

My ladies return. "Fetch me writing materials," I order. There's more fluttering, the ladies competing to fetch the inkpot and sharpen the quill, one unrolling a sheet of vellum that's the same ivory as bones. One lady sets a dish of scented lilac wax next to a candle, ready for the seal of my heavy gold ring. My desk sits facing the window, with a view of the castle's gray stones and soaring turrets and the gloomy winter sky. Lady Marguerite lurks nearby like an owl, blinking at me.

"Please don't think me impertinent," she says, "but I wonder—is this a letter that will leave the castle grounds? Or is it something that will be delivered to His Majesty or one of your advisors on the Small Council?"

"I don't see why the destination of this letter should concern you, Lady Marguerite," I tell her. "I have everything I need here, and I'll summon a page when I've finished my correspondence. You are dismissed."

"Of course, ma'am." Another curtsy. She's facing the floor, her veil drooping onto the flagstones, when she speaks again. "I'm just concerned for your well-being. Deeply concerned."

The fire crackles and spits. I tap a sharpened quill against the wood of the desk. It sounds like the beak of a woodpecker, drilling into a tree.

"I don't understand," I tell her, sounding as impatient as I feel. "What is the reason for this concern?"

"I'm just thinking of your safety, ma'am."

"Well, at this moment I am simply writing to my mother, as I do every week. Unless one of you has poisoned the ink, I don't see why this letter compromises my safety."

"Of course. I just fear that since . . . the incident." Lady Marguerite peeks up at me. "When you rode out with the king. I fear that not all support you as they should. I would not wish the letter to fall into . . . enemy hands, as it were."

"The enemy, whoever they may be, would be very bored with this letter," I tell her. "From daughter to mother, with no matters of state discussed or anything of import. Unlike, I presume, the missive that arrived this morning and was sent directly to His Majesty."

"Your Majesty." She backs out of the room, almost stumbling on the hem of her dress. I wait until the heavy door clangs behind her before I turn back to my desk and the blank sheet.

I can't write a word. I'm seething. Apparently I'm the queen of this realm, but important letters arrive for Hansen's perusal only. If something is happening in Stavin, it should be considered by both of us. And now I can't even sit down to write a letter without being interrogated about its destination. What does Lady Marguerite think—that I'm writing a love letter to the Chief Assassin? Who is this "enemy" who plans to pounce on a letter to my mother?

Maybe she knows more, sees more, than she reveals to me. Perhaps I'm wrong to discount the opposition to me in Montrice. I must be careful about what I write, I suppose, and keep in mind that anything I send to my mother may be intercepted and read—or misread—and used against me.

This is so frustrating. I write to my mother on this day every week, and now I feel as though I can't write a word. Still, she'll be expecting something from me, and I mustn't delay. It's a difficult journey for the messenger, for Renovia is a place of secrets and deep hollows, of misty moors and damp gullies. Even expert travelers can find themselves disoriented and lost in its miles of dense scrub and birch forests.

I dip the quill into black ink and start to write—benign drivel, really. Even if I had no fear of the letter being intercepted, I wouldn't want to tell my mother about the ride with Hansen when the people expressed their displeasure. Where *I* was booed, and villagers looked at me with horror and disgust, as though I were a witch. I won't endorse the story about the lilac ice in the village of Stur by committing it to vellum. It's unlikely to be true, and even if it were, the sight is evidence of black magic, not malfeasance on my part. If this letter is intercepted, or falls into the wrong hands in any way, nothing in it must suggest I'm afraid.

So I write to her of the new marble in the floor of my chapel and the bustle of troops training in the courtyard below my window. The king, I tell her, is in his usual good health. I assume that this is true, because I would surely have heard by now if he was ailing in any way. Lady Marguerite, at the very least, seems to know the gossip.

Outside my window a crow caws, and even though I'm wrapped in a shawl spun from fine Argonian wool, I shiver. The sun is weak and all the warmth seems to be leaking from the day. There's something about the castle here in this rocky city of Mont that makes it feel like a prison. When songbirds of summer are gone, we're left with nothing but grim crows, the same color as the ink in my pot. They swoop onto my windowsill and glare at me with beady eyes, as though they're my jailers. The sound of them sets my nerves on edge. Some days it feels like we have more crows in the castle than soldiers patrolling the parapets or rats scurrying in the cellars. I'm tempted to pluck my bow from the wall where it hangs near the window and scatter a few well-aimed arrows across the courtyard. No one would miss those crows.

And I still never miss a shot.

Writing this letter reminds me of how much I miss my mother and her wise counsel. I ask her if she's seen my aunts, Moriah and Mesha. I trust their wisdom and instincts more than anyone's—perhaps even more than Cal's. They know the world of Deia, our great and ancient goddess, and trained me from childhood to be present and alert in the natural world—in forests and rivers, in mountain caves and treetops and thickets. *Look and look and look again*, Moriah would tell me. *Then close your eyes and listen.*

If only we could travel together to the northern region of Montrice, to investigate and speak to the people there. The best way to banish mistrust of me, I believe, is to meet people face-to-face, and let them see that I'm not a monster.

My aunts raised me to be a Guild member, not to live some kind of useless, cosseted life. They brought me up to fight and to respect the power and danger of magic. The more I think about this, the more I'm convinced we need to go north, to stand in the place where magic hijacked nature and brought terrible suffering to the people there. But how can I trust this to ink and vellum?

The doors to my chamber burst open and I'm out of my chair, quill brandished like a knife. If I have to, I can take out an eye with its needle-sharp nib.

A man stands before me, out of breath and startled to see me holding a weapon at his throat.

It's Hansen—my husband, the king.

Chapter Six

Lilac

"PUT THAT THING DOWN!" HANSEN'S handsome face is pale and he is visibly irritated after being startled. The pages close the doors behind him and we're alone. "I'm not here to attack you."

"Then can't you knock like a normal person?" I throw the quill onto the table.

"I'm not a normal person. I'm the king."

"And I'm the queen, in case you'd forgotten."

"Well. About that." Hansen starts pacing in front of the fire. For someone who's such an avid sportsman—truly happy only when he's riding to hunt or galloping in a jousting tournament—he wears the most elaborate and fussy clothes. Hansen has more lace in his wardrobe than all the ladies of the castle combined. Today his long robe isn't just edged with ermine; it's embroidered with gold thread. I suspect he takes longer to dress than I do.

"Well," he says again.

"What? Is something wrong?" Hansen never visits me in my apartments. I think the last time he was here was to throw something out the window as a joke, pelting one of his idiotic courtiers with a dead pigeon or squirrel carcass. Hilarious.

"Not wrong exactly." Hansen stops pacing and stands, hands on hips, blocking the heat of the fireplace. His fair skin is red, either with heat or embarrassment. "But something we have to do."

"Travel north?" I say too quickly. Perhaps my aunts could meet us there. It's as though Hansen, for once, had read my mind.

"Travel—what? No. We have to stay here. Don't you remember what just happened, only a short ride from the city walls? The people hate us. We got married, they loved us, and now they've turned on us."

"I think that's an exaggeration."

"Do you?" Hansen shakes his head, the expression on his face incredulous. "You have a short memory. All this business down south, in that remote village with the name I forget—"

"Stur."

"Right. Never heard of it until last week. Anyway, this business with the snow and the black and the pond, and the children dying, and the lilac frost or whatever it is."

"We don't know if that last part is true," I say. The very mention of it makes me wince.

"True or not, everyone's saying it. Everyone. A letter arrived this morning from our ambassador in Argonia, and he knows all about it."

I pace before the window, trying to calm myself. "I need to see that letter as well. I am your equal as ruler. It's time the ambassadors of Montrice—the whole court, in fact—understands this and stops treating me as a mere consort!"

"But see, that's the thing." Hansen steps closer. "That's what we have to address. And I'm not just saying this because the Duke of Auvigne told me to."

I roll my eyes. Clearly the duke told Hansen to visit me and make this incoherent little speech.

"You can look as cross as you like, Lilac, but we have to face facts. Our marriage won us popularity and united the kingdoms and added gold to the coffers and that was good. You and I agreed . . . well, somehow we agreed to keep our lives separate in private, and in public put on a good show. Smiles and waves and such. And that was working. Until it stopped working. Now we have to put a stop to the things that are being said about you."

"Isn't that why the soldiers are training outside?" I say, waving my hand at the window.

Hansen twists his face. "Soldiers can't kill beliefs or rumors. And anyway, from what I hear, these boys are hopeless. They'll march north and be killed at once by black snow or whatever it is. One crack of lightning and they'll all fall over. But ten armies won't change people's minds about you being in league with the Aphrasians."

I hate to admit it, but Hansen is making sense. With one hand I grip the edge of the shutter pulled back from the window, in part to steady myself for whatever he's going to say next.

"The Small Council wants to see us," he tells me.

"Since when do you care what the Small Council wants?" I snap. Hansen can barely be bothered to attend meetings. I usually go alone. Now he looks hurt.

"I'm not completely oblivious, whatever you may think. I can listen to sense. My whole life, I've lived here, either in Mont or at the summer residence in the mountains. Everywhere I've gone in the kingdom—villages, towns, shepherds' huts, fishermen's cottages, grand manor houses, you name it!—I've been loved. Everyone has always loved me."

I believe him. He's a handsome young man, and was no doubt a handsome boy. He was the heir and then a young king, and for all his dull predictability and obsession with dogs and hunting, Hansen doesn't have a cruel bone in his body.

He's pacing now as well, playing with one of the ornate rings on his fingers. "Now we ride out together and I'm despised." He shakes his head, as though he can't believe it.

"It's not you they loathe," I say.

"No, I suppose not," he says thoughtfully. "They think you're still harboring the Aphrasians in that damp, mysterious country of yours."

"But that is not true!" I protest.

"It doesn't matter what's true or not. We know that, don't we? Our marriage hasn't been 'true'—not for almost a year now. That's why the Duke of Auvigne says, and I agree, that it's time to put the kingdom first."

"Kingdoms plural." I can't resist correcting him. I've never heard Hansen talk like this. Usually he says that the Duke of Auvigne is a bore. This is the longest conversation we've ever had.

"Exactly. We have a duty to our joint kingdoms, however unpleasant it might be. To us."

I can't speak. I don't want Hansen to say another word. I don't want to hear what he's about to say, the thing I've always dreaded. And yet I know he must.

"Lilac, I am as sorry as you are that it has come to this. Perhaps, like you, I had hoped we could continue this way forever. But an heir will tell the world that we're a real marriage, a real union, and there is nothing to fear from their queen, as she is the mother of my child."

He doesn't look at me when he says this, which is a blessing, as I'm too shocked to reply. I knew this day would come—but not so soon. Not today.

"It will send a strong message through the kingdom that I support you and that our two kingdoms will be united forever through our heir. Or heirs, if we have more than one child, and it is hoped that we shall. Several children will mean more possible alliances through marriage. We can secure the futures of our kingdoms, and all the kingdoms in Avantine."

Deia, give me strength. Hansen is still talking. The Duke of Auvigne must have blasted him for hours about this. I clutch the shutter for strength. No, no, no. This can't be happening. Hansen can't be going back on all his promises to me. He said we could wait. He said there was no hurry. He said he would never ask me for something I did not want to give.

"So that's why . . . ," he says, walking to the fireplace and leaning against the mantel. "That's why . . . I've agreed to cast aside Cecilia. Lady Cecilia."

His current favorite, the one who giggles too loudly and wears black-feathered masks that scandalize the castle servants. Hansen doesn't need to say the word *mistress* for me to understand what he's saying. I don't like the way this is going.

"She shall remain in court, of course," Hansen continues. His face is even pinker now; he's too close to the flames. I'd like to think he is ashamed of himself, but that's probably inferring too much. "However, she will no longer share the rooms next to my own."

"I see," I say. I feel sorry for Lady Cecilia; she no doubt imagines that Hansen is her devoted and adoring lover, but he's prepared to dispose of her the moment the commoners no longer admire him. "How generous of you."

Hansen sniffs, as though my sarcastic comment isn't worthy of a reply. He thrums his fingers on the mantel, and I wonder if I've angered him. But no.

"The thing is," he says, hesitant now—sensing, perhaps, that he's on more dangerous ground—"the thing is, Lilac, you should be, *ahem,* seen to be alone as well. The Chief Assassin, I think, shall have to vacate the castle."

"The Chief Assassin?" I echo. "What does this have to do with him?"

The thought of Cal leaving my side makes me shudder—with rage and with fear. An instant longing for him, for his touch and his smell, the masculine presence of him near my body and in my bed, ripples through me. I think of his deep olive skin against my white sheets, and my whole body aches for him.

Hansen looks at me meaningfully. "I believe you know why."

"No! We're not talking about him," I say, my voice rising even as my blood thunders in my temples. If the king knows—*and the king knows*—then our lives are forfeit. There is nothing to stop Hansen from ordering our deaths for adultery and treason.

Instead, Hansen is simply asking me to do what he has done. To cast aside a favorite.

But Cal is not a diversion like Cecilia. Cal is . . . Cal is . . . What are the words? Cal was right, there are no words for our relationship but those of an illicit nature. He is no one to me; he has to be no one. I am married. I am the queen.

"And yet we must discuss this!" Hansen smacks his hand on the mantel. "Be reasonable! You know very well that Holt has to be somewhere else if we're to . . . conceive a child. One that everyone *knows* is a royal child."

Disbelief gives way to something much nastier, something that makes me feel queasy. He knows. The Council knows. Our secret has not been a secret at all, but something the king and his counselors have tolerated until now . . .

If Cal is sent away and I conceive a child, no one will be able to say the king is not the father of his own royal heir. Hansen gives up his mistress, but she can stay in court; she just can't live next to him anymore. Meanwhile, I have to give up my lover—the love of my life—and he must be sent away on a mission, just so all the judgmental, gossiping courtiers in Mont can be assured that any child I bear is the king's.

My heart is pounding. "Can't we wait?" I ask, desperate. "We've only been married a few months."

"Wait for what?" Hansen's tone is weary. "Wait for people to start loving us again? Wait until we've been married more than a year and everyone is talking about us, wondering what's, uh, going wrong? That the king is . . . un-un-unable? Or the queen is infertile? Rumors flying that you're a witch or an empire builder, refusing to give me an heir? Think about it." He looks me square in the face. "Lilac, we should have a child, and the sooner the better."

I see now that Hansen isn't the bored regent I had taken him to be, or a spoiled and vain boy. He is a king, and he must do his duty, as distasteful as it is, and he is being as kind as he can be.

"I am truly sorry," he says now, "but we are not children. We must put away our toys."

He puts a tentative hand on my shoulder, and I force myself to look him in the eye. "Am I as repulsive as all that?" he asks. "I do not ask you to love me. I only ask that we do what is best for the kingdom."

Close my eyes and think of Renovia, is that it?

And send my lover away.

But I hold my tongue. I slump into a chair. I have no fight left in me. Rhema exhausted me physically during the training session in the courtyard, but this is far, far worse. It's a malaise sweeping over me, a feeling of powerlessness that I despise. Intensely I wish that I was still Shadow, the girl who grew up in the forest and meadow glade, rather than the fine lady trapped in a castle, hectored about obligations.

My pulse is racing, as though my entire body were in rebellion.

"So," says Hansen, as though we'd had a chat about new tapestries for the summer residence. "That's that. The Small Council is planning a special meeting and we should both be there."

I have no words, and I just stare at my feet. I suspect I look as defeated as I feel. Cal sent away. Hansen in his stead. A child—a child that isn't Cal's. How could I love such a child? Maybe I really am a monster.

"I know this is difficult to accept, but it is probably for the best. Holt is of much more use to us out in the field than shackled to court. Your assassin is a man of action. He's not going to be happy to be some glorified guard or training a slew of fresh recruits. His job is to keep you from danger, and the sooner you bear my child, the safer you will be." He squeezes my shoulder in a sympathetic manner. His kindness just about kills me.

I stare into the flickering fire, unwilling to meet Hansen's gaze. "You have said your piece. I shall see you at the council meeting."

Hansen leaves without another word, pulling the door open himself rather than tapping and waiting for the pages to open it. I've never seen him do that before. I always thought he was too lazy, too pampered. Then I realize he does this so that the pages feel they have done their job. It is a privilege to serve the king.

Hansen isn't as detached and oblivious as I thought. He's capable of politics. He's capable of manipulation. And to hear him talk, he's capable of setting his feelings aside in order to have this heir.

I've been deluding myself in these months since our marriage. The rumors are true, after all: My mother's dream is to unite all four kingdoms of Avantine once more. Hansen and my marrying was the first step. The next step was having children who would grow up to marry the heirs to Argonia and Stavin. A new Dellafiore dynasty, she told me. I listened, but I suppose I didn't really hear. Or I thought that when the time came, it would be a bearable duty, not something that intruded on my relationship with Cal. My love for Cal, my devotion to him.

I had promised him that my husband would be no true husband to me. I thought I could keep this promise.

The crows outside caw, laughing at me. Everyone knows everything here in this cold, miserable castle. Everyone wins. Everyone but me.

It's time to grow up, I know. Time to face the Small Council and my husband and accept my fate as queen.

Chapter Seven

Caledon

When Cal is summoned to an emergency meeting of the Small Council, it's almost dusk, and the day's training in the yard is winding down. Exhaustion and incompetence have finished off most of the recruits, and Cal can't help but feel the entire day has been an elaborate waste of time.

The meeting, he assumes, is about the scribe's belief that an Aphrasian monk stalks the narrow staircase of the tower. Cal has already set a guard outside, and the evening search of the building will begin soon. After all the scribes—and Father Juniper, Lilac's personal priest—are in their chambers for the night, the tower will be locked, soldiers standing guard until daybreak. Another search will take place then. The captain of the guard has promised a thorough search of the entire castle, in fact, to make sure no gray monk is harbored in any servant's chamber, or lives secreted in the catacombs or cellars.

The captain of the guard, Cal suspects, believes that Daffran's sightings are the terror-fueled imaginings of a doddering old man. Given the unreliability of the witness, Cal wasn't expecting the

Small Council to take this matter so seriously, but after what happened in Stur, perhaps they feel an incursion by the Aphrasians is a distinct possibility.

He sprints up the curving stone staircase that links all the floors in the building of royal enclosure. It feels strange to use this grand public thoroughfare, when he's more accustomed to the narrow stairs from the cellar that lead to the Queen's Secret.

The Small Council meets in an impressive chamber, wood-paneled, with a decorated ceiling so high, the room requires two large fireplaces to keep it warm. Darkness is settling outside, and the table is ringed by tapers on ornate stands. The place reminds Cal of some kind of Montrician hunting lodge, particularly as King Hansen's enormous hounds lie sprawled across the floor, their long tongues lolling.

The presence of the dogs means that Hansen's here—that's the first surprise. The second surprise is that Lilac is here as well, sitting at the opposite end of the table, facing the door. The sight of her face, beautiful but troubled, knots Cal's stomach. He wishes he could rush to her and kiss her sweet, soft lips. Instead he merely bows and maintains his usual expression, emotionless and staunch. Lilac doesn't meet his gaze.

The only member of the Small Council who looks pleased to see him is Daffran. The Duke of Auvigne sprawls in his chair, the usual scowl on his face, his fat fingers twitching because he isn't holding a tankard of mead. Cal doesn't trust the duke—not because he suspects him of being an Aphrasian, like Duke Girt before him—he doesn't believe Duke Auvigne supports or cares about Lilac. She's a political pawn to him, not a real woman.

Today even the wheezy old chancellor, Lord Burley, has taken his place at the table, though these days he must find it difficult to climb the stairs. He seems uninterested in Cal's arrival. Cal stands near the high window, waiting to be addressed or summoned forward. When they want to confer with him or dispense an order, they'll know he's there.

The stairs aren't the only reason that Lord Burley isn't often at these meetings. In the tortured Montrician hierarchy, he outranks the entire Small Council and usually advises the king in private, in the royal audience room near the chancellor's own apartments. Cal rarely sees him. Lilac barely sees him, either, from what she tells Cal, though occasionally Hansen summons her to these private meetings, so he doesn't have to pay attention himself. Too occasionally, according to Lilac. She's told Cal that Lord Burley doesn't—or won't—remember that she's a joint ruler, and not a consort. Apparently they still like to do things the old Montrice way.

But the Montrice way isn't her way, and it's not Cal's way.

"I've told all this to the Chief Assassin," Daffran is saying, gesturing at Cal with an ink-stained hand. "He knows what's going on."

"What you *think* you've seen," says the Duke of Auvigne, his mouth settling into a dissatisfied sneer. "You saw a cloak you imagine is gray, but you saw no black mask. You smelled no feral stench. Why would an Aphrasian monk haunt the stairs of the tower, of all places? Nobody important lives there. And there is only one way in and one way out. No cellars or dungeons or passages. And the chapel window on the ground level is too small for a man to get—"

"Perhaps," interrupts Lord Burley, "it is one of your scribes playing a merry prank."

"I can assure you that the royal scribes do not play pranks."

Daffran sounds mortally offended. Cal has to suppress a smile. "We take our work with the utmost seriousness. We are not jesters or fools!"

"There's the priest as well, of course," says the duke. "Father Berry, or whatever he's called."

"Juniper," Lilac says, in her most imperious tone. Even in the room's twilight, Cal can spot the impatient flare of her nostrils. She looks much more distracted and unhappy than she should, he thinks. He thought that this morning's training would have helped her shake off the doldrums of the aborted ride to the harvest festival, but clearly it wasn't enough.

"Aren't the guards doing everything the guards should do?" It's Hansen's turn to be impatient. He seems no happier than Lilac to be here. "I don't see the point of discussing this over and over. Searches will take place, and whatnot, and anyone threatening will be tortured in the dungeons, in the usual fashion."

"Quite right," the Duke of Auvigne says. "Your Majesty has it. The guards are investigating. They will make sure that the Chief Scribe and his underlings—"

"And Father Juniper," Daffran reminds them.

"Yes, yes. The scribes and the priest—all will be guarded and protected. If a gray monk has managed to infiltrate our stronghold here at a time when we have an unprecedented number of soldiers training in the yard, not to mention various apprentice assassins selected by the Guild, then he will be found." The duke's tone makes it clear that he believes no such infiltration has taken place.

Cal's not sure why he had to be summoned, when everyone at the Small Council seems to know of the steps taken to investigate Daffran's complaint.

"Now," says the duke, turning in his chair so he no longer has to look at the scribe, "to more essential business. Holt! Please step forward."

Cal steps from the shadows, and bows.

"Look here, Holt," Hansen says, and Cal is startled by the sound of the king's voice. Hansen never speaks to him or seeks him out. They maintain a distance at all times. Cal notes that Hansen is addressing him but not looking at him.

"I will explain," says the duke, who clearly doesn't trust the king to deliver instructions. Not surprising, Cal thinks. Hansen slumps back in his chair, like a child who's been reprimanded. "The recent events in Stur are more than troubling. They are despicable and suggest a terrible danger to our people. We have heard, as you know, that the Duchy of Stavin has been similarly beset. We cannot have such terror and violence inflicted on Montrice. It is insupportable."

Cal says nothing, though the duke has stopped talking. None of this is news. The reason he's spending all his days in the yard is to train an army to march north and restore order.

"Chief Assassin," warbles Lord Burley. "We need you to undertake a special mission."

Cal's heart sinks. So there it is. They're sending him north with the farm boys. No wonder Lilac looks so glum.

"Whatever is happening or not here in Mont, the Aphrasian Order remains a threat," continues Lord Burley, settling his dark robes around him. "They are abroad, spreading their black magic and exploiting the sacred knowledge of the Deian Scrolls to their evil ends. But all intelligence continues to point to their homeland of Renovia as a base of operations, if you will."

Lilac's face is thunderous.

"They're still there," says the duke. "We know they are. You probably know they are. They're somewhere in those swamps of Renovia, holed up with the scrolls, concocting their next magical act of terror. You know the lay of the land well."

"Yes, sir," Cal says. It's true. He knows Renovia as well as anyone alive can know it—though all this means is that he knows to be wary of its traps and alert to its dangers.

"Then you must go at once," the duke says. "Take a small team with you—the best of the best. All others will remain here in Mont to guard Their Majesties or travel north with the guard to stick the boot into any adversaries there."

"The quest must be successful, you understand." Lord Burley's hands are shaking, either with age or fear—Cal's not sure. "The autonomy of our kingdoms depends on it. The lives of our people."

"The reputation," says the duke, "of the queen. Until we rout the Aphrasian threat, our people will believe that Renovia is complicit. While they and whoever directs them remain at large, aspersions are cast on Her Majesty."

Lilac says nothing. She's fighting back tears, Cal thinks. He wants her to stay strong. He doesn't want to leave her, but this is certainly a better use of his skills than training soldiers. If the Aphrasians are still entrenched in Renovia, he's the person to root them out and destroy them once and for all.

"You should leave in the morning," Hansen says, adamant, his voice hard. "First thing."

Even the duke looks surprised by Hansen's sense of urgency.

"Your Majesty, perhaps we can give the Chief Assassin time to get his team in order," he tells the king. Hansen makes a face.

"He'll take that boy—Jander—the one who used to be mute. I hear him talking to horses down in the stables now, so he seems to have his voice back." He looks at Cal with undisguised distaste. "Am I right, Holt?"

"Quite right, Your Majesty," Cal says coolly.

"You need another fighter with you, Holt," the Duke of Auvigne says. "That boy has the strength of a feather. You'll want someone highly skilled in combat. You'll face strong opponents, I fear."

"Cartner, sir." Cal says Rhema's name without thinking twice. "She's new, from the mountains here in Montrice. The best fighter and tracker of any of the apprentices. And with Guild knowledge, like Jander."

"Well, that's that." Hansen sounds pleased. "Everything is settled. Take the best horses in the royal stables. Ride out in the morning. I've already sent a messenger, to the queen mother in Serrone, to send word that you're on your way."

"You have?" Lord Burley looks astonished.

"Yes," Hansen says, pink in the face. "I sent someone immediately after my conversation this afternoon with Queen Lilac. My wife."

He gestures to her at the other end of the table, in case anyone was in doubt about her identity. Lilac stares back at him as though in a daze.

"You should have sent two messengers," the duke mutters. "Or even three. It's a damned dangerous road and Renovia itself is one giant sinkhole, from what I can gather. Holt, ready yourself for the journey. There'll be coin for you, of course. And any other provisions you need. You'll be gone for some months, I expect."

Some months. The words hit Cal like a sock to the gut.

"And by the time you return," Lord Burley says, a fake smile plastered over his cunning old face, "you will bring us good news, and we will have good news of our own here in Mont."

"Sir?" Cal doesn't understand what he's getting at.

"Why, an heir, of course." The Duke of Auvigne is smiling as well. When he bares his teeth this way, he looks like an animal rounding on its prey. "Their Majesties have just told us that they plan to start a family. By this summer we hope to have an heir to the thrones of Montrice and Renovia."

"And the Aphrasians squashed at last," adds Lord Burley. Cal feels as though he's just been punched. *Their Majesties have just told us.* When was Lilac planning to tell *him*?

"All as it should be," Hansen says, pushing back his chair. "All as it should be. My dear?"

He gestures to Lilac, and she rises slowly. The members of the Small Council stumble and scrape, hurrying to stand. Hansen is on his feet as well, waiting for her to process around the table—the far side of the table from Cal, never meeting his eye. Then she takes Hansen's arm and they leave the room, heads high, the model of an imperial couple.

The three members of the Small Council take their chairs again, but Cal remains standing, glued to the spot. He's to be sent away on a long and dangerous mission. Lilac and Hansen will be sharing a bed, and begetting a child.

Their secret nights are over. Reality has set in. Lilac is the queen, and she has a duty to perform. He understood that the day she decided to marry Hansen—and save Cal's life. She made a huge sacrifice so Cal could live.

But now it feels like too high a price to pay. Today's meeting of the Small Council reminded Cal that he will always be nothing but the queen's servant—the assassin. He must obey orders. The day she was married, Lilac's allegiance was bound to another man. Cal's been a fool, pretending his intimacy with the queen would continue indefinitely.

They made promises to each other, pledged their hearts, but in reality there is nothing that keeps them together but a small key to a secret room.

His duty is to go where the Small Council sends him. And Lilac's duty is to her realm—and her husband.

Chapter Eight

Lilac

I'm not certain that Cal will visit tonight. So much time passes after my ladies retire that it seems unlikely he'll seek me out. Perhaps he's leaving so early there's no time to waste: He must prepare for the journey.

But he can't possibly consider leaving without saying goodbye. Without one last night in my arms. Can he?

Out on the battlements the watchmen give the call for midnight. I climb out of bed and walk to the window, gazing up at the moon. It appears and then disappears behind tumbling gray clouds. The good weather of autumn is gone, I think. Perhaps yesterday was the last day of sunshine. Mont in winter has steel skies and too much rain.

Renovia will be foggy, I realize, and its winter mists will settle on Cal's skin like a layer of slime. This is the worst possible season to be undertaking a mission. But I do understand that there's little time to waste, when the Aphrasians seem to be so rampant.

And Hansen wants Cal out of the way, so there are no questions about the paternity of a royal heir. I shudder at the very thought.

I could send another letter to my mother, asking her to intervene in some way—in any way. But there's no point; my mother would agree with Hansen. She would tell me to endure the obligations of my marriage with grace and fortitude, and after I've had a child or two, Hansen and I can resume our separate lives.

It all sounds so clear, so rational. So hateful.

Tap-tap-tap. I almost run to the door, hitching up my trailing linen nightdress so I can leap over a footstool, skidding my way across the floorboards. When I open it, Cal is there. He doesn't take me in his arms. My eyes have adjusted to the room's darkness, but it's hard to make out his expression. Something in the way he stands, so stiff and unyielding, makes me step aside to let him in. Instead of walking to the bed, he heads for the fireplace and pulls off his jacket, flinging it onto a chair.

I want to ask him what's wrong, but it's a stupid question. Nothing is right. Cal is going away, and we may not see each other for months.

Cal drops into another chair and runs his hands through his hair, a sign that he's agitated. He kicks a stool out of the way. He makes no effort to take off his boots.

"So," he says, his voice flat. "You and Hansen, playing happy family. Were you planning to tell me about this, or was it your idea that the news got broken to me in a public place?"

"That's not fair," I say, marching over to him and giving the stool another kick, for good measure. "When could I have spoken to you this afternoon? It was a surprise to me, as well. I had no idea they were planning to send you away."

"You didn't look very surprised." When he looks up at me, his eyes are dark and narrow. Suspicious.

"Well, of course I knew before the meeting itself."

"I see. You knew, but didn't tell me."

"How could I tell you? I can't summon you in on a whim for a personal audience, not with the castle on edge and suspecting the worst of me. Hansen came to see me this afternoon, very upset, saying we have to . . . *do* something about the way the people here have turned on us. And to him that means having an heir, to change public opinion, to cement the alliance between our two countries. So I'm no longer seen as an outsider. Hated as an outsider."

"That sounds like a speech written by the Duke of Auvigne," Cal says, and I could smack him. He's being so difficult about this.

"We both knew this day would come," I say, trying to placate him. "We just hoped it wouldn't be this soon."

"You seem to have made up your mind very quickly." Cal is not placated. "The first time Hansen raises the issue, you capitulate."

His words make me cringe. "I hate the idea. Hansen's not happy either."

Cal sits shaking his head. "Hansen has a different mistress every month. To him you're just another young woman he sleeps with, another notch on his royal bedpost. But you . . ." He turns away, and I hear the break in his voice.

"You are everything to me," I say. Why won't he listen? "Hansen is nothing. We are obligated to each other, no one else. One royal heir, and everyone is happy."

For a while, at least, I think, but I don't have to talk about having other children with Hansen. Cal is broken enough as it is.

"Everyone?" Cal echoes pointedly.

"Don't be jealous," I tell him. "I am as trapped as you are. You are being stubborn and emotional."

He sighs, leaning back in the chair until his head lolls. Why won't he be reasonable? Isn't that what Hansen said to me? Be reasonable?

"Just admit," he says to the ceiling, "that you're relieved to get me out of the way, so you can be queen, and be the wife to Hansen you so obviously want to be."

"Is that what you think?"

Before he can answer, I continue in a rush. "Why don't *you* admit that you're happy to be leaving this castle that you hate and this capital that you hate and this country that you hate, so you can ride off with Rhema?"

"Ha!" Cal's laugh is forced, and there's a nastiness to it that I've never heard from him before. "Now who's being jealous and emotional?"

"You're impossible," I tell him again, crossing my arms tight. "And you're not answering my question. Why, when you have so many apprentice assassins at your disposal, can you not wait a moment to blurt out her name to the Small Council? The duke tells you to pick a strong fighter and you practically shout her name across the room."

"You trained with her this morning!" Cal sits up, indignant. "You know she's a good fighter."

"And she's the only fighter you have, apparently. I remember a time when you didn't want a 'girl' trailing around with you. Now everything's changed when some pretty thing from the mountains rides into town."

"Are you accusing me of something?" he demands.

"Not at all," I lie. "You will have your companion, and I will have mine."

"What?" Cal looks incensed. "So Hansen's your *companion* now?"

"Why not? We'll be sharing a bed, after all." The more I talk, the more out of control this conversation becomes. I know that deep down, but I can't stop myself. Cal is right—I am jealous of Rhema *and* highly emotional. Never in a thousand years would I admit this to him. Not while he's being so rude to me. How dare he question my devotion? I risked everything for him. He knows I love no one but him.

"I'm not Shadow anymore," I tell him. "I can never be that girl again. I'm Queen Lilac now, and for the rest of my life. You have to accept that."

Cal stands up. "The only thing I have to do," he says, his tone curt, "is go."

"You're really leaving?" I ask, and he looks puzzled, almost impatient.

"You heard the Small Council. You heard *your husband*, the king. I must ride at once to Renovia. There's no choice in the matter." Cal reaches for his jacket, the only item of clothing he's removed tonight.

"I mean *now*," I say in a softer voice. I don't want this to be our goodbye. I don't want the last words exchanged between us to be angry and jealous.

I don't want to sleep alone tonight—not when I may not see Cal for months.

"Days are short," he says, matter-of-fact, as though he's sniping at a stable hand. "We need to be on the road at daybreak, and there's a lot to prepare."

I open my mouth to protest, but no words emerge. Instead I just stand there, defeated. Cal's already gone—I can see it in his eyes. The mission has taken over; he's imagining the winding trails through Renovia, its secret highways. And he's angry with me—angry with me for being the queen and agreeing to perform the queen's duty. Angry because of the things I said tonight.

"Be safe," I manage to say, and for a moment I imagine that his eyes have softened. He stands at the end of the bed, ready to go.

"You too," he says. "Take care, Lilac. Trust no one."

Cal doesn't even kiss me before he leaves. He just disappears into the chamber's far corner, and I hear rather than see the door open and close. I wait, hoping he'll change his mind and return. But too much time passes, and when I clamber out of bed to look through the window at the courtyard below, I can make out a tall figure stalking toward the stables.

I lock the door to the Queen's Secret, and resettle the heavy tapestry that covers it. Who knows how long it will be before I hear a knock at this door again?

Perhaps I never will.

Chapter Nine

Caledon

THEY SADDLE THEIR HORSES BEFORE dawn, the animals' warm breath misting in the cold courtyard. Cal notes the guards outside the tower door and strolls over.

"Any activity during the night?" he asks, and they say they've heard and seen nothing. Cal sends them in to search the tower earlier than planned. If something—or someone—is found, it's better that he's here to deal with it.

The tower has eight floors but few rooms. The ground level is almost entirely devoted to the chapel. Guards swarm inside, and in the morning quiet of the yard, Cal can hear their boots stomping up the long staircase. The old scribes won't be happy to be woken this early, but the priest, Father Juniper, emerges from the building in his white robes, looking unhurried and calm, as though he were already up and ready for the search. In the early light, his robes look pale as the waning moon.

"Chief Assassin," he says, with a bow in Cal's direction. "Thank you for overseeing this. I know you must be eager to be on your way. You have a long journey ahead, I understand."

"Yes," Cal says. It's hard to look at Father Juniper without thinking of Lilac; he's her personal priest, presiding over her personal chapel. Last night's argument with Lilac was a stupid mistake, and it solved nothing. But it's too late now to do anything. With so many people up and about, Cal can't visit Lilac without detection, and it's not safe to send her a note.

"We will pray to Deia for your safe return," the priest says, turning to survey the tower. Some guards have already emerged and loiter near the front door. They can't have seen anything untoward.

"And you," Cal says quickly, realizing this is his one chance to get a message to Lilac, "you'll take good care of the queen, I hope."

"Of course." Father Juniper bows again.

"Perhaps you could let her know, when you next see her, that I pray for her safety and will have her happiness and security in the . . . forefront of my mind during this mission to Renovia."

"I will pass that message on, Chief Assassin," replies Father Juniper, and Cal bows. Even if he could see Lilac alone right now, he wouldn't have much more to tell her. They said ugly things to each other in the night. Lilac seemed eager to remind him she'd be sharing Hansen's bed. Her show of jealousy about Rhema—surely she wasn't serious? Rhema is his apprentice and nothing more. Perhaps Lilac was merely feigning jealousy to cover up the truth.

Perhaps she's looking forward to sleeping with Hansen. Perhaps she is curious about him. He's good-looking. He's a king. She's already married to him. Perhaps she was only waiting for this moment to tell Cal the truth, that she's weary of their arrangement. She saved his life, sure, but her heart is no longer his. If only his own wouldn't break so.

The rest of the guards pour out of the tower, and their leader walks up to Cal. Father Juniper steps away in deference, to leave them to their conversation.

"All is as it was last night, sir. Just the residents. Nothing extraordinary."

"Holt!" An old man is calling his name. Daffran, the Chief Scribe, scuttles toward him, a blanket wrapped around his blue robe. "Are you sure these men have checked thoroughly?"

"Under every bed and in every cupboard, sir," says the guard, glancing at Daffran in amusement.

"And up every chimney?" Daffran asks.

"Yes, sir. We were most thorough."

Daffran sighs and pulls the blanket tighter around his hunched shoulders.

"It worries me," he tells Cal, "that you are leaving Mont when the gray monk I most clearly saw, with my own eyes, on more than one occasion, has not been apprehended."

"I'm sorry that I have to leave," says Cal, and that, at least, is completely true. "But the captain of the guard has assured me the night watches and searches will be continued, and a thorough search of the castle will begin today. There will also be additional security measures to vet anyone entering or leaving through the gates."

"The gates!" Daffran mutters. "I don't think a murderous Aphrasian monk will come walking up to the drawbridge. Do you? Wearing his black mask and nodding to the guards, mm-hmm? They have secret ways and means. You should know that better than anyone."

"I do, sir. And you must keep the captain informed of anything you or anyone else sees," Cal tells him. He feels sorry for the scribe.

Daffran is getting quite old, and most residents of Mont are nervous and unhappy these days. Everyone is spooked by shadows, imagining the worst. "I wish I could do more, but I'm afraid we must ride now."

"Do as you must," Daffran says, downcast. His fingers twitch, seeking out his bag of seeds, but he doesn't have it with him.

"Sir." Cal bows to him, and heads back to the horses. Rhema and Jander are wrapped up for warmth in the muted cloaks that assassins always wear into the countryside. They need to blend in with the hills and trees, and always be ready to hide. Even their horses are a uniform seal-brown color, selected for their steady temperaments and endurance.

They all tie up saddlebags and check for essential supplies. Rhema is trying to stuff a sheath of arrows into a bag already bulging with knives and other weapons. Her auburn-red hair is tied up, keeping it clear of the short spear she wears strapped to her back. Cal wasn't lying when he told Lilac that she was a fighter.

"We should be going," Jander says to him—faithful Jander, never complaining—always ready for the next mission, however dangerous.

"I've never been farther than the mountains," Rhema announces with a grin. She almost bounced off the stable walls when Cal told her she'd been selected for the mission.

"Then you haven't lived," Cal tells her, swinging up onto his horse. He allows himself one last look up at Lilac's window, but it's still shuttered. She's not looking out at him, not waving goodbye. He'll have to carry the memory of her beautiful face with him, and hope the image won't be muddied by the anger of last night, or the pain of what she's going to be doing while he's away.

Chapter Ten

Lilac

Cal is gone. I know it the moment I wake, stupidly late. My ladies bustle in to pull back the curtains around my bed and the shutters at the windows, and a dull sunlight seeps into the room. He will be miles away by now, and I've missed the chance to say goodbye to him. Already I long for his touch, for the taste of his kiss.

Why did we have to argue last night and spoil everything? It's so utterly infuriating. And now he's ridden off with Rhema Cartner, not just an impressive fighter but a beautiful girl. He can't expect me to be sanguine about that. Cal is a young man, fiercely attractive, charismatic. She'll be in love with him before they reach the border, I predict, if she isn't already. And a long journey like this, a dangerous quest, brings people together. I know that better than anyone.

After my breakfast I feel listless, tired to my bones. I'm still not permitted to ride anywhere, and I don't have the spirit for a training session with whatever Guild member is left in the castle. I stand like a limp doll while my ladies dress me and do something elaborate and unnecessary with my hair. Morning drags into afternoon, and the sun begins its drift downward. I can't settle to anything; my mind is too feverish, bouncing from regret to jealousy to fear. Finally I can't tolerate sitting around anymore.

"Lady Marguerite," I say, summoning her from the corner where she's embroidering elderberries and holly on the hem of one of my nightdresses. "Please alert my guards. I'm going to visit the chapel."

The castle settles into gloom at this time of year, its galleries in permanent dusk. I make my way down the long staircase out into the brisk courtyard, still busy with training soldiers. Lady Marguerite walks ahead of me, in case I trip on the ludicrous velvet folds of my gown and tumble onto my face. The other ladies rustle behind me, hoods up to keep the draft from their cold noses and ears. We must look like a procession of pantomime monks, I think, on our way to prayers. We scuff through the yard's dirt to the portico, the guards keeping the servants and soldiers of the yard at bay, and one opens the heavy door to the tower.

My ladies, who always escort me to the chapel in a skirt-swishing battalion, remain outside. They arrange themselves on two benches outside the chapel's wooden door and I step in, throwing my hood back.

I have my own priest here, Father Juniper. He's soft-spoken and gentle, and although I resisted the notion of having a priest at all—it's the Montrician way, not the custom in Renovia—I soon found my visits to the small chapel in the tower a comfort. A distraction, I suppose, from the clamor of the court and all the people who surround us, fussing over us, every moment of the day, and month of the year. With Cal gone, Father Juniper may be the only person I can talk to.

The chapel itself is plain stone, its pillars white and smooth as bone. The ceiling is rounded and flawless: It reminds me of the moon on a clear night, and when I sit gazing up at it, I feel some kind of peace. The only seating there is a plain wooden bench, just for me. No one else uses the chapel, and Father Juniper always seems to materialize when I arrive.

A single taper burns on its golden mount, the one item of royal ostentation in the place. I know that Father Juniper will hear the clunk of the main door and slip in from his small vestry, the place he spends his days reading. Today I'm not sure what to say to him: He's not really a confidant, more a quiet presence who makes me feel some kind of peace. We'll pray together, perhaps, to Mother Deia, and in the murmur of our voices something will be offered up to the universe—a plea, a supplication, even if it's not an explicit request. Like *Bring Cal home*. Like *Ask Cal to forgive me*. Like *Save me from the duties of a royal bride.* The last is impossible, I know.

I settle on the bench, sniffy with the chalky dust in the air. The only window in the chapel is small and paneled, high in the wall. It's not usually dusty in here: Father Juniper keeps it clean, I know, but I heard that guards searched the tower last night and this morning, and they no doubt tramped in dirt from the yard.

The taper carries with it the scent of lavender and thyme. If I close my eyes, I can imagine I'm back in my aunts' herb garden, bees buzzing around me, on a sweet spring day in Renovia. If I could go back to my girlhood and its freedom, I would. But that's never possible: Life pushes us forward, into more complications than we ever imagined as children. Even when I first fell in love with Cal, I never imagined the pain we would cause each other or the obstacles we would face.

I look toward the vestry's door: It's painted white, to fit the rest of the chapel's plain décor, and is smaller than the main door. The arch shape reminds me of a shield. As though he can sense my gaze, Father Juniper emerges, a slender figure in his white robe.

"Your Majesty," he says in his soft voice, and bows his head. "I'm so pleased you've come. Shall we sit together?"

I nod, relieved to have his calm presence next to me. My ladies wind me up, I think, with their fluttering and gossip, their infernal deference. We sit looking at the taper, watching its narrow, dancing flame. Deia is light, I tell myself. She shows the way when all seems dark and mysterious. I pray to her for strength, and I pray for the villagers in Stur who lost their lives. The children trapped beneath the ice. The people washed away in the terrible torrent of melting snow. My personal unhappiness seems so selfish by comparison. I've been too petulant, I decide, the very spoiled royal I was always determined not to become. Yes, I miss Cal, but I have to think of others, not myself. I shudder. It's drafty in the room, the fire not enough to warm me.

We sit in silent contemplation for so long, I grow stiff on the bench and wriggle like a schoolchild.

"Your Majesty grows cold," says Father Juniper. "I'm sorry there is no fireplace here in the chapel. Or in my vestry where I read and write."

"How do you manage all winter?" I ask him.

"My own bedchamber is on a higher floor, and that has a large fireplace. As winter progresses, I spend more time upstairs, I confess, than down here. Every room up in the tower is like that—small windows but large fireplaces. In winter it is very comfortable for me, and for the scribes who live here as well."

"Yes! Daffran and his workers. I've heard about the sightings he reported. A gray monk, he says. But you've seen nothing of the sort, I trust?"

He shakes his head. "Nothing. We all hope that the scribe is, in this instance, mistaken. Certainly, the guards have found no evidence, and they will be searching the tower tonight, once again, and securing it. We feel quite safe here, I can assure you."

"Well, I've been told to trust no one," I say, and Father Juniper gives his shy smile.

"You can trust me, I hope," he replies. "And, Your Majesty, may I pass on a message I was given this morning, by the Chief Assassin?"

"Ah—yes," I reply, trying to steady my voice, though my heart is bounding and jumping like a fawn in the woods.

"He requested that I take care of you, ma'am, and I assured him that I would."

"Very kind." I lower my head, tears prickling my eyes.

"And he also wished you to know that he is praying for your safety, and will be conscious at all times during this mission of protecting you and ensuring you are both happy and secure."

I can't speak. I would squeeze Father Juniper's hand to thank him, but that would be quite the scandal in Montrice. Poor Father Juniper would probably jump out of his skin. So all I can do is send a silent message of thanks to him, and to Mother Deia, for giving me a moment of peace in an otherwise bleak day.

Chapter Eleven

Caledon

FOUR DAYS OF HARD RIDING takes Cal and his assassins across the border into Renovia—the place he misses, the place he grew up. The place he and Lilac met, and could have lived happily ever after, if her royal identity hadn't intruded.

The first swamps they encounter are so familiar to him—their mists and hollows, the fumes that rise from them late in the day, the long-legged birds stalking among the reeds, and the birch forests that stretch in every direction—Cal knows them as well. Sometimes, if the sun is at just the right angle, the birch trunks glow a ghostly white, imparting their own kind of magic. Even in winter there's a special kind of light here, one that doesn't exist in Montrice.

Knowing a place doesn't mean you can trust it, and Cal maintains his respect for the great emptinesses of the Kingdom of Renovia. Wild animals lurk here, unseen, and now, in the early winter, they're still active and already hungry. At night their screeches and rumbles echo through the trees. Some people call this the dead time of year, but Cal knows how much life, and how much danger, teems in these wild places.

At one point they ride close to the border with Argonia, but that realm with its great seaports and foundries, its elegant capital and courtly manners, may as well be thousands of miles away. Once the great swamp begins, civilization ends. That's what the Montricians think, anyway, and maybe they're not entirely wrong. After just a day riding through Renovia, the endless trees and marshy waters begin to look like a dream to Cal, a never-ending dream in which every other person has disappeared.

Almost every other person.

His two companions ride behind him most of the time, but sometimes they take the lead when the path ahead is clear. Jander says very little, and occasionally pulls over his bay mare to forage for berries or herbs. Cal never worries about Jander getting left behind or lost, because he has more sense about how to survive outdoors than the entire population of Mont. But there are dangers hidden in the trees that even Jander, with his sharp wits and natural knowledge, wouldn't be able to fight. In an attack, he'll need Cal and Rhema to step in.

Rhema. Sometimes Cal regrets bringing her. The first day of their journey, she was the girl who wouldn't shut up. She had so many questions, Cal wanted to gallop away and leave her behind. In fact, that was one of the reasons they'd made such speedy progress in Montrice—he didn't want to hear another word from Rhema.

Two nights of hard riding and sleeping in or under trees and taking turns to watch at night so nobody got mauled or pounced on seems to have knocked some of the chirpiness out of her. She's still, Cal muses, the one most likely to wander too far from camp or ride too hard in pursuit of some marshy phantasm.

"Chief," she calls. "Over there, due west. There's higher ground, just a patch of it. Maybe a good place for tonight, if you're ready to stop."

Cal doesn't reply, but he nudges his horse in that direction. Rhema can never wait for him to find the best route, or for him to find a place to rest. Her mind's always spinning, thinking about the next thing, the next danger. It's a good quality, he guesses, but an exhausting one.

"I'll ride on ahead," she says, passing him on her bay horse. Cal glances back at Jander, and the boy shakes his head, picking through the long grass on his own horse, suppressing a smile.

"At this pace, we'll reach Serrone tomorrow," Cal tells Jander, and he's right. Not long before nightfall the next day, the forest breaks and fields stretch before them, all the way to tumbles of houses, smoke wisps rising from every chimney, and the palace of Violla Ruza towering above them.

Rhema whistles with appreciation.

"Nice castle," she says.

"It's a palace," Jander rasps, and Cal is surprised to hear him speak about anything but directions or the weather. Maybe Rhema is getting on his nerves as well.

"Do we get to meet the queen?" she asks, undaunted by Jander's tone. "Or is it just you, Chief?"

"Just me," says Cal.

"I've heard about the palace windows," Rhema says. "One of the cooks told me that she worked in the kitchens there as a girl. She said that in the great hall of Violla Ruza, some of the windows have actual colored glass. Can you believe it? And there's a rose on each one, with three circles around them."

She was talking about the Renovian royal seal. Cal knew it well.

"The three circles symbolize eternity," he tells her.

"Shame it's not four. Four kingdoms and so on."

Cal picks up the pace. He doesn't want to think about the four kingdoms right now. They just remind him of dynasty and duty, and all the things keeping him and Lilac apart.

Lilac. It was in the palace of Violla Ruza that Cal first saw her in princess guise, rather than her other identity of country maiden Shadow. He'll never forget the day he was ushered into Queen Lilianna's receiving chamber, so ornate and intimidating. Giant doors with gold scroll handles, like something in a storybook. A high arched ceiling and tall windows. The queen sat on her throne, and next to her was the mysterious princess that few members of the public had ever seen. Lilac was impossible to recognize as Shadow: She wore a silvery white wig that resembled a giant cake, and a feathery white mask obscured most of her face. Cal didn't recognize her that day.

Sometimes he thinks he doesn't recognize her now.

The gates open for Cal: He and his assassins are expected, so Hansen's messenger must have arrived. Cal's humble apprentices, as he predicted, aren't permitted onto the palace grounds. They're hustled off to the stable block, and Jander, at least, seems relieved. They'll sleep tonight with a roof over their heads, after eating a supper they haven't had to kill or cook themselves. Cal's not sure how long they're expected to stay in the capital, but their horses certainly need a rest.

Jander and Rhema lead the horses to the stables, and Cal is directed to the palace. He asks for time to clean up before his audience with the queen, but her captain of the guard is insistent: Her

Majesty wants to see Caledon Holt right away, the moment he arrives in the palace grounds. Here Cal is conscious of his grubbiness, of the dirt crusted on his boots and in every crevice of his face, in a way that he never is in Mont. Maybe he cares less in another country. But Renovia is his homeland, and Lilianna is his queen. Before he was Lilac's right hand, he was the Queen's Assassin of Renovia, taking the place of his famous father.

His late father. What would Cordyn Holt say if he knew the kind of life that Cal lived now, as the secret pet of another man's wife? What would his father say about Cal's failure to stamp out the Aphrasian rebellion or find the Deian Scrolls?

It's strange to be back here inside the palace, entering its impressive entrance hall with the walls covered by portraits of the kings and queens of Renovia. Cal glances to his right, where the portraits of King Esban, Lilac's father, and Queen Lilianna, painted when she was a young woman, hang side by side.

He's startled to see that the small portrait of Lilac as a baby has been replaced with one of Lilac on her wedding day, in her crown and other finery, beaming with regal happiness. He almost stumbles at the sight. It's as if Lilac were in the room with him, but not the Lilac that Cal knows. In this portrait she's Hansen's happy bride, ascending to the joint thrones as though it were the thing she wants most in the world.

Perhaps she does, he thinks. Perhaps her life as Shadow was always just a dream, a play. In the hall here she's surrounded by portraits of her storied ancestors, all the way back to cruel King Phras with his pointed beard and narrowed eyes. The legacy of the Dellafiores is power, not love.

Not love with a lowborn assassin, that's for sure.

Guards lead him up the sweeping staircase and open doors after doors: The corridors in this palace feel endless, bright with the light from tapers. The flames reflect off the gold detailing along the floor and ceiling. It's a beautiful place, Cal thinks, and he's not surprised that Lilac finds the castle in Mont to be so dreary and uncomfortable by comparison.

The final set of doors swings open to an apartment that's well-lit and all white, even the floor. The Dowager Queen Lilianna is before him, and Cal drops to one knee, head bowed.

"Caledon Holt! Please, take a seat. The messenger from King Hansen arrived only late this afternoon, and he said you would not arrive until tomorrow at the earliest. We are glad to see you."

"We might have overtaken him, Your Majesty, as I am familiar with the Renovian landscape," Cal says, waiting until the queen settles herself into an ornate gold chair. He then sits down on another, and it's so soft he wonders if it's stuffed with goose feathers. "We had a good journey, a good ride. Myself and my two apprentices."

"Good, good." The queen sounds distracted. She is still a beauty, though of a more austere kind than her daughter. Her cheekbones are high and sharp, and her dark skin is luminous in the firelight. She still wears white, the color of mourning, though her husband has been dead for two decades. There's something sad about her, Cal always thinks. Perhaps she's lonely here in this sumptuous palace, her only daughter living in another kingdom.

"We're at your disposal, ma'am," Cal tells her, and the queen gestures to one of her ladies for what looks like a ragged piece of vellum.

"A letter," she tells him, "arrived today from the guards at the obsidian mines around Baer Abbey. Holt, the timing of your arrival could not be more fortunate."

Baer Abbey, the old Aphrasian stronghold. Cal braces himself for bad news.

"The guards report—in a very ill hand, I am sorry to say, barely readable—anyway, they report there have been some small but highly unusual events. Please read this yourself and see what you make of it."

She hands him the letter, and Cal struggles to make sense of the scrawl.

> *There is talk of strange noises underground. The men say it is a deep whisper, far below the earth. Well underground, and they are afraid to return to the mine. Also disturbing us are flashes of black lightning in the sky. These occur every afternoon. None of us have seen anything like it. No one will work, and most have left to return to their homes.*

"So now our Renovian miners have stopped removing the obsidian," Queen Lilianna says, her voice weary. "They have grown too afraid, and who can blame them? I believe that a similar black lightning was observed in the sky in northern Montrice, when that unfortunate village was flooded. It strikes terror into the hearts of our workers. News spreads fast, as you can imagine."

"Yes, Your Majesty. Even in a place like Renovia where roads are so few." Cal surveys the letter and its inky scrawl. Word of any new supernatural activity at the abbey may mean that the Aphrasian order—or whatever is left of it—has returned to the place they began.

"They attack in Stavin, then in Montrice, and now here," says the queen.

"Never in a town or city," Cal observes. "Only villages or out-of-the-way places like the abbey ruins."

"They risk discovery or interception in a larger settlement."

"Indeed, ma'am. But perhaps they're testing their strength before mounting a larger attack on a city."

"Or a palace." The queen raises her eyebrows. Sometimes she looks so much like Lilac. Cal wonders why the queen hasn't mentioned her daughter at all or asked for any word of her health. Perhaps she's making a point. Cal is the Chief Assassin, not an intimate of Queen Lilac's. Officially, they have no private relationship at all. Queen Lilianna has always been a stickler for protocol, alert to appearances. She was the one who insisted on Lilac's marriage to Hansen. Nothing is more important to her, Cal thinks, than restoring the primacy of the Dellafiore dynasty.

Not even her daughter's happiness.

"We'll rest overnight, ma'am, then be on our way."

"There is no time to lose," the queen agrees, and she stands, holding out a tapered, elegant hand for Cal to kiss. Still not a word breathed about her daughter.

Cal backs out of the room, and the large mahogany doors open as if by magic. This palace may be beautiful, but he can't wait to get down to the stables, to Jander and Rhema, and tell them about the next—and dangerous—step of their mission.

Chapter Twelve

Lilac

CAL HAS BEEN GONE FOR just a few nights, and I can't sleep, too restless and agitated to settle. In the fire tonight I saw a dancing vision, the flames shaping themselves into broken towers, like the silhouette of a ruined castle. At once I recognized it: not a castle, but Baer Abbey. Is this where Cal is drawn in Renovia? Is this where my mother will send him? Nothing good can happen in such a place.

My days seem so empty now that I can't look forward to holding Cal in the quiet hours of darkness. Rain falls in the courtyard, turning the dirt between flagstones to mud. Some of the recruits have already begun to march north, and more have taken their place in the impromptu training ground. The mornings are loud with their shouts and moans.

I'm in such low spirits that Lady Marguerite suggests I return to the chapel to see Father Juniper. Maybe he can give me wise counsel again, though he's unlikely to have another message from Cal. The messenger sent to Serrone has yet to return, and the Duke of Auvigne is sure he never will. Montricians like to think of Renovia as wild and dangerous. The duke would be amazed if he was to see our palace there, a place of beauty and refinement. Maybe there'd be less swagger in his step if he realized the sophistication of old Renovia.

Even my ladies are flagging, feeling the damp in their bones in this castle, swishing along behind me with little enthusiasm. It must be cold for them, sitting outside the chapel to wait for me, on those hard benches with no fireplace to warm them. I won't be long today, I tell them. I'll just spend a little time sitting with Father Juniper, hoping for peace of mind.

The usual herbal scent is missing from the chapel, as though it'd been closed up since I last visited. The taper is unlit. This is not like Father Juniper.

I sit on the bench and wait. Usually the priest is alerted to my presence by the sound of the great door opening and closing, but today he doesn't appear. Time passes in frigid silence. I don't want to call for him: This is a place of silence and quiet contemplation, not for an imperious queen summoning her servant.

I walk over to the small arched door to the vestry and place a gloved hand on it. At first I can't see any kind of handle, but on closer inspection I spot a narrow rail, also whitewashed. I was right about this door: It's solid and heavy, and I have to push hard to make it budge.

It opens with only the slightest of clicks, as I expect. Father Juniper always seems to emerge into the chapel without making any fuss. I never hear him scraping back his chair, or clearing his throat.

The room is cold, of course, because no fire is ever lit there. I expect to see Father Juniper sitting in his chair, hunched over a manuscript, or maybe even bundled up and dozing on this gloomy, wet day. But he's not there. When I push the door farther, it sticks on something. I have to wriggle into the room in order to step inside.

Not something, I see in a glance, but someone. Father Juniper lies faceup on the flagstones, his body still. Not moving, not breathing.

I drop to my knees and press my head to his bony chest, but I know from a glance that he's dead, and has been dead for some hours. His thin hands are stiff and frozen, and his mouth is wide-open, green eyes staring. There's a chalky blackness around his mouth, some kind of powder. When I bend to sniff it, there's no odor. It's not ink. It's not ash. But I don't dare investigate any further. Dear Father Juniper is dead, and I don't know why there's a strange powder on his stark white face.

I try to hold one of his hands, but they're too rigid now, not to mention cold. I want to sit there, sobbing in this freezing room, but that will do no good at all. I learned a long time ago that tears don't save lives. All they do is blur your vision. So I drag myself up and hurry back through the chapel. For once, my ladies can be useful. They can summon more guards, and fetch the court physician. They can send messages to the king and every member of the Small Council, to tell them that death has visited Castle Mont.

—•—

The court physician is named Martyn, and he's as round as Father Juniper was lean. He crouches by the body, sniffing at it like a cat who's caught the scent of a bird. His flowing gown is white and plain. I think that's one of the reasons I like him. He's not one of Hansen's usual courtiers, caring more about appearance than his profession. He's a serious person, particular about things.

"I'm not sure what to say, Your Majesty," he tells me. I'm seated on Father Juniper's chair, my hands trembling in my lap. In front of everyone else I must seem poised, more concerned than upset, but here in the small room with only the physician present, I don't have to hide my shaking hands or worry if I am tearful. The quiet of the chapel is spoiled by the guards and their thunderous footsteps, people coming and going. But here there's just me and Martyn, and poor Father Juniper.

"You'll take him away and examine him?" I ask.

"Of course, yes. It certainly looks like some kind of poison. But I've never seen anything quite like it. It will take time to determine what it is, and we must all be quite careful, for the residue could release further contamination." The physician sniffs at Father Juniper again. "It might be some potion of roots and herbs, but there is something else to its smell that I can't place. Earthy and damp, yes, but more like a feral animal than something dug up from the ground."

I sit forward, eager to hear more. "You mean it's more animal and less plant?"

"From the smell of it, more creature. Yes." He nods, and rocks back on his heels. "A strange thing. Impossible. Perhaps it is some kind of fungus."

"A magic thing, perhaps?" I suggest. "You don't think . . . you don't think the scribe really did see a gray monk?"

"How is it possible?" The physician shakes his head. "The door to the tower is guarded at all hours. The window in this room is small, and there is no fireplace. The only entry is through the chapel. Still, I will speak to the captain of the guard about searching the building again."

The entire castle has been searched daily, I think, and nothing—and no one—found, apart from an illicit litter of pups that one of the pages had hidden in the cellar, and a stash of summer wine, stolen from the royal stores, in one of the barrack rooms.

The physician stands, dusting off his hands. His nails are always short and clean; I've observed them before. I wonder if he'll bandage his hands before examining Father Juniper's body in more detail.

"The dark arts are not my area of expertise, ma'am," he tells me. "I can only work within the confines of the material world and my knowledge of the human body. When the material world is warped or infiltrated by greater forces, not subject to the usual mechanisms of my practice . . . well."

"Well indeed," I say. My aunts, Mesha and Moriah, would be able to help the physician, I know, though I don't say this aloud. One thing I've learned here in Castle Mont is that the powers of Guild women are not always respected. Sometimes, I suspect, they are feared.

"With your permission, we will remove the body from the tower to my chambers," the physician says. "My assistants and I will do our best to test this alien substance and solve the mystery of its composition."

"But not the mystery of how it might have been ingested," I say. "Or who might have administered it, and when."

Martyn says nothing for a moment. His eyes meet mine, and I realize we share the same guarded look, the same careful approach. Neither of us uses the word *murder*, even if that's what we're thinking.

"I can only diagnose and, if the patient is alive, treat him. If the patient is dead, I can look for causes, but not reasons. Or conspiracies."

"I understand," I say, getting up with as much dignity as I can muster.

"Any other investigation is the domain of the captain of the guard, Your Majesty," he says, and bows his head. "And at the behest of the Small Council. They're in session now, you know. After this . . . news."

I feel myself redden. This is insupportable. Irritation must have registered on my face, because Martyn bows again.

"I'm sure they assumed you were upset, ma'am, about the death of your priest, especially as you were the person to discover his body."

"No one," I say, in my most imperious voice, "should ever assume anything about me. I shall go to the Small Council."

The physician bows again, and I sweep past. I don't glance down at poor Father Juniper, because the sight of his rigid body and shocked face still has the power to upset me. If only Cal were here.

If only Cal would come back.

⚜

Chapter Thirteen

Caledon

At this time of year, the ride to Baer Abbey is a hard one. The ground is either frozen and hard to negotiate, or thick with mud, so it's even more difficult to make progress. Impatient Rhema learns the hard way that galloping can mean getting mired in the sludge, not to mention flecked from head to toe with dirt.

Rain starts to fall, so ice cold it's almost sleet. The raindrops feel like pinpricks on Cal's face, and even Rhema rides slowly with her head bowed.

When the path widens in a valley, Jander's horse appears alongside Cal's.

"A suggestion," Jander shouts; the rain is loud, pelting against the grass and trees, bouncing off the horses' backs. "We could turn at the end of the valley and stop at the cottage. They may have something we can use."

Cal nods. It's not a bad idea. The "cottage" Jander is talking about is the home of Lilac's aunts, Moriah and Mesha, surrounded by their gardens and apiaries. The women may have a spell or potion of some sort for them, something that can help them at the abbey.

Cal has a deep respect for Guild knowledge, and for the skills and intuition of the two women who raised Lilac.

"Lead the way," Cal shouts to Jander, wincing as sharp rain stings his eyes. It's too wet for further conversation, and Rhema follows Jander without question. She's new to Renovia and doesn't know the route they're taking to the abbey.

Perhaps, he thinks, it might not be a bad idea to sleep on the straw of Moriah and Mesha's barn tonight, rather than the damp ground. From here on there'll be nothing but forests, gullies, and swamps.

Although he can't see Jander's face, Cal knows the boy will be murmuring an incantation, in case the couple has a protective spell surrounding their cottage and gardens. Mesha, whom he recently learned is his aunt and his mother's younger sister, entrusted him with this Guild knowledge. Sometimes, Cal thinks, Jander's more her apprentice than his.

Whatever Jander is chanting must be working, because it's not long until a welcome sight emerges from the blur of gray: the gravel path winding to the little house deep in the forest, past lines of beehives and the orderly spread of garden beds, covered or tilled for the winter. Their cellars, Cal knows from memory, will be packed with dried herbs, sacks of potatoes and parsnips, dried meats and fruits.

"Where are we?" Rhema shouts, but Cal is already off his horse, throwing his hood back so the aunts can see his face.

"Cal!" Moriah is at the door, her smile wide and hair even more silver than the last time he saw her. "Come in, come in! Jander too! And . . ."

"Rhema Cartner, my new apprentice," Cal tells Moriah, and

doesn't miss the look that passes over the older woman's face. Something between surprise and suspicion.

After the horses are stabled, they all huddle in the cozy kitchen, drinking steaming cups of elderflower tea and enjoying cheese and bread and honey. Rhema gazes around her at the hanging dried herbs, at the bleached rabbit skull that sits by the basin.

"Aunt!" says Cal, still feeling shy, as he has not had family since his father's death, but Mesha gives him a solid hug and puts him at ease. Mesha fusses around them, picking leaves and twigs from Rhema's damp hair when she thinks Rhema isn't looking. Mesha's long braid may be almost white now, but she's no little old lady. Neither of them is. They're expert members of the Hearthstone Guild.

Jander looks even more pale and intense than usual, huddled over his tea. Though it was his idea to come here, Cal thinks, now that they're all inside the cottage, the boy seems uncomfortable.

"Cartner, Cartner," Moriah says to Rhema. "Any relation to Sarena Cartner?"

"My great-aunt," Rhema says with a proud smile.

"Ah!" Mesha exclaims. "A great Guild member too. A woman of knowledge. She visited Serrone once some years ago, to share with us the wisdom of the mountain regions of Montrice. Very interesting. Quite a fighter in her day too, I understand."

"She taught me," Rhema says. "It's because of her that I grew up wanting to be an assassin. I was always better at fighting than forest knowledge, but I do try to listen to the earth, and tune in to the messages of Deia. That's more Jander's thing, though."

"Dear Jander." Mesha squeezes his spindly arm. He murmurs something to her about learning how to make different kinds of poultices from ground minerals, to take with them to the abbey.

"Not the abbey again!" Moriah's face falls. "That place should be dug up, every last stone, and its underground passages blocked. It brings Renovia nothing but trouble."

"Too much obsidian there," Cal observes. "It's so valuable, the mining will continue. As long as it's not terribly dangerous."

"And it's highly dangerous now, from what we hear," Moriah says, her voice weary. Mesha and Jander have moved to the kitchen fireplace, where a heavy kettle dangles from an iron spit. She moves toward the shelves across, lifting clay pots from the mantel and uncapping them so Jander can sniff the contents. "Black lightning. I don't like the sound of that. Everything is getting worse again, just as we thought there might be respite from Aphrasian skullduggery for a while."

"We'll see what we find there," Cal says. He's distracted by Mesha heaving open the trapdoor to the cellar, and Jander clattering down its rickety steps.

"May I go down as well?" Rhema asks, curious as ever.

"Ah, no, dear," Mesha says, about to follow Jander. "It's very small and there's not really room . . . Just give us a little moment or two. We'll be back."

Moriah shoots her wife a bemused glance. Cal's less surprised. Mesha is a good judge of character, and she probably doesn't want Rhema with all her questions when she and Jander are discussing ingredients for a poultice.

"I didn't realize when we arrived that this was *your* house," Rhema says to Moriah. "The aunts of the queen! You're famous, even where I come from in Montrice, where very few outsiders visit."

"I wouldn't say famous," says Moriah archly. "We have very few visitors."

"But you know about the black lightning at the abbey," Rhema says, screwing up her face. Cal wants to kick her. Rhema needs to learn when to keep her mouth shut. "So someone must have come to tell you about that."

"We sometimes *receive* messages," Moriah says. She gives Rhema her most imperious look. "But that's different from hosting visitors. Like you."

"We won't trouble you much longer," Cal says. He doesn't want to postpone the ride to the abbey. At first light they should be there and ready to investigate, rather than lolling around a barn. They need to press on, however unpleasant the rain drumming on the cottage's thatched roof. He's edgy about what's waiting at the abbey but aching for some kind of confrontation—some kind of result.

"Are you sure you can't stay?"

"Her Majesty the Dowager Queen Lilianna wants us to reach the abbey as soon as possible."

And this house, he thinks but will not say, reminds him of Lilac in the days of her happy girlhood, when she could climb out the window and scamper through the woods, free as a bird.

Moriah dispatches Rhema to the root cellar to fetch more provisions for their journey, then unfolds a square of waxed cloth on the scrubbed table. She places two freshly baked loaves of bread in the center and wraps them.

"We've had no news from Lilac this week," Moriah tells him in a low voice. "Is there anything we should know?"

Cal shakes his head. "Nothing you don't know already, I'm sure."

"Really?" Moriah scrutinizes him. He can't meet her gaze. But he also can't avoid her questions. He's never been able to lie to the aunts.

"I believe," he says, "that the king and queen intend to begin a family."

Moriah seems unsurprised.

"Well," she says, and pauses. The faint sound of Mesha's voice downstairs merges with the rain and Rhema's rummaging in the cellar. "It's to be expected. Isn't it?"

Cal nods. There's nothing he can tell Moriah. Of course it's expected. But that doesn't make it any easier.

"You must think of your own future," Moriah says quickly, leaning close to Cal. "Your position means you must die for the queen if duty demands, but you should not live for her. I know you've sworn not to marry or beget children until your quest is complete, but when it is—and it will be, Cal, for I have faith in you—then, at that time, you should think of your own happiness, not just that of Lilac."

"I can't . . . ," he begins, but he doesn't know what to say. He doesn't know what Moriah is saying either. Is she telling him to marry someone else?

"You two may have promised each other all sorts of things," she whispers. Her blue eyes are kind, but holding her gaze makes him uncomfortable. "There are some promises that cannot, and should not, be kept."

"I don't see it that way," he says.

"Not now, perhaps. But if you return to the court to find the queen with child, what then?"

A lump settles deep inside Cal, its pain pressing hard at him from within.

"Think about your own future, Cal." Moriah pats his hand. "You're young now. Strong. But there are other possibilities for you, remember that. Other assassins, perhaps."

Moriah glances out the door. Rhema, he thinks. She's suggesting he transfer his affections to Rhema. Has she gone quite mad? He could never love anyone but Lilac.

If you return to the court to find the queen with child . . .

"We should go. Jander!" he calls. "Rhema!"

"Coming!" the girl shrieks from outside, and in a moment she's hurtling into the kitchen, holding onions and potatoes, a bag of carrots, walnuts, and apples swinging from her wrist. Jander emerges from below with his own sacking bag.

"And the rain seems to have stopped," Mesha says, stepping up into the kitchen and lowering the trapdoor. "The heavens are with you, for now at least."

Outside, fetched from the barn, the horses stamp and whinny, as though they know, as well, that this next phase of the journey will be crucial, as though they can scent a battle ahead.

"I was hoping you'd suggest staying here overnight," Rhema says, arranging the food sacks into side bags across her horse to keep them dry.

"No time," Cal says in a gruff voice. The days are short at this time of the year; after dark, they would make little progress in the marshes. In a few hours they'd need to find a dry place to camp, but those were hours they couldn't afford to lose if they were to reach the abbey soon.

"Jander! Take this." Mesha runs to Jander's horse and hands him a small bag of oiled cloth, bound with a dark ribbon. "Farewell to you all. Safe journey. May Deia protect you." She blesses and gives Cal a warm hug.

"And you," Rhema says, astride her horse now and tugging at its reins.

"Be safe, Aunt," says Cal.

Jander is looking at Cal, his serious eyes intent on him. Jander always knows when something is up. He is like the son Mesha and Moriah never had, attuned to the small motions and deep currents of the earth.

They ride away fast, as though they are being chased, and Cal doesn't look back to the little house or the women watching them go. The thundering of the horses' hooves on the hard winter ground helps drown out the ringing in his ears. But it can't do anything for the swelling anger inside him. Perhaps the aunts know more than they are saying, and that's why Moriah was telling him to turn his attentions to someone else.

Cal leans forward on his galloping horse, pressing the bay stallion's strong flesh with his knees. Dirt sprays up around him, and the cold wind bites at his face. Before them lies the darkness of the marshes, shadowy with wild animals and other unknowable threats. All Cal wants to do is ride and ride and ride. Anything that dares to cross his path won't last long.

He feels a feral surge in his body. He's more animal than person now, away from Lilac, away from the sham of their secret life together. It doesn't matter anymore if he makes it out of this mission alive. There's nothing waiting for him back in Mont.

Nothing and nobody.

Chapter Fourteen

Lilac

I march into the Small Council meeting, and they all seem surprised to see me. Except for Hansen, who is sprawled in the seat close to the largest fireplace, his dogs panting around him.

"Now that *you're* here," he says, his face relieved, "I can go. I mean, it doesn't need two of us, does it? Her Majesty knows much more than I do about . . . all this business."

This is an appeal to the Duke of Auvigne. The duke's pursed lips suggest he would much rather the king remain in the room.

"But, Your Majesty, please!" protests Daffran. His face is puffy and flushed, as though he's been crying. "You must take this matter seriously. I warned you all of a gray monk, and now—"

"Yes, yes," Lord Burley interrupts, with an impatient wave of the hand. "Don't hector His Majesty! He knows best."

Hansen has the grace to look sheepish at this. Even he would agree that knowing best is not one of his strong suits.

"I'm afraid that I have urgent business elsewhere," Hansen says, and nods to me. "Her Majesty is more than capable of representing our views and setting a course of action."

For him, urgent business means the stables or the dog kennels, I suspect, where a new horse or hound has arrived. The Winter Races loom, I'm told, though all these Montrician festivities are new to me. It's a series of horse races that sound chaotic and dangerous, and it's one of the highlights of my husband's year.

"The queen and I are in perfect agreement on all issues now."

He flashes a significant glance at the duke, who looks smug.

"We're on the same part of the scroll, as it were. Everything moving ahead with us in harmony on all things. Are we not, my love?"

I just look at him.

Hansen whistles to his dogs and they rise and stretch, shaking off sleep, tongues lolling. They're handsome beasts, really, but I hope they're more active when Hansen is out in the forest, riding to the hunt. In the castle they're like overgrown pups.

I take Hansen's seat and wave him away when he tries to push my chair closer to the table.

"Gentlemen," I say, before the Duke of Auvigne can launch into one of his pompous speeches. "As the Chief Scribe has said, something strange and terrible has happened in the castle. My personal priest, Father Juniper, has been murdered—"

"Found dead, Your Majesty," says the duke, because he can never resist interrupting me and showing the others that he knows better.

"Murdered," I repeat, nose in the air. "It has been confirmed by Martyn. There's a black chalkiness on Father Juniper's face that the physician believes might be a new form of poison. Or the result of dark magic."

I see the long glances exchanged between the duke and Lord Burley.

"Just as I warned!" says Daffran, indignant. "I told you that dark magic was afoot, and now we have paid the price for our complacency. Poor Father Juniper. Someone must have slipped past the guards. They should be put to death!"

"We can't afford to lose any more fighting men," the duke snaps. "The priest might have eaten bad food or inhaled some of that foul ink you all use. Maybe one of your scribes is to blame!"

"My scribes are men of the utmost integrity," Daffran says, his face shocked and his eyes, the color of weeds, bulging from his head. "I have been inhaling that foul ink, as you call it, for years, with no ill effects."

"Really?" The duke leans back in his chair. "There must be some reason all of you in the tower seem to be losing your hair."

"Gentlemen!" I say in my sharpest tone. "Whatever the cause, Martyn will identify it. But we appear to have a serious breach of security to confront. The sanctity of my private chapel has been violated. Someone close to me has been killed, not long after Daffran reported suspicious activity in the tower. We will investigate the murder immediately."

The duke makes a strangled noise that he pretends is a cough. I know that he would much prefer to be the one ordering investigations. He's used to Hansen being compliant and disinterested. Too bad. I'm not Hansen, and it's time I asserted my regal authority.

"If my own Assassin was here," I say, trying to keep my voice calm. "If he was here, he would be the most fitting person for this role. In his absence, we will have to make do with the captain of the guard. It's to him that my orders have been issued."

The duke's response is not at all what I was expecting.

"Very wise, ma'am," he says. "This is indeed a serious matter. Your safety is of utmost concern to us."

I make no reply. The duke is up to something. He's never agreed with me once since my marriage to Hansen.

"Utmost concern," Lord Burley echoes. "I'm so glad that Your Majesty grasps the peril that surrounds you."

"Surrounds *us*, surely," I say, and they all nod over and over, in an almost dizzying way.

"Surrounds me in particular, as I live in the tower," says Daffran. "And therefore I'm in immediate danger. Which everyone here seems to be overlooking. Not you, Your Majesty. Apologies."

"Earlier, when His Majesty was here," Lord Burley continues, "he told us the very happy news that you wish to begin a family as soon as possible. We are delighted with this news."

"Delighted!" the duke shouts, and Daffran jumps with fright at the noise of it.

"That is why it's essential that you remain in your chambers and venture no more to the chapel or the yard, anywhere you can be intercepted or attacked."

"You wish me to remain inside?" I can't believe my ears.

"It *is* getting quite cold," says Lord Burley, who always avoids discomfort. "It is much worse for you to be out of doors, with the rough soldiers—"

"And the gray monk!" Daffran interjects.

"And . . . anyway . . . I have quite lost my train of thought." Lord Burley scowls at the scribe.

"The point is," the Duke of Auvigne says, his tone wheedling, "that we are all eager, including the king, for Your Majesty the Queen to be well-protected at this difficult time. An heir means the cementing of our alliance. Just what the two kingdoms need at this difficult time."

Difficult time seems to be the saying of the day, I think, fuming. They're using the death of my priest to keep me in my chambers, a virtual prisoner.

"Rest assured," booms the duke, back to his usual domineering form, "that the Small Council vows to ensure nothing disturbs or threatens Your Majesties. Guards at the castle and outside your personal residences will be doubled. We will all be waiting—"

"For the captain of the guard to conduct his investigation," I say. They smile at me, patronizing, as though I were a little girl.

"For the happy news of an heir," says Lord Burley.

"They want to lock us in together until a child is produced? This is insupportable," I say. "What of the . . . what of the Winter Races? His Majesty will not allow those festivities to be canceled, however *difficult* the times may be. The people of Mont would resent any such curtailment of their annual pleasures and pastimes. And I cannot be locked in the castle if my husband attends a public event. It would look very bad to our people."

"Quite right," agrees Lord Burley. "An exception can be made for the races—don't you think, Auvigne?"

"If only by then we had happy news to share with the people of Mont," the duke says. He gives me that nasty teeth-baring grin again. "What a celebration that would be!"

"It would be far too soon to make such a delicate matter public!" I snap.

"So, we are not to discuss the gray monk anymore?" asks Daffran, and the duke gestures for him to be silent.

"The investigation has begun, as Her Majesty indicated," he says. "And now she and the king will turn their attention to happier matters. Their *immediate* attention."

Whatever strange battle we're fighting in here, I think I've lost.

Chapter Fifteen

Caledon

RHEMA IS ALMOST OUT OF sight, her auburn hair a flash of color in the foggy gray of the marshes. Cal is impressed with her energy, as well as her tracking skills. Even Jander seems impressed with her Guild training. Rhema may have told the aunts that she's a fighter rather than a tracker, and not skilled in nature the way Jander is, but now he sees that she was being modest. It's impossible not to admire the way she's able to listen to the earth, to read signs that are invisible to most other people. Despite her overabundance of energy, she's extremely intelligent, and now she seems to be talking less, asking fewer questions. Perhaps the prospect of a showdown with Aphrasians at Baer Abbey is preoccupying her. They'll all have to have their wits about them.

It takes Cal and Jander a half hour to catch up with her. Rhema wastes no time: She's tethered and wiped down her horse; built a fire on a small patch of dry ground, near a stand of old trees; and is gathering wood—kindling and logs for the fire and longer branches for a makeshift shelter. The night fogs here are damp.

Usually they stretch animal skins over a basic twig frame to keep dry while they sleep.

"You two are the slowest riders," she grumbles, dumping a bundle of kindling on the ground. Jander's still tending to the horses, the thing he likes doing best. When he's finished, he'll sniff out a spring so they have fresh water. Cal doesn't need to tell him; Jander knows what to do.

"No reason to get stuck in a bog," Cal says. He pulls out his ax to split some of the longer branches. "We know this region better than you do, remember."

"You keep saying," Rhema says, then stomps away, muttering under her breath. Rhema is spoiling for a fight, he knows, a real fight, not with some snuffling creature of the night, but with a shady Aphrasian or two.

If and when it comes time to fight, Cal knows that Rhema will be an asset. When the Guild suggested her as an apprentice, Cal had his doubts. At first he thought she was just a too-smart girl from the mountains with the typical Montrician arrogance. At her age, she couldn't possibly be expert as a tracker and fighter. But, like Shadow before her, Rhema has skills that belie her age. She's expert in sensing danger and smelling fear. She might not be very tall, and she's slim as a reed, but she's certainly nimble and tenacious. Rhema can climb a tree like a wildcat. Cal is certain she'll be able to fight like a wildcat as well.

It's hard to look at Rhema without being reminded of Lilac, back when they were roaming together. This would be the kind of mission the old Lilac—Shadow—would relish. But the new Lilac doesn't go on missions. She's queen of two kingdoms.

Cal is king of none.

By the time Cal and Rhema have a basic shelter in place, Jander is back with a bladder-skin bag of water and a handful of herbs to cook with what's left of the venison they were given in Serrone, along with one of the aunts' onions and the mushrooms he foraged earlier in the day. Rhema has plenty to complain about, but she never makes a peep about Jander's cooking.

They eat in darkness. Cal would prefer to eat in silence as well: He and Jander like a companionable quiet. But tonight Rhema is back to her old questioning self. With each day, as she grows more comfortable with Cal, she has more confidence.

"So," she says, after she's licked her fingers clean, "you told me about the black key you're carrying—"

"Nope," says Cal. "You assumed that. I haven't told you anything."

It's a piece of obsidian shaped like a key, but Rhema doesn't need all the details.

"Yes, you did. You've got a key that can open the Deian Scrolls, just in case we find them. Which is unlikely, but it would be brilliant if we did."

Jander winces at the mention of the scrolls. He has a vested interest in finding the scrolls and destroying the demon king, but at this moment they are there to investigate and quash any Aphrasian rebellion, yet again. The search for the scrolls remains there in the background, the thing that Cal has to do if he's to be released from his father's blood oath so that he can live his own life. He needs to be ready at any time, alert to the slightest hint, the most distant clue.

"I heard," Rhema continues, and then pauses. She's busy picking at her teeth with a hunting knife. "I heard that the key was discovered by Queen Lilac in Duke Girt's library. Is that true? She's a good fighter: I experienced it firsthand the other day. They say you've known her for a long time—is that true?"

"Bed for me," says Jander, standing up and stretching. He gathers food scraps and ties them in sacking, to be hung from a high branch overnight. There's nothing like food on the ground for attracting wild animals.

"Bed for us all," Cal says. There's no point in barking at Rhema to be quiet. That'll just make her more curious. The less she knows about him, the better.

Rhema gives a long sigh, to show Cal how frustrated she is with the blank wall he presents.

Frustration. Cal knows all about that. His whole life has turned into a frustrated quest, and he's been faced with one thing after another that he can never have or never find or never vanquish.

Another night without Lilac. She'll be in Hansen's bed by now. By the time he returns, she may be with child. She may even be a mother. Her fealty will lie with her family, no matter what her heart might want. There will be no way to deny her duty and her love. For of course Lilac will love her child, and in time, perhaps she will come to love the father of her child. Which means nothing, absolutely nothing, can ever be the same between them again.

Chapter Sixteen

Lilac

Lord Burley may look like an old man who finds it difficult to breathe and walk, but I see past all that. He's a cunning operator. He seeks me out in my apartments on some pretext—to reassure me that the captain of the guard is doing all he can, and so on. But we both know why he's here.

Because I've started playing *his* game. If it's too dangerous for me to leave my chambers right now, if I'm such a precious flower that I must be protected at all times, then I can act the part. I will pretend to be so shattered that I can do nothing more than languish. Such a delicate flower cannot be summoned to the king's bed.

When I heard he was on his way, limping along the long gallery, I had my ladies arrange me on the bed, as though I were an invalid who's too weak to sit up. At the last moment, Lady Marguerite draped a damp cloth across my forehead, for added dramatic effect. When Lord Burley clunked into the room, panting like someone who'd just climbed a mountain, he was forced to sit on a stool next to my bed and grasp my limp hand.

"It's so awful," I say, and sigh. "Since the death of Father Juniper,

I feel terribly sad. And worse than that, I feel scared. Truly scared for my life, and for that of His Majesty the King. I can barely eat or drink. Today I've had nothing but a spoonful of honey."

"Your Majesty, you must keep your strength up," he says in his wise-old-man voice. I don't think I'm fooling him, but that's all right. He can look at me reclining here, shaking with feminine terror, and know that I'm taking a stand, however short-lived it must be. It's about time he realizes I'm from Renovia, where monarchs hold the power, not Montrice, where interfering courtiers have muscled their way into high office. If I can't be a useful member of the Guild, on a mission or fighting an enemy, then I'm not going to be some decorative item in Castle Mont, to be moved around—or locked away—as the Small Council sees fit.

And if there's any possible way I can solidify my position as ruler here without sharing Hansen's bed and bearing Hansen's child, then I need time to devise a solution. I will not be hurried by a gang of old men.

So for now I must lie on my bed and play sick.

"You have seen the Chief Physician, I hope?" he asks.

"Oh yes"—I utter another theatrical sigh—"Martyn believes that peace and quiet is what I need at present, without any excitement or disturbance. After poor Father Juniper's murder, my nerves are shattered."

"Quite." Lord Burley nods and looks solemn. I assume he understands what I mean by "excitement." There's no way I can visit Hansen's chamber to start producing royal heirs, not in this—admittedly fake—state of nervous collapse.

"Bed rest and quiet, that's all I ask." I had no idea I was so good at playing a weak woman.

There's a knock at the door, and Lady Marguerite slips in, curtsying low to Lord Burley.

"I'm so sorry to interrupt, ma'am," she says. "But the physician has given us strict instructions to limit all visits to a few minutes. He is deeply concerned for Your Majesty's well-being and future . . . health."

I have trained her well.

Lord Burley is the one sighing now, sounding more grumpy than wheezy. He mutters something about my future health being of utmost importance to the two kingdoms and then creaks his way out of the room. I give a few pathetic coughs before the door closes. The only bad thing about this ruse, of course, is that I have to give up training and can't be spotted shooting at anything from my window. But this is a small price to pay for a reprieve from my "duty."

I wait long enough for Lord Burley to have stumbled his way to another part of the castle. The guards outside the door have strict instructions not to admit anyone apart from my ladies: I am sleeping now and not to be disturbed. The shutters have been closed across the window, and the only light in the room is from tapers and the flames twisting in the fireplace. The burning wood cracks and settles. I slip my feet into fur-lined slippers and wait in an armchair by the fire.

Earlier in the day, when Martyn visited me, he told me about an old woman named Varya. She often comes to the castle to bring herbs and poultices from her garden to the physician, and he summoned her after the death of Father Juniper to consult with her about the nature of the black powder and the possible sources of the poison.

"She is on her way to see me now," Martyn told me. "I feel she may have a greater sense of what caused the priest's death. Her knowledge is more ancient, shall we say."

That's when I realized this Varya must be a member of the Guild.

Lady Marguerite is instructed to do my bidding. After Lord Burley leaves, she scampers away to the physician's chambers to intercept Varya before she finishes her business there and departs the castle.

I would prefer it if Varya could climb the secret staircase to the Queen's Secret and tap on the door. This way the guards wouldn't see her, and no spies lurking in the gallery could report on a stranger's visit. But I'm mindful of Cal's instruction to trust no one, not even Lady Marguerite. She cannot know about the secret passage and staircase. Not yet, anyway.

Instead, Varya is to disguise herself by putting on the lilac cloak my ladies of the bedchamber wear on cold days. Anyone watching will assume she is a colleague of Lady Marguerite's, and that they are both on their way at my request. All Lady Marguerite knows is that Varya has come from town to help the physician.

"She is a skilled nurse and midwife," I say. "I wish her to consult with me as I prepare to begin the royal family."

The more people who think I'm planning to have Hansen's child, the better.

The time I spend waiting in that chair feels endless. I worry that Varya has already left the castle, or that they've been intercepted by the Duke of Auvigne and his spies as she follows Lady Marguerite up the stairs and along the gloomy gallery lined with paintings of dull old Montrician nobles.

At last the doors creak open and Lady Marguerite appears, another woman behind her. Both push back their hoods and stand before me. Varya is old but not elderly, I see. The physician exaggerated her age. She is slight with erect posture, her gray hair in a long braid, her gown the color of spring mud.

"Thank you, Lady Marguerite," I say. "You may go."

Lady Marguerite looks disappointed. Did she really imagine that I would have a medical conversation in front of her? Perhaps I should be concerned that she grows too bold in her intimacy with me and fancies herself more deeply in my confidence than she can ever be.

Varya stands quite still, saying nothing until Lady Marguerite has left the room. Then she takes a step closer to me.

"You look just like your mother," she says. No "Your Majesty," no curtsy. It's almost a relief after all the false fawning I usually have to endure in this place.

"You know my mother?"

"I've seen her rather than known her. I'll never forget the sight of her on her wedding day, when we all danced outside the palace of Violla Ruza, lavender ribbons in our hair. Everyone waving lilacs. I've never seen such a sight. She was so beautiful. She and your father were very much in love, you know."

"So I understand," I say. I don't remember my father at all. He died in battle, fighting the Aphrasians, when I was a baby.

"And of course I know your aunts," Varya says, her voice matter-of-fact, and I lean forward, surprised.

"Really?"

"Yes. I grew up in Renovia. Moriah and I turned thirteen around the same time, and she lived nearby. The stones were cast, and we knew what lay in store for us."

The Seeing Stones. I have so many questions for her.

"Please, take a seat," I say, and I draw up a small table between us for her stones.

"The stones were cast for me the night of my own thirteenth birthday," I tell her. "But my aunts wouldn't tell me what they said."

Varya smiles and raises one bushy eyebrow. "The stones may see, but that doesn't mean that we must tell. Each reader of the Seeing Stones must judge for herself."

"It disappointed me at the time," I say. I'm still disappointed, really. Aunt Moriah had drawn a circle with a chunk of coal, and thrown the smooth disks of translucent rose quartz onto the floor. I didn't understand their symbols, picked out in gold leaf. And I didn't have time to try to decipher them, because my aunt gathered them back into a pouch and refused to say another word. At that time, they wanted my destiny to remain unknown to me. They thought they were doing the right thing.

Varya settles back in her chair and closes her eyes. For a moment I'm afraid she's about to drift off into sleep, until she starts speaking in a low, steady voice.

"The Seeing Stones will not help us with this mystery," she says. "The stones see into the future, but we need to know the past. Who killed your priest? *What* killed your priest? Was this the work of man, or the work of magic?"

"The Chief Scribe believes he saw an Aphrasian monk in the tower a day or two before Father Juniper was killed. He swears to this, but nobody has found such a person. A gray monk, he says. The guards searched the entire castle, and the tower is guarded at all times. It was guarded on the day my priest was killed."

"And there is no other way in or out, I understand from the physician," she says, her voice soft. "Just one door."

"What should we do?" I ask her. The warmth of the fire is so lulling, and soon it feels as though some kind of trance is overtaking me. Varya leans forward and takes my hand. Her grip is strong and her skin feels surprisingly hot.

"What do you see, there in the flames?" she asks. "What do you see in the shapes of ash, in the points of light?"

We both gaze into the fire, and I try to focus. At first I see the usual colors—red and vivid yellow, a deep blue at the heart of the flame—a brightness that's almost white flickering like a spirit up the chimney. Then there's something darker, a shape rather than a color.

"You see it, yes?" Varya nods in the direction of the strange shape. "I'm not surprised that it's there, right in the heart of your private chamber, right in the center of your fire. It's a darkness that has infiltrated the castle."

"What is it?" I ask stupidly. We're still holding hands, and the heat has spread to me now as well. I can feel the warm throb of her pulse.

"I'm not sure," she says. "But I do know that it has the same shape of a man I have dreamed about for the last two nights. I wasn't surprised when Martyn sent for me to help examine Father Juniper's body."

"A man? Someone you recognize?" I stare again at the dark figure in the fire, but I can't make out any particular features.

"I'm not sure he's a real man. What was it that your scribe said? A gray monk? I've been thinking of this figure in my dreams as the Obsidian Monk."

As soon as Varya says this, I can see the shape of a hood in the fire shadow, the swoop of a gown. Among the bright colors of the fire, this darkness shines like a polished pebble.

"Does the man in your dreams wear a black mask, as the Aphrasians do?" I ask her, and she shrugs.

"The face is unclear to me. Or at least, the features look strange, not like those of a regular man. Perhaps he wears a mask."

"Could an Aphrasian monk—or a gray monk, an Obsidian Monk—really be at large in the castle?"

"Or perhaps he is a magic creation," she suggests. "That is why we see him, and then we do not. Why your scribe insists that he is there, but the guards find nothing."

I'm conscious now of a different sensation, a chill creeping up my legs. There's something about this shape in the fire that makes me fearful. I would smash it with the poker, the way I would an ember that's jumped onto the outer hearth, but I know it would do no good. The figure there among the flames isn't real. I suppose that is why it's so unsettling.

"Martyn told me something interesting," Varya says. She releases my hand and nestles back into her chair. "From the captain of the guard's report about the death of your priest. In one corner of the chapel they found a shard of black glass."

"Black glass? But Father Juniper wasn't stabbed."

Varya nods. "The captain decided that the shard came from a weapon used in the murder, but as you say, the corpse bears no stab wounds. The only thing the physician can find is the black marking around the priest's mouth."

"Made from black obsidian?" I ask, thinking of the monk in

Varya's dreams and the dark shape twisting in my fire. "But if obsidian is ground, it won't create a powder, will it? Or a poison."

"If magic is involved," Varya says, "anything is possible. Now, I should go, and you should return to bed. Too long a visit from me will raise suspicion among your ladies."

She stands, smoothing the dark folds of her gown. Nobody is supposed to stand before I do, but I like that she treats me as a fellow member of the Guild.

"Would you . . . ," I begin, not even sure of what I'm asking. "Would you . . ."

"Get word to your aunts? Of course, Your Majesty."

"I worry that if I write to them, the letter will be intercepted and read." I stand up, too, and draw my shawl around me. "I really don't know who to trust in this castle, and certainly I feel I can trust no one in Montrice beyond the walls."

Varya smiles at me, and I can see that she pities me.

"I see," she says. "Safer for me to carry word to your aunts of this Obsidian Monk than an official missive from you. I'll work out a way to do this. Don't worry."

"I really need their advice," I tell her, and now that I'm disconnected from Varya's hot touch, I feel shivery and almost tearful. Being near a wise woman from the Guild reminds me of the women I love and miss.

Varya drapes the lilac cloak about her, and waits while I climb back into bed. I have to resume my invalid's posture: It's my only weapon at the moment. She opens the door and I hear her speak, followed by Lady Marguerite's voice. The door closes again and I am alone.

It's such a relief to meet someone who knows my aunts. Someone who actually saw my parents get married. Renovia seems so far away—and with it my mother and my aunts. Cal. Everyone I love most in the world is there at this moment, and I'm stuck here, alone, in Montrice. I can't see a way out of any of this, especially when the figure of a dark monk dances in the flames of my fire, taunting me, taunting us all.

Chapter Seventeen

Lilac

Two days after Varya's visit, I'm rigid with boredom. I can't stand being cooped up. It's bad enough to be confined while actually sick, let alone when just pretending. I'm itching to take some exercise and practice shooting or fighting—anything but idling away one dim winter's day after another.

When one of my ladies flutters in to warn me that the Duke of Auvigne is approaching, I'm practicing spear thrusts by the fire. Since Varya's visit, I haven't seen the apparition in the flames again or heard any more about the shard of obsidian discovered in the chapel. When I asked for the physician to visit, he told me that no progress had been made with identifying the substance that killed Father Juniper.

Somehow I know that the duke is not visiting me to discuss the ongoing investigation.

There's not much time to strike my usual invalid's pose, and I have to dash to get to my bed. I lean back on the soft linen of my pillows, hoping my cheeks aren't too flushed with exertion. I've managed to kick the spear under my bed, and even if the duke spies it,

I hope he'll assume I keep it there in case I get attacked in the night, not because I like to rehearse my own attacking skills.

After the usual bowing and false, impatient inquiries into my well-being, the duke gets to the point.

"It has never been more important, Your Majesty, than it is now, with so many questions about the future of our kingdom—our joint realms, of course—and so many doubts about the security of our villages, not to mention the safety of your own person and the person of the king—"

I can't take any more of this waffle. "What has never been more important, Auvigne? Please get to the point."

He looks surprised at my question and indignant at the interruption.

"I mean the Winter Races, of course. I mean, Your Majesty." Another bow of the head, probably to hide his irritation.

"The horse races?" I ask. I have to pretend I don't really care about them, because anything that looks like pleasure for me ends up being taken away or canceled. And I don't really care about them, of course. When I first heard about them, I told Hansen they'd be more pleasant if they were held at a warmer time of year. Hansen was outraged. He bleated on about it being a tradition since his great-grandfather's day, and something that every Montrician from prince to peasant views with eager anticipation.

"As we discussed at the last meeting of the Small Council," the duke says, looking at me as though I've gone soft in the head, "I believe it's vital that we hold them as usual."

"I believe that I was the one who argued that very point," I say. If I irritate the duke, he irritates me twice as much.

"Quite true," he says with a grimace masquerading as a smile.

"We should not needlessly alarm the citizens of our capital city, as you so succinctly pointed out in our meeting. If we cancel the great tradition of the Winter Races, then we deprive our people of great pleasure."

"Not to mention depriving the king," I observe. Hansen loves horse races. He loves anything where he can place bets and—usually—lose money, anything where he can enjoy himself without being in personal peril or discomfort for a single moment.

The duke chooses to ignore my comment.

"It's also an opportunity for you and His Majesty to appear in public together, to reassure your people that you are safe and happy. Very much a united front. Despite—everything that has occurred."

"Of course the king and I will require extra guards and protection. It's unfortunate that you've sent the Chief Assassin away."

"We will ensure your safety," he replies with a bow. I decide to torment him some more.

"Though I believe it is my duty as queen to attend the Winter Races, and be seen at the king's side, you must understand that I remain quite unwell." I sink back into my pillows with a breathy sigh.

"I think you look very well indeed today," argues the duke. "Quite rosy in the cheeks, if I may be so bold as to venture the observation. And you may be a little fatigued by being cloistered here in your chambers, unable to enjoy the brisk fresh air. A change of scene, just for a short while, and the entertainment offered by the races—"

"Yes, yes." Of course I'm tired of being stuck inside. But the duke was the one who stuck me here and told me it was too dangerous even to walk in the yard. I'd rather be riding a horse than watching one race past me, but I can't pretend to be feeble *and* be seen galloping around the place.

"So it's settled," he booms, clapping his hands. The doors pop open, because the guards outside think he's summoning them. "We have just a few days to prepare, but that is a trifling matter. I will order the carpenters out immediately to build the usual scaffolds for seating."

Scaffolds make me think of a public hanging, but I don't mention this to the duke. He's cheered up considerably at the prospect of his silly race day. No doubt he has a new horse he wants to show off or a new lady of the court he wants to impress. And then there's Hansen and me, his puppets, to display to the public.

"You think they will cheer?" I ask him. "The king finds it very distressing when it is the opposite."

The duke turns red in the face.

"Anyone who demonstrates even the smallest amount of disrespect will be arrested and imprisoned," he says, his voice rising with anger. "I will not have it! Not in our own capital city."

"Very good," I say. "You must leave me this instant and attend to this important business of scaffolds and arrest. I just hope that I will be well enough to attend."

The duke stands by the open door, frowning at me.

"I would very much hope so, Your Majesty. We will have triple the usual number of guards in your detail. Anyone who dares to boo you or His Majesty—well, I shall run them through with a sword myself, on the spot."

"That sounds quite illegal," I say, and sink back into my pillows, starting up my usual fake cough.

Really, I do long to leave this room. The only things required of me at the races will be smiling and waving from the platform. Hansen and I can make a show of things, reassuring the suspicious

Mont public that the union between king and queen is loving, and that I am not a monstrous witch or a conniving outsider, but a dutiful wife.

How much longer I can postpone the actual duties of a royal wife, I don't know. I live day to day, waiting for the next terrible thing to happen.

Chapter Eighteen

Caledon

To the untrained eye, Baer Abbey looks like an overgrown ruin.

Cal's horse picks its way across slick flagstones that are tangled with withered vines. Jander is in the distance, near the riverbank, his own horse navigating a tumble of fallen trees. Impatient Rhema is off her horse and crouching on the ground, sifting soil through her fingers and sniffing.

Cal's already signaled to the guards, who huddle in a disconsolate group by the mine entry. As he makes his way toward them, their expressions—of boredom, anxiety, and relief—become clearer. Their uniforms are ragged and dirty. This is no crack team, he suspects. Out here, so far from anywhere, guard duty is a punishment, not a reward. Perhaps even a peril.

He questions them without getting off his horse. Cal likes the vantage point it gives him. He's had nothing but bad experiences at the abbey in the past—surprises, attacks, near-misses, condemned to imprisonment for assassinating a traitor.

"No miners here, sir," the stocky captain tells him. "They're too afraid. Packed up and left days ago. We've been waiting here for reinforcements, or you, sir."

Eight wan, grubby faces stare up at him. Like many Renovians, they know that Caledon Holt is the Queen's Assassin, the son of the great Cordyn Holt. Strange, Cal thinks, to be back in a place where his name means something. In Mont it was easier to hide, to slip in and out of the shadows.

The captain fills him in: One man was found in a mine shaft, savaged by some unseen animal. He was still alive when his colleagues came across him, blood dripping from his blackened face, but everything he tried to tell them, in blood-frothing gasps, was unintelligible.

"Looked clawed to death, sir, when they carried him from the mine. One of his eyes gouged out and a hand torn off. Horrible sight. None of the miners would go back down after that."

"You saw nothing down there when you investigated?" Cal asks, and the guards look sheepish. None of them will meet his eye. None of them, Cal realizes, look much older than Jander or much stronger.

"We went in," says the captain. "Well, we went in a short way, to where the body was found. The miners said they heard some kind of whispering deeper in the mine, where they'd been working. But we didn't hear anything. To be honest, sir, we didn't explore much beyond the place the body had lain. It was pitch-black and our torches kept blowing out. And we didn't have the . . ."

"The what, Captain?" Cal asks.

"The weapons, sir," replies the captain, head down. "It's a narrow space and . . ."

He can't finish, and Cal doesn't press. He has no interest in humiliating the guards. He's seen things before in Baer Abbey that no ordinary soldiers could fight.

Cal beckons Jander and Rhema over. All the horses are jumpy, sensing something they don't like—an approaching storm, maybe—because the sky has turned into a turbulent mass of rolling gray clouds. With an almighty crack, black lightning splinters the sky. Magic is still here at the abbey; the place is clearly potent with evil. The guards drop to the ground in terror. Rhema, hands on hips, whistles.

"Never seen that before," she says, sounding pleased rather than frightened. "Heard about it, but never seen it. How something can be both black and bright at the same time—wow."

The captain glances up at her. Yes, Cal wants to tell him, she's a strange girl. Strange is what he needs right now. Strange and brave.

Jander isn't wasting time: He's pulling a tinderbox from his saddle bag, ready to light torches. From the pouch around his neck he produces a white stone that's new to Cal.

"Mesha gave me this," Jander tells him. "If the torches go out, it'll glow."

"At last," Rhema says under her breath, just loud enough for Cal to hear. He knows what she means. After their long trek, it's time for a fight.

Before they enter the mine, Cal turns one last time to the guards.

"Don't think of taking the horses," he says to the captain. "They won't let anyone but their true rider onto their backs. And if you manage to rope them, they'll drag you to your deaths. They train with the assassins."

"Wouldn't think of it, sir," says the captain, and Cal wants to laugh. He's seen the soldiers eyeing up the horses, and they'd be fools if they hadn't considered plotting a speedy escape.

The three of them step into the entrance and clamber down steep wooden steps, Rhema leading the way and brandishing a torch. The passageway here is narrow, and Cal knows that below-ground here is a vast network of similar passages and tunnels. The flame flickers and buckles, threatening to blow out, but they still have light when they reach the first landing area. This is where the miner's body was found, and the flame picks out a wild spray of blood on the stone walls.

Jander, small and sharp-eyed, scours the area, running his hand along the crevice where wall meets dirt floor. Rhema sniffs the blood.

"Human and something else," she says. "But not an animal. Strange. Didn't they say the miner was killed with claws?"

"What looked like claws," says Cal. He's listening for the deep whisper that the miners reported, but hears nothing. It smells of damp soil and blood, and maybe rotten flesh. They're going to have to venture deeper into the labyrinth below the old monastery.

"Look," Jander says, walking into the light. He's holding something small in his hand. It looks like a tiny piece of coal, or maybe a lump of the obsidian that's mined in this region.

Cal steps close to Rhema to examine it. "Looks like a tooth?" he asks. "Maybe it flew from the mouth of a miner when the creature—whatever it was—attacked him."

"No, it's some sort of animal tooth," Jander tells them, and Cal realizes he's right. It's a blackened tooth that's much larger than any human tooth.

"Monster tooth," Rhema agrees, her face bright in the torchlight. "Definitely not human. Hey!"

She spins around and Cal is in shadow; he can't see past her.

"Black robe!" Rhema cries. She takes off at high speed, the torch flames dancing.

"Rhema!" Cal shouts at her disappearing back. This isn't the place to run off. It has all the twists and turns of a maze. But she's almost out of sight, so there's no choice but for him and Jander to follow in the twilight of her wake.

He can't see anything but Rhema's sprinting form ahead, but Cal can hear the fabled whispers now, louder than his pounding heart. It's like something between an incantation and the sound of a field of corn bending in a breeze. He turns a corner at high speed, bashing his elbow against a wall, and the whispers are now loud as a windstorm.

Black robe, he's thinking—is that what Rhema saw? An Aphrasian monk here in the mine?

They turn again and again, and again, the whispers echoing louder and louder. Cal can no longer make out the pounding of Jander's footsteps behind him. Rhema is a sliver, an arrow of light. That girl can run, he thinks. But what will she do when she finds what she's chasing?

The answer is around the next corner, where the passage hits a dead end. Rhema's not running anymore: She's cornered, flattened against one wall, sword in hand. A giant black jaguar, twice as large as an ordinary one, growls and paces, its eyes glowing amber orbs.

Rhema's torch flickers and dies, but Jander is there, right on Cal's heels. He holds up the white stone and the glow illuminates the cavern. The whisper Cal's been hearing, deep and urgent, is now a roar echoing off the walls.

This beast reminds him of the jaguar Lilac had to fight in the forest near the abbey, but even bigger. Its haunches are enormous, its head the size of a wagon wheel. Its gleaming teeth are longer than Jander's head, and sharper than their swords. It's more mythical creature than animal.

"Steady," Cal says in a low voice. "Stay still, Rhema."

"I thought I was following a monk," she says, eyes fixed on the beast. "I swear I saw his black robe. Then he transformed into this."

The creature growls again, then lunges at Rhema. Her sword is ready, but Cal can't see if she's managed to drive it into the beast. All he can hear is the cacophonous whisper and Rhema's scream. He plunges his own sword into the beast's neck and is conscious of Jander, to his right, clutching a fistful of fur and hauling his skinny frame up its back. Then he loses hold of the stone, which plunges everyone into darkness. Cal stabs again and again, the only thing in his line of vision the blackness of the animal and the viscous spray of its blood.

"Rhema!" he shouts, because she's not screaming anymore. The creature thrashes, and he glimpses Jander clinging to the scruff of its neck, then driving his dagger down in a straight line. Cal's close to the head now, close to the slavering jaws. His sword smashes into one of the giant gleaming teeth and bounces back with a clang. He has to aim higher.

Cal leaps with strength he doesn't realize he has, sword gripped in both hands. He's screaming now—not with pain but with fury—willing himself to land a blow that counts. With everything he can muster, Cal thrusts his sword into the beast's eye socket. It explodes into black pieces, sharp as hail: Cal recoils from the pain of the dozens of small hits.

With a hiss the creature shrivels and disappears. Nothing is left of it but black shards—obsidian, Jander says, picking one up with a shaking hand.

Rhema lies up against one wall, streaked with blood.

"I'm alive, Chief," she manages to say. "Don't worry."

"We're all alive," Cal says. His breath sticks in his throat. This was too close a call.

They stagger back to the entrance of the mine, Cal propping up Rhema. She's limping badly, and one leg seems pretty useless. Jander leads the way with the glowing white stone. Cal offers up a silent prayer of thanks to the aunts. Without that light, they would have had to fight the beast in utter darkness, deafened by the wall of whispers.

Outside, the guards are gone, but their horses are still there, whinnying and stamping. Cal ties a tourniquet around Rhema's leg while Jander busies himself making a poultice for Rhema's wounds: He grinds turmeric with witch hazel and other herbs that Cal doesn't recognize. He even grinds the blackened tooth they found in the mine and adds that to the mix. Cal doesn't ask him why. Jander has been alive for a long, long time and knows more about the natural world than Cal ever will.

Rhema's trying her best not to moan, but the grimace on her face shows how much she's hurting. Like Lilac, Cal thinks, back when she was Shadow and just as fierce and impetuous. She slumps on the cold ground, leaning against a fallen tree, and Jander hovers over her, dabbing at her cuts with the thick herbal paste. Rhema winces with every touch. Her left leg is going to need a splint, and Cal starts looking for wood to bind what might be a fracture.

The beast down in the mine was created by dark magic, he thinks.

They need to get out of this place, or at least regroup. If there's a legion of these dark beasts, all his skill as a fighter won't be enough to outwit the demon king's powers. One thing's certain: The Aphrasian order is living on, here at the abbey. The magic they're concocting seems even more powerful, even more deadly than ever. This time he and his apprentices have escaped with their lives, but they may not be so lucky again.

Chapter Nineteen

Lilac

On the morning of the Winter Races, the courtyard below my window hums and clatters with noise. My ladies and I watch the activity—guards marching, horses straining at their ropes, stable hands and tradesmen bustling about. It's a cold day, though the sun is bright, and the wind whips the banners positioned along the castle's battlements.

Some horses are being readied in their colors, the ribbons and saddle mounts that announce the identity of their owners. Lord Burley's horse, a chestnut with a bad temper, is dressed in red and gold ribbons, his colors of choice.

"Ostentatious," Lansha, one of my ladies, declares with a sniff. "He seeks to outdo Your Majesties, as though he's the most important personage in the land."

"If Lord Burley needs pretty ribbons to impress us with his power and authority," I say, "then I don't think we need worry about him."

They're laughing when a groom in royal livery leads a handsome white horse into the courtyard. It whinnies and tosses its mane, sparkling as though kissed by frost.

"Such a beauty!" Lady Lansha declares. "And such a present for you, Your Majesty, from the king."

I say nothing, though I like watching the horse stamp on the cobbles, asserting its place in this throng of men and animals. Yes, this is supposed to be my gift from Hansen, as I learned first thing this morning, and it's about to be decorated with lilac ribbons and a lilac sash that swoops over its sleek belly. But I know that it's the Duke of Auvigne who bought me the horse. Hansen would never think of such a thing. He's too wrapped up in his own horses, not to mention placing his own bets. I don't think it would enter his head that I might like a horse to race on my behalf, or that it would be a political act to have a gift from the king decorated in the queen's colors. We haven't spoken a word to each other since the day I attended the Small Council, and then took to my bed. He must think I'm really ill, because he hasn't bothered me once with his demands to begin a family, and beget a miniature Hansen or Lilac.

Another horse is led into the courtyard, this one as black as mine is snowy white. It's a handsome beast, with powerful haunches and a long, proud face, but something about it unsettles me. The gleam of its hide reminds me of the obsidian found in the chapel, and the shining dark figure that materialized in my fire.

"That's a fine animal as well," I say. None of my ladies reply. Each one is quiet, gazing out the window. "Don't you think? To whom does it belong?"

More silence, and a few uneasy glances exchanged. I have no idea what's going on.

"Is it the king's horse?" I persist. That would be a neat pairing; my white horse, his black horse, racing against each other. My ladies say nothing, but I see another groom approach with a tray of ribbons to decorate the bridle. Hansen's colors are green, taken from the Montrician coat of arms with its three pine trees. He loves green, he told me once, because it reminds him of childhoods spent at the summer palace high in the mountains, and the rustle of the trees in the forest surrounding them.

The ribbons used on the black horse aren't green: They're black.

"So if it's not the king's horse, whose is it?" I ask. "Come now, ladies—I seem to be talking to myself."

After a few more significant glances, Lady Marguerite clears her throat.

"I believe," she says, "that the black horse belongs to Lady Cecilia. Cecilia Bedyne."

Lady Marguerite looks back out the window, trying to avoid my eye. The others are all transfixed, it seems, by the activity below.

I know exactly who Lady Marguerite is talking about. Hansen told me he planned to cast off Lady Cecilia, to give her up as his mistress, so he and I could Do Our Duty. Now I know why he hasn't come knocking at my door. The casting-off has yet to take place.

"The black ribbons," she says. "They are her color."

"A severe color for such a young woman," I suggest. Something is seething within me, more than irritation. Not jealousy—of course, not that. How are we to give a public impression of unity when his mistress is so obvious to everyone at court? Why is he buying her a horse as fine as the one he gives the queen? I was wrong when I thought that Hansen had grown up and understood the political ramifications of our public behavior. He's still a stupid boy, reluctant to give up his favorites, whatever he tells me.

"She thinks that black flatters her fair complexion," blurts one of my younger ladies, Fiar. "She thinks it makes her look more pale and ethereal."

I've seen Lady Cecilia: She's certainly a beauty, and she's certainly fair-skinned. She looks as though she'd never spent a day outdoors in her life. I wish her no ill, and in different circumstances I would be glad for her keeping Hansen distracted. But these are not normal times. The people of Montrice are looking for another reason to turn on me. Without Hansen's support—in public, at least—I'm stranded and exposed.

"I had no idea that Lady Cecilia was so wealthy a woman," I say, trying to keep my tone measured. "That horse is very fine—even more fine, I think, than my own. She is young, and her father is a gentleman, but not rich. How do you think she could possibly afford such an animal?"

Silence again, interrupted only by the crackle of the fire, and the noise of men shouting and hooves clopping in the courtyard.

"It's possible," says Lady Marguerite, sounding hesitant, "that the horse was a gift to Lady Cecilia, Your Majesty."

"A gift?" They don't even murmur in response. "Hmm."

Of course that fine black horse is a gift from King Hansen to his favorite. Now I understand why the duke bought me a horse and tried to persuade me it was from the king. Otherwise today would have been too humiliating—the ribbons of the king's mistress decorating the most handsome horse, and the queen with no animal and no colors at all.

We're spared more of this conversation by the arrival of Hansen himself, bursting into my apartments with a ruddy face—suggesting he's already been drinking—and a wide smile.

"Come along, my . . . ah, dear," he says. He's wearing the most extraordinary costume of green trimmed with delicate lace, sleeves slashed to reveal bulges of linen and mink. Drooping from one sleeve, I notice, is a black kerchief. Hansen never wears black. This must be a love token from Lady Cecilia, a reminder of whose horse he must cheer for when the races begin. Another humiliation for me. Does Hansen have absolutely no sense of propriety? I can only imagine his rage if I acted this way in public with Cal.

My ladies arrange my sweeping train and fur-lined hood so I can descend the stairs in the most impressive manner possible. The cloth of my dress is lilac, naturally, and the white flowers from the Renovian coat of arms are embroidered along the hem. My kid gloves are soft and white. I feel like slapping Hansen in the face with them.

But I understand restraint, even if he doesn't. I grit my teeth and take his proffered arm. We walk out of my chamber and along the gallery, flanked by armed guards and trailed by an excess of scurrying courtiers. Anyone watching would think we were the picture of an elegant and devoted married couple.

"I know you were lying to me," I hiss at him. "About Cecilia."

"No idea what you're talking about," he whispers back.

"No idea about a certain black horse with black ribbons, and the black rag you have dangling from your sleeve?"

"It's not a rag." He's hissing now as well. "It's a linen handkerchief."

"Dyed with badger fur? Or maybe pig blood?"

"What is wrong with you?" He jerks his arm to pull me closer.

"We're supposed to be doing that united front thing today, smiling so the people don't, you know, rebel. Or feel afraid of black fingers breaking ice lakes. Or talk about *lilac frost*. You know."

"All I *know*," I almost spit into his ear, "is that you gave me a big speech about making personal sacrifices. But what you really meant was that I had to make sacrifices, and you would just carry on with your life. And with your mistress."

Hansen pouts. We're walking down the grand stairs now, the cold wind from the courtyard blowing toward us. This wasn't quite the fresh air I'd hoped for.

"What, you've just discovered that life is unfair? That the virtue of the queen is more a concern for the people than the virtue of the king?"

"Stop tugging my arm," I snap. I don't even care if the guards can hear our conversation. "And stop making a fool of me. I'm the queen of my own realm, not some consort you've married to be a broodmare."

"I love it when you talk about horses," he says. We emerge into the courtyard, and the gathered crowds—soldiers, servants, courtiers—sink as one into curtsies and bows. This gives me a moment to adjust my face into a smile, though I hope it doesn't look as pained as it feels.

"By the way," he whispers, while we head toward the iron portcullis of the castle. The portcullis creaks as its chains are cranked up, protesting with groans and squeaks. "Now that you're up and about, there can be no more excuses. Tell your ladies I will be paying you a visit tonight."

So now I understand why the Duke of Auvigne was so keen to hold the Winter Races this week. If I'm well enough to process through Mont with Hansen, then I'm well enough to share his bed. The thought of it makes me feel sick.

Hansen coughs, and I dig my fingernails into his arm. If he feels anything, he doesn't betray it. This is, perhaps, the first act of physical bravery in his entire life.

Chapter Twenty

Lilac

It's bitterly cold out on our scaffold, even with burning braziers creating a fiery barrier behind us, even sitting on thrones draped in fur. I'm still ready to snap at Hansen, because he is so duplicitous. He keeps his mistress and orders me to his bed, just another woman he can control and manipulate.

I also resent being made the object of court pity. Everyone sitting around us knows why Lady Cecilia is simpering and fluttering her kerchief at the black horse. At least nobody is booing us today. The people of Mont really do love their horse races, and for a few hours, at least, they can forget that a Renovian witch sits on the throne next to their beloved King Hansen.

Before the races can begin, we have to sit through an endless parade of horses and riders, of marching guards with their banners and swords. The seats for the people of the court have been built above a fountain—currently frozen over—in Mont's largest square, which has a ten-foot-tall statue of the young king. This is the start and end point for the final race, I'm told. We won't see most of the running, but Hansen cares only about winning, not about the race itself.

People hang from windows around us, and crowds line the streets that radiate from the square, packed tight and held back from the impromptu racecourse by guards. Hansen and I smile and wave, and I try not to shiver too obviously. The streets have been scrubbed with salt, to prevent the horses from slipping if ice forms, but the waiting crowds are stamping their feet from the cold, huddled under hoods and coats, clearly eager for the races to begin.

Early on, Hansen leans over me, as if sharing a secret with his beloved wife.

"You need to smile more," he murmurs, and then lifts one of my gloved hands to kiss it. A half-hearted cheer rises from the people stationed closest to our dais. "You look as though you just ate something rotten."

"I *married* someone rotten," I reply through gritted teeth, trying to turn it into a smile. Hansen sighs. He waves up at the people packed into windows in the tall stone houses that surround the square, and they wave back. I understand what he meant when he told me that the people of Montrice have always loved him. Long ago he was a golden-haired child who rode his pony in this very parade. Now he's their handsome king, as excited as they are about the races.

I'm alert to the noise of the crowd, listening for any boos or shouts about the tragedy in Stur. The Duke of Auvigne, sitting nearby, has one hand on the hilt of his sword, ready to make good on his promise to see off any sedition-spouting onlookers. Daffran sits in the front row; he seems to have nodded off. I doubt that horse racing is his thing.

"Where's your son and heir, sire?" a woman calls from a nearby window, and Hansen laughs. This is how he's playing it, I see. "Montrice needs a young prince again!"

"You hear that, my darling?" Hansen leans toward me again. I'm conscious of the black kerchief peeping from his sleeve, and wonder how many others around us notice it—and know what it means. "They love me here, and now they want another, just like me."

"Surely one of you is enough, *darling*," I reply, and the grin on his face is so smug and irritating that I can't help myself. I tug the kerchief from his sleeve and use it to dab my lips. "You don't mind, do you?"

Hansen's smile disappears, and I can see he's struggling not to snatch the kerchief back. I toss it to the ground next to my temporary throne, out of reach. It's petty, I know, but I feel he's driven me to this. They've all driven me to this.

Of course, these people—the duke, the courtiers, the ordinary folk of Montrice—don't care if Hansen has one mistress or ten. Kings are allowed to have mistresses, but queens cannot stray. That's the rule. Kings need to have heirs, and everyone needs to know that those heirs are legitimate and not the children of some handsome Renovian assassin.

Cal. I wish I knew he was safe. Our messenger returned from Serrone to say Cal had made it there and had an audience with the queen, my mother. He headed off for Baer Abbey, where trouble had been reported at the obsidian mines.

Baer Abbey, the most dangerous place in Renovia.

While I'm fretting and anxious, I can't help making things worse.

Rhema Cartner. Why did Cal have to select her, of all possible assassins, to accompany him and Jander? She's young and ambitious, just like the girl I used to be, agile and smart, ready to fight, quick-witted. If Cal forms a bond with her during this mission, it wouldn't surprise anyone, least of all me. Perhaps one day he might choose to marry her. He could never marry me.

Now I have to struggle not to cry. The cold wind bites at my cheeks, and I pull the hood closer to my face. The sky's blue is cruel, promising sun but delivering no warmth. I've changed my mind: I'd rather be in my chambers watching the Obsidian Monk dance in my fireplace than out here in the frigid town square, pretending to be happy.

The races begin, the first set with groups of six horses and riders, colored ribbons fluttering, each jostling for position before they take off around the square and then down a narrow street that leads toward the river. People are packed too tight in these streets, and collisions are inevitable. During the second race, screams and gasps filter up to us, along with the wild neighing of a horse.

"Someone's got squashed!" shouts the Duke of Auvigne, as if this were the happiest possible outcome. Last year, my ladies have told me, three onlookers were killed and two horses needed to be put down. The duke was delighted. Montrice is a strange place. I had no idea that horse racing could be a blood sport.

The sun is low in the sky before the final race is scheduled to begin. I know that my new white horse will be racing, and I assume that Lady Cecilia's black horse will be running as well, because both animals have yet to make an appearance.

What I don't realize until the crier makes the announcement is that they'll be running head-to-head, with no other horses in contention. It's also been decided, at the last minute, that they'll be making six circuits of the square, rather than dashing through town like the others. The horses are expensive thoroughbreds, and I wonder if neither Hansen nor the duke wants to see his investment run into an unruly crowd down by the riverbanks.

"Six is my lucky number," Hansen informs me. He's spent much of the afternoon alternately crowing about the winning horses on which he'd placed bets and sulking after the races when his pick lost—or, in one case, not finished at all. The rider straggled up the hill without his horse, and the lord who owned it looked furious.

The white horse and the black horse, ribbons fluttering and riders crouched low on their backs, stamp and circle at the start line.

"That's my horse!" Lady Cecilia cries over and over, in case anyone could have any doubt. "His name is Raven."

Raven—Raven—Raven: The name is passed through the crowd, and I can hear it murmured from all sides of the square.

Lady Cecilia is entirely dressed in black apart from a green sprig pinned to her hood—obviously a reference to Hansen and his own royal colors. I hope my own white horse flies around the course like a blizzard, beating every possible record.

"What's your horse called, my dear?" Hansen asks me, pretending to be interested.

"The winner," I reply, and he looks away. I hope he's placed a lot of money on Lady Cecilia's horse, and that he loses every penny.

Even before the race begins, it's evident that the crowd has decided to cheer for Raven rather than my horse. The murmurs have grown into shouts. There's no doubt who the people of Mont are supporting in this race. It's the black horse that belongs to a minor member of the nobility, not the steed in the queen's colors. They have not forgotten the attack in Stur and the way I was implicated. They still don't trust me, let alone love me. If I need any proof of the lack of affection for me here, the lack of respect, then today's providing it yet again.

Off the horses race, clattering on the stones of the square, necks stretched forward. The corners are dangerous: Both horses skid and slide, and the crowd gasps. I rise from my seat, too excited to sit still. The horses are fine runners, and they're neck and neck for the first circuit, the second circuit, the third. The crowd is still calling out to support Raven, but horses, I've long believed, don't care much for what people think of them. They race because there's a wild spirit inside of them. They race for the thrill of the gallop. They race because they want to be the fastest.

By the fifth circuit I think the horses must be tiring. Their riders are hanging on, gripping the striding, leaping bodies. Raven's rider almost falls at one corner, then my horse's rider almost slips off at the next. I can't hear their pounding hooves anymore; the roar of the watching crowd drowns them out. There's nothing between one horse and the next. This race will come down to the final moments.

But on the sixth circuit Raven pulls ahead—not even by a length, but enough to win. Hansen is on his feet as well, bellowing and whooping. I wish I'd given my horse a name, so I'd have something to shout, but all I can do is watch and will the white horse to win. Win, win, win.

"Come on!" I call, though I know the horse can't hear me. Raven pulls even farther ahead, and now there's only one corner left. If my horse doesn't overtake the black horse here, it's all over.

The final moments of the race play out like a dream—a bad

dream, a collective dream—that all of us gathered here are forced to witness. On the last corner, just before the final stretch, my horse rears up and throws the rider to the ground. He bounces on the hard stone and rolls into the crowd.

"Yes!" shouts Hansen, because this means the race is over. All Raven and his rider need to do is cross the finish line. The white horse is disqualified. I flop back down on my makeshift throne, trying to compose my face. I must appear to be a gracious loser.

My horse is still running, because it doesn't know the race is lost. I squint at it, then blink, because I seem to be seeing things. The white horse is changing color. Its lilac ribbons and the binding for its racing saddle drop to the ground, as though someone's untied them. The horse is gray; now it's the color of a bruise, the color of a rain cloud. It has four legs; now it has eight legs. Now it's lifting off the ground, swirling through the air toward the black horse and its rider.

We can hear the black horse's hooves now, because everyone in the courtyard has fallen silent; there's a jumble of voices from people stationed in the streets, but they sound distant, unformed. My white horse is a horse no longer. It has transformed into a whirling tornado of iron-like claws, dark and furious, spiraling toward its opponent.

I stand up again, and Hansen clutches at my arm, mouth hanging open. The clawed tornado thumps into the black horse, and the rider is hurled high into the air. With a sickening crack, he lands on the stones. The black horse is no longer running—no longer standing. Strips of black flesh and bloody innards fly through the air, and people begin to scream. The black horse is decapitated and its head lands at the feet of Lady Cecilia. She shrieks, a bloodcurdling sound, and falls away in a faint. The Chief Scribe has collapsed as well, and Lord Burley is on his feet, moaning and swaying, propped up by attendants.

What we're all witnessing is sickening, extreme. It's impossible to make sense of it. The black whirl of the tornado slices through every piece of the horse. Strands of its tail and mane float through the air like spring pollen, and people duck to avoid it or scream as a piece falls onto their clothes. Moments ago two horses were racing. Now there are no horses. One has transformed and enacted terrible violence on the other. Raven is in pieces now, his huge heart lying on the cobbles, still throbbing: It is purple and grotesque.

Hansen is looking at me, his eyes wide with horror. Neither of us can speak. Some people are running away, scattering; some are screaming or crying. Around me the people of the court are on their feet, except for the prone Lady Cecilia.

They're all looking at me. The foreigner, the interloper, with a horse that's turned into a terrible demon. And I know, without anyone saying a word, that they think I'm behind this attack, and that the dark magic of this afternoon is my monstrous creation.

Chapter Twenty-One

Lilac

Nobody wants to go near the shredded and broken body of the dead black horse. What remains of its corpse lies in pieces, strewn around the square, as though the body were attacked by a thousand knives. The dark tornado that was once my white horse has disappeared. No one saw where it went. Maybe it dissipated in the chilly air, an apparition. An obsidian cloud.

I'm shaking, struggling to pick a strand of horse hair from my mouth. The dais where we've been sitting is dusted with these black strands, thick and tasting of dust and death. Hansen stares at me as if I were some terrifying stranger. There's a glob of horse blood on the white froth of lace at his throat, and when I reach over to brush it away, the blood smears the fabric.

"I had nothing to do with this," I say to him in a low voice, and take his hand. He doesn't resist. I wonder whether he's scared of me now. I have no idea what we do next, what happens next, how we make sense of everything.

The Duke of Auvigne looms behind Hansen, his face thunderous. I refuse to let him blame me for any of this. He was the one who brought the horse onto the castle grounds. I refuse to let him have the first—or last—word.

"Auvigne, where did you get this horse?"

"I . . . I . . . ," he splutters. "It was brought to my home by a traveling horse dealer. My marshal and the farrier were impressed with the horse and wanted us to keep it, but then His Majesty needed something for you . . ."

He looks at Hansen, his mouth open, unable to finish his thought. Hansen is speechless. Perhaps both the duke and the king are starting to realize how implicated they are in today's events. How they've been used by the darkest forces of magic and have allowed them to infiltrate the castle.

And now around us there are angry and confused people—courtiers, guards, the citizens of Mont. Men, women, and children—terrified by what they've witnessed and terrified because the black magic that killed other Montricians in the north has exploded into the capital city. Once again, it involves me.

Some have fled, but there are still thousands of people in the streets. They've come for a day of pleasure, and instead they've been confronted with something bloody and mystifying. A crowd this scared and unstable might riot. I feel the glare of eyes on me, the hostility of a people who've never warmed to me, people who want answers for the violence they've seen. Perhaps they see this as a show of power—of black magic—by an unloved queen.

"We must return to the castle," I say to Hansen. "We need the guards around us—a double guard. We need the utmost protection right now. Do you understand?"

Hansen says nothing. He and the duke are both useless. Lord

Burley is slumped in his seat again, weeping as though he were under personal attack. If enemy troops had charged us in the square, the duke would have risen to the occasion, I'm sure, with sword in hand, shouting orders to the guards. But a magic force can't be fought with a sword or an army. The duke doesn't have the knowledge of the Guild or their insights. He can't take on the Aphrasians, who must be responsible for the terror today.

If only Cal were here. He would know what to do. He would protect us.

A woman's voice near us moans in a spine-chilling, otherworldly way: It's Lady Cecilia, on her feet now, but supported by other ladies of the court. The moaning changes into a hiccup-sob, and even a few bursts of hysterical laughter. She's splattered with blood and gore. I can't ignore her, though Hansen is doing just that. She's supposed to be his favorite, but he seems unconcerned by her fainting spell, or her behavior now. What's happened here at the Winter Races has entirely unhinged Lady Cecilia.

"Witchcraft!" she shouts, tearing at the black ribbons tied around her wrists. "No . . . no . . . my lovely horse. No! Killed my horse!"

"Can't you do something?" I ask him, bending close so nobody else hears. Hansen looks dumbfounded.

"Didn't you see it?" he replies. "Something bad killed the horse."

Hansen is white and shaking, oblivious to the cries of his favorite, oblivious to the people watching him. His last ounce of courage, of presence of mind, has gone.

"Witchcraft!" Lady Cecilia shouts again, so loud that people still in the square can hear her. The whisper of "witchcraft" moves through the crowd and down the lanes. Someone boos, and a moment later I can hear hissing as well. This is not good. If Hansen is useless, and the duke is blustering, I need to take charge of this situation.

"The guards," I say again to the duke. "Rally them, this moment. The king needs their protection. And someone must remove Lady Cecilia before she incites the crowd."

The duke signals to the guards, and I see my own Lady Marguerite with her arms around the sobbing Lady Cecilia, hushing her and attempting to lead her away.

"In addition, we need immediate help from Renovia," I tell the duke, my voice louder than I intended. "You must send for my aunts. They know how to deal with this black magic."

"If it is magic—" he begins, and I hold up an imperious hand.

"Clearly it is magic. This is no time for arguments. There are no 'ifs' about any of this."

I wish I could demand the immediate return of Caledon Holt as well, but I don't dare. Even with Hansen in this pathetic state, trembling with fear and shock, I can't push it too far. He and the duke might think I'm behind this in some way, using the knowledge I learned from the Guild to summon a demon. All just to get my Chief Assassin back in Mont.

If only.

"Guards!" I say. The duke is just standing there, looking unhappy while the boos and hisses of the people mount around us. So much for his promise to run through anyone who disrespected us with his sword. "Rally to us. Rally to the king!"

The guards hurry into position, forming a barrier around me and Hansen, a walking shield. Hansen is still a quivering wreck. He's grown up too sheltered, never exposed to anything more dangerous than hunting wild boar in a party of armed men and baying dogs. He's never had to fight in his life, and he's never been directly exposed to black magic. I'd feel sorry for him if he wasn't my idiot husband.

"Hold on to me," I hiss at him, linking my arm through his and wedging my body against him.

"Didn't you see . . . didn't you see . . . ," he mutters. He's shaking, and his face is deathly pale. I have to keep him on his feet and moving, even if it means dragging him back to the castle.

"I saw," I tell him. "Everyone saw. Come on, Hansen, you have to walk. We must get to safety."

"It wasn't a dream?" He turns his boyish face toward me, and I feel both impatience and pity. "And you saw?"

"One step, please." He's tall, but I'm strong, despite too many days languishing in my chamber recently, pretending to be ill. "Please, Hansen. You're the king. I'm the queen. We must return to the castle. Now."

I feel like I'm speaking to a child, and at last Hansen complies, like a little boy agreeing to go to bed. He leans on me and somehow we manage to move, the guards shuffling around us, weapons drawn. The walk back to the drawbridge feels endless—cold, damp, slow. I keep waiting for the noise of the crowd to abate, for their angry boos to fade. But even when we're in the castle and the portcullis is lowered behind us, I can still hear the rage of our people. Everyone is frightened. Now no one feels safe.

"What's to be done, Lilac?" Hansen asks me, his earnest tone out of keeping with his usual glib, smug self. He's lost his swagger and his clothes are a party costume—foolish and out of place—in this more dangerous reality.

"I don't know." I'm being honest. At this moment I have no idea what happens next, or what we should do. Wait for reinforcements, I want to tell him. Wait for guidance. Our world here in Mont is shot through with darkness, and none of us in the castle, with all our weapons and horses and arrows, are strong enough to fight it.

The Royal Palace

- Violla Ruza, Renovia -

To Her Majesty the Queen Lilac R,

My darling girl, I am writing in great haste. The messenger is already on his horse, waiting for this letter to be placed in his hand.

Something terrible has happened. Our beloved Violla Ruza palace has been burned to the ground. I was woken late last night, quite overwhelmed by smoke, and taken to Liona Manor as a place of sanctuary. From here I can see smoke hanging like a dark cloud over Serrone. The high turrets are completely gone. The air smells acrid.

I'm told that our citizens in the capital and surrounding villages are confined to their homes, with the royal guard enforcing a curfew. Surely this is the work of the Aphrasians, who grow bolder and more violent by the day. I have summoned Caledon Holt from Baer Abbey to investigate this fire.

The council believes this place is no longer safe for me. I can see no other choice but to return to the land of my birth. Please expect me in Mont within the week.

These are not the circumstances in which I imagined our reunion.

Your loving mother,
The Dowager Queen Lilianna

— II —

The White Against the Gray

Chapter Twenty-Two

Caledon

As long as he can remember, the white stone palace of Violla Ruza had towered over the rest of Serrone, its royal banner snapping in the wind. Now all Cal can see is smoke and charred remains, the famous turrets collapsed like children's blocks. Jander, Rhema, and he approach the capital from the west. At every hamlet and village they pass, people stand outside in silent awe, gazing at the pall of smoke clouding Renovia's most famous landmark. The palace has fallen.

The three of them ride in silence, mouths covered with cloths to keep the smoke at bay. What is there to say? Cal knows that something like a kitchen fire, or a knocked-over taper in a stable block, wouldn't be enough to fell the entire complex. This is a work of arson, complex and well-planned, ensuring utter devastation.

Queen Lilianna spoke of this when they met just a week ago. The Aphrasians were growing bold again, she said, and though their recent targets had been small settlements, there was no reason to think they didn't have larger prizes in mind.

Perhaps all the soldiers at Castle Mont made this kind of attack too difficult to execute in Montrice. So instead they'd struck at the heart of Renovia, the center of power for the Dellafiore dynasty. It was just luck that Lilac's mother had survived. Many of the palace's hundreds of other inhabitants were not so lucky, trapped in burning turrets or smoke-filled cellars.

As they near Serrone, all traffic is traveling in the opposite direction. The merchants and townspeople are leaving, their own homes destroyed or scorched, the air of the capital no longer fit to breathe. Cal passes wagon after wagon heaped with whatever the citizens of Serrone could salvage from their houses, stalls, and workshops. Some people sit or lie on the wagons, their burns bandaged. Almost everyone is coughing or wheezing, sad and afraid. Richer inhabitants rattle along in carriages, even though some of those carriages are scorched or missing doors or pieces of their roofs. The fire is an equalizer, Cal thinks, voracious and all-consuming. It doesn't care if the houses it burns belong to a lord or a peasant, the mayor or the rag collector. Neither did whoever lit the fire—or fires. They wanted to destroy Serrone and its palace and its inhabitants. And its royal household, most of all.

Wintry rain begins to fall, ice cold, and at least, Cal thinks, that will tamp down whatever is left of the embers in the palace ruins. The fields that surround the capital are gray with ash and littered with debris. Their horses pick their way along the slippery cobbles of the roads up the hill, along streets that Cal can barely recognize. The market square is a jumble of collapsed roofs and rafters, the doors in any remaining building black with soot. The gleaming white capital now resembles a rotten tooth, black as the one they found underground at Baer Abbey.

The gates to the palace are melted and twisted, like jail bars bent by a giant. Cal signals to one soldier picking through rubble near the old guard's box. A white cloth is tied around his arm, and at first Cal thinks it's a bandage. But it's tied over his sleeve, and that's when Cal understands: It's a makeshift version of a white mourning ribbon. The entire place is in mourning.

"Your captain?" Cal calls, and the man shakes his head.

"Missing, sir. Half of our number are gone. The sergeant left with Her Majesty, to escort her to safety."

"To a manor house, yes?"

"On their way to Montrice now, sir. To her daughter, in the capital."

"Who is leading the operation here?" Cal asks. The guard gazes up at him, his face gray with ash.

"You, sir. We've been waiting for you to get here."

Cal mutters an oath under his breath. The name of Holt is still a potent one in these parts.

Jander and Rhema are still silent—expected for one, but not in character for the other. They must be overwhelmed by the sight of this devastation. Cal stays on his horse, so he can better survey things, but it's hard for the creature to find a way through the tumble of stones and burnt wood.

Cal remembers what his father told him of the war against the scheming monks that followed King Esban's death. Queen Lilianna was in grave danger then too. The Aphrasian rebels wanted to eliminate the entire royal family, including the baby Lilac, Crown Princess and sole heir to the Renovian throne. That time they failed. Maybe this time they'd succeed.

He circles his horse back to face Jander and Rhema. The lingering smoke stings his eyes, and he has to squint to get a good look at them. One of Rhema's legs is still bandaged from her encounter with the beast at the abbey, but she hasn't complained once, even when they removed the splint so she could mount her horse for the journey back here. She's tough, Cal thinks. And maybe she came too close to losing her life—so close that she's a little chastened now. Fighting in the castle yard is not quite the same as taking on a magical creature with claws like knives, and teeth as sharp as swords.

"We can't stay here long," he says, and draws his horse closer to theirs so he doesn't have to shout. Smoke rises like steam around them, pelted by the cold rain. "There's nothing we can do but organize the recovery squads and any parts of buildings that remain standing."

"Didn't the queen want you to investigate?" Rhema asks, wincing and shifting in her saddle. It's been a long, cold ride to get here.

"We'll talk inside," Cal says in a low voice, leaning toward them. The main entrance to the palace is still intact, though above it the higher stories have burned through to a charcoal-and-stone skeleton, and the charred great doors that Cal stepped through a week earlier are wide-open, revealing what's left of the sweeping staircase. They ride their horses in, the animals negotiating the outside stairs—slick with rain and ash—with some difficulty. He never thought the day would come when he'd ride into Violla Ruza rather than walk. The marble floors are smutty and cracked. Rain falls through a jagged hole in the ceiling, and Cal can hear crows cawing and swooping overhead.

"Look," Rhema says, nudging her horse farther into the cavernous space. She's pulled down her mouth covering: Damp ash is smeared across her face. "The paintings."

Paintings of royal Renovian ancestors still hang in place, but the canvases are torn and the paint blistered, the faces now unrecognizable. The gilt frames are intact, so it looks as though someone held a flame to each one in turn, making sure each image was destroyed. The effect is eerie.

Jander is shaking his head, his horse stopped. He has one hand pressed to the cloth covering his mouth. They can't stay in there long, Cal knows. As well as rain, there needs to be a strong wind to carry this foul smoke away.

He follows Rhema along the line of portraits, stopping where she does, in front of the last, hung near a blown-out window. It's the portrait of King Phras.

The picture is completely unharmed. The gilt frame is yellow as the sun. His sharp face glares out, marred only by drifting ash. It's been left by whoever burned the palace, whoever took the time to destroy each of these paintings in turn, wiping out the image of every Dellafiore ancestor.

A message from the Aphrasians, Cal thinks. A message of intent.

He pulls on the reins of his horse and wheels away from the painting.

"This is a sideshow," he tells the others. "We have to go."

"Go where?" Rhema asks, an edge in her voice. Maybe she thinks they're returning to the abbey and its underground horrors.

"The queen is on her way to Mont," Cal says. "The royal families of both kingdoms will be there together, with us away and most of the guard already headed north. We can't waste time here."

Rhema turns her horse as well, her face still pinched with pain, but with a new blaze in her eyes that Cal hasn't seen over the last few days.

"Let's get these squads organized," she says. "And then we ride. We can sleep on the horses if we need to."

Cal manages a grin, but there's nothing in this burned-out, defiled place to bring anyone any happiness—anyone but Aphrasian rebels, neither dormant nor hidden any longer. He is about to defy an order from Queen Lilianna to investigate the destruction of her palace. But if Cal's mission in life is to defend the crown, he needs to follow the crown to the place where it's in imminent danger. The assassins have to get back to the Montrician capital before it's too late, and—like Violla Ruza—Castle Mont is burned to the ground, too, with the entire royal family in it.

Chapter Twenty-Three

Lilac

For days I've been waiting for the thunder of horses riding into the courtyard, and the creak and sway of the Renovian royal carriage, and here it is, at last. My mother is back in Mont—safe and sound—if any of us can be considered safe these days.

It's strange to think of Mont as being familiar to her. Long ago, she was supposed to marry the Crown Prince of Montrice, Hansen's own father, and this castle would have been her home. But instead she eloped with my father, and the story of the four kingdoms changed again. All these years she's been the strong presence holding wild Renovia together. But now she's had to flee, and the dream palace of Violla Ruza, in all its towering beauty, is gone. Nothing lasts forever. Like Baer Abbey before it, Violla Ruza is a heap of ruins. The Aphrasians have had their revenge at last.

It's a cold day and the sky is heavy, threatening snow or icy rain. I pull up my fur-lined hood and lean out the window, my ladies begging me not to lean too far or expose myself to the cool wind. I ignore them. To see the Renovian carriage clatter in, with its gilt and purple decorations—not to mention the coachman's livery—is a welcome sight. It's selfish to be pleased that my mother is here, given the circumstances, but I'm desperate to see someone who I know is on my side.

Lord Burley has sent word that he will greet my mother and then escort her directly to my chambers. There is no need, he says, for me or the king to expose ourselves to illness and discomfort by loitering in the courtyard, slipping around the icy cobbles. I protested, but was overruled.

"There is the issue of your safety, Your Majesty," he said, with one of his obsequious bows, and I couldn't argue with that.

So instead I lean out the window, the tip of my nose icy, and peer for the first glimpse of my mother. She emerges from the carriage in her usual elegant way, though she must be stiff from the long journey in such inclement weather. Her flowing robe is purple as heather, a woven wool that's one of the specialties of Argonian craftsmen. Her hood falls back, and I can see the glint of silver in her black hair, the warm honey of her dark skin. Even exhausted and anxious, my mother is always regal.

I want to shout to her, but she wouldn't approve of that kind of behavior. I'm not a farm girl anymore. Instead I have to make do with leaving my apartments and rushing down the long gallery, past the dreary portraits of inbred Montrician ancestors, and enjoy the flurry of guards and ladies who sprint along with me. We all tumble to a halt at the top of the grand staircase, to wait for the dowager queen.

"You shouldn't be out here, you know." It's Hansen, arriving from his own apartments. He has twice my entourage and twice my guards. He's also wearing twice the amount of clothing: For someone who loves riding through damp forests, Hansen really does hate the cold. A fine woolen scarf is wrapped around his head and neck like some strange, bulky kind of bandage. "We've been ordered to stay put."

"Orders you haven't obeyed, either," I point out. I haven't seen Hansen since the incident at the horse races. We've kept apart in some kind of unspoken pact.

"I wanted to greet the dowager queen," he says, and sniffs in a theatrical way. Perhaps he's been ill. Half my ladies have had colds, but all that powerful herbal medicine fed to me by my aunts when I was growing up has made me hardy and resilient, unlike these feeble Montrician nobles.

"As ever, we think alike," I reply, and I smile, but Hansen doesn't smile back. I wonder if he's ashamed about how he crumbled at the races, so terrified he could barely walk. Or perhaps he's scared of me, convinced—as so many others here seem to be—that I'm the source of all the dark magic.

Downstairs there's the noise of doors opening and closing, guards smashing their spears on the flagstones, and—from outside—a half-hearted attempt at a fanfare on a single hunting horn. Castle Mont really is in disarray these days. My mother enters and begins to climb the stairs, taking her time rather than sweeping up as she always did at home in Violla Ruza. There the grand staircase is marble. *Was* marble.

My mother wears her hair in a simple bun rather than in her more usual elaborately pinned braids. Her smile is weak. She's tired, I think. Sick and tired.

I drop into a curtsy and my ladies follow suit. I glimpse Hansen bowing, but it's not a deep-enough bow for my liking. When my mother pauses at the top of the stairs to curtsy, an impressive puddle of regal purple in this bleak taper-lit gallery, I can barely wait for her to stand again so I can embrace her. Meanwhile, Hansen seems to think protocol has been observed and looks eager to return to the warmth of his chambers.

"Welcome, twice welcome, Your Majesty," he says, the words sounding stilted, as though he were reading a prepared speech. Hansen was too spoiled as a child and took over the throne on his father's death without sufficient preparation. He can only ever manage the most basic of civilities. "You are most welcome here. Please treat this castle as your home. Because, you know, your own home is . . . is . . ."

My mother waits to see if he's planning to finish his sentence. "Burned to the ground?" she offers, and he nods, with what he no doubt imagines to be a sensitive grimace.

I hustle past him to embrace my mother. She pats my back rather than hugs me, conscious as ever of public shows of affection. When we kiss, her cheeks feel cold. Her hands are cold too. It's the worst time of year for such a long journey.

"I'm so relieved that you've arrived safely," I tell her, and lead her back to the warmth and privacy of my own chambers. Hansen makes no attempt to follow us, and I'm grateful for that. For now, our courts can continue to remain separate. Our lives can continue to remain separate.

"I thought we would never get here," my mother whispers, leaning into me. The silver in her hair looks painted on, like lacy frost on winter trees. "I was fretting the entire way. The countryside in Renovia is a sad sight, the roads thronged with people and all their belongings."

"People from Serrone fleeing the capital?" I ask her, and she nods.

"I wonder whether many will move to Argonia," she says, "abandoning Renovia forever. Many seem to be headed here to Montrice. Our kingdom will struggle to recover from this blow."

"At least you're here and you're safe." I touch her arm, and try to sound reassuring. But I don't really believe this. None of us are safe—not here, not anywhere.

In my chambers, the queen mother and I settle by my fire. She doesn't say anything, of course, about how rustic it is here, but these are not the fine royal apartments she's used to in Serrone. I'm conscious of the dark wood on the floor and the walls, and the wooden shutters hung within the window casements to keep the draft out. Everything is fine here and well-made, but it's not the marble and gilt of Violla Ruza, or the gleaming white stone of the palace buildings. Montricians care more about their personal finery than their homes, spending a fortune on wardrobes and wigs. There's no stained glass here, no polished timber from Argonia. There's money here in Mont, but little elegance.

Then I remind myself that everything I remember of the finery of Serrone is gone. The palace is destroyed. It's hard to believe. When my mother talks about being awoken by swirling smoke, and how her ladies and guards risked their lives to get her out of the palace before the roof caved, it sounds like a bad dream.

I dare not mention Cal's name, though I know she had an audience with him after he arrived in Renovia, and in her letter she said she was summoning him to Violla Ruza to investigate the blaze. He must be there now, I think, with Jander. And that Rhema Cartner. The thought of fire reminds me of her hair, the same color as flames, but more beautiful. I wonder whether Cal finds her beautiful.

I'm startled back to my mother's story by the mention of his name.

"At least Caledon Holt is in Renovia," she says, pulling her robe tight to keep out the draft. The shutters are not quite as effective as they might be, especially on these windy winter afternoons. "He will find the culprits. I cannot understand how this could happen while Violla Ruza was so well-guarded. Either the ranks of my guards were infiltrated or powerful magic is to blame. The Aphrasians grow very bold. This business in Baer . . ."

"What business?" I sound overeager, I know. My mother's eyes narrow. She is always measured in the way she speaks and the way she moves. I wonder if she still disapproves of me, in a way, and thinks I rush about too much. But my wild childhood, growing up with my aunts in the countryside, was her decision, not mine.

"The mining at the abbey has been abandoned. A miner was killed there and I still have no intelligence on the cause. Holt was sent to investigate, but of course when the palace burned, that took precedence."

Baer Abbey. The place is so potent in my memory that its very mention makes me shudder. I think about the day I stumbled upon it, out on one of my illicit adventures. I had a vision of the great battle there where my father died at the hands of a monk in a black mask. And I almost met my own end there as well; I was about to be run through with a sword when Cal saved me.

I knew exactly who he was, though I'd only glimpsed him in the flesh once before, at his own father's funeral. Cal was famous already, despite being so young, and I was just Shadow, afraid of getting into trouble with my aunts.

My mother is talking about black lightning strikes seen at the abbey. I need to pay attention rather than drift off into my own memories, into events that were such a short time ago, really, but feel like an eternity away now.

"The guards sent me reports of black lightning, which I found to be impossible to fathom. They've never seen such a thing in their lives, and neither have I. But it has such similarities with that horrible incident in the north of Montrice, and the King of Stavin had told me of such things as well. You have seen it here?"

I tell her about the bewitching of my horse at the Winter Races, and how it hacked another horse to death. My mother shakes her head, her hooded eyes almost closed.

"Aphrasian magic is infiltrating Mont," she says. "And once again, my darling, you are its target."

"But who could possibly think I would be involved in burning down Violla Ruza?" I ask her. "Why would I want to destroy the palace where my mother lives, where my parents were married, where my own portrait hangs on the wall?"

My mother leans forward to take my hand. This is a rare act of affection from her, and it reminds me of sitting with Varya and seeing the vision of the Obsidian Monk in the fire. Unlike Varya's hot hand, my mother's is cold and limp. I know she loves me, but she's never been demonstrative. Luckily, I grew up with plenty of hugs and kisses from my aunts.

"Such strange times," she says at last. "Rather than attack you directly, the magic has been used against you in a more sophisticated way. But this attack on our palace is something quite different, I agree. I'm sure the Chief Assassin will have his theories when he writes to me. We must wait and see."

Waiting. That's all I do, I think. Wait for good news, bad news, any news.

"This attack at the races," my mother continues. "How is the king taking it?"

"He's afraid . . . and confused, as we all are. If the Aphrasians want to get rid of me, then why target those around me, like my priest or a horse in a race, instead of just attacking me directly?"

"You are better protected, perhaps," my mother says, dropping my hand. "In the meantime, you are made to look culpable for what is happening. Enmity is stirred between Renovia and Montrice. And Renovia and Stavin."

"When Hansen and I rode out to villages this autumn, the crowd turned against us. Well, against me, really. They see me as a foreign witch, rather than the queen."

"So," my mother says. She looks me straight in the eye with that intense gaze of hers. When I was a girl, I thought she could see into my mind and read all my rebellious thoughts and shortcomings. "You must understand how important it is for you and the king to form a strong bond, a strong marriage. The aim of such dark magic may be to persuade the king to reject you and cast you aside. Aphrasians won't want you to bear a child who unites Montrice and Renovia. This is just the way they reacted when your father and I married, and had you. Violence was unleashed throughout Renovia. Remember, the Aphrasians are the sworn enemies of the Dellafiore dynasty."

While my mother talks, my heart is sinking. My mother may have married for love, but I wasn't permitted to. Everything to her is about the dynasty, the succession, the political alliances. There's no way I can tell her how strenuously I've been avoiding sleeping with Hansen since our wedding day.

She's away on the usual subject, the possibilities for future marriages and alliances with Stavin and Argonia, uniting the whole region one day through intermarriage.

"All it needs now is for you and Hansen to have children," she says, staring me down. "Then Avantine will be one again, and much stronger as a result. Stronger even than the Aphrasians."

"We've barely been married a year." I squirm in my seat. Something about my mother always turns me into the sulky child, the reluctant princess. My mother raises one perfectly arched brow.

"That is ample time," she says. "People will talk, Lilac, and that's the last thing you need. Now, tell me what is happening between you and the king. I sensed tension out there on the stairs."

"Well, maybe there's a little," I say, eyes darting to the fire. I'd take another Obsidian Monk sighting in the flames over this interrogation. "Hansen was very upset by what happened the day of the races."

"Then you must be the one to comfort him," she replies, her voice firm. A knock on the door heralds the arrival of refreshments, and there is the usual fuss of drawing up tables and adjusting our chairs.

My mother is lucky, I think—or she was lucky, at least, when she fell in love with my father. He was royalty. Not the royalty she was supposed to marry, but still, a king.

I don't love Hansen and I never will. He'll never love me. I can't say this to my mother because I know she'd just tell me again that the future of our two countries is more important than our personal preferences. This is the life into which I was born. Privilege comes with responsibilities and obligations, not a selfish life doing as I please.

My mother waves away everything but a thin crust of bread spread with the merest trace of preserved gooseberries. The pages have brought mead instead of wine, and I send them away for something more suited to my mother's refined palate.

When it arrives, the wine is carried in by Lady Marguerite, rather than a page. Her hands shake, and I wonder if she is intimidated by my mother's presence. I know I am.

When Lady Marguerite places the tray on a low embroidered stool next to the fire, I worry that the silver ewer of wine will end up on the floor. My mother reaches a hand to steady the tray and glances at me, frowning. Lady Marguerite appears to be on the brink of tears. She curtsies so deeply, I worry again, this time that she won't be able to get up.

"What on earth is wrong?" I ask her, reaching out to haul her to her feet. "Have you heard news of some kind?"

Lady Marguerite shakes her fair head. Her eyes are red and her face is puffy, as though she's been weeping.

"No news, Your Majesty. I mean, Your Majesties." She sinks into another unnecessary curtsy. "It's just . . ."

"What?" Her silence is even more irritating than her sniffles.

"It's just, I have a terrible sense that something bad might happen."

"Something bad *already* happened," my mother says drily. "My palace was attacked and burned."

Lady Marguerite twists her face. "I know, Your Majesty. But I mean, something else. Something here. I fear that your own palace was destroyed in Renovia simply to force you to Mont. Could you be under threat here?"

"I doubt that," my mother replies, imperious. She has never been one to take counsel from courtiers. But worry tautens her already gaunt face. When I was younger, I found her hard to read: She seemed so serene, immune to strong emotions and always measured in her actions. But now her hooded eyes are as bright as a bird's. Perhaps she is alarmed by Lady Marguerite's suggestion, even while she dismisses it.

"You have no intelligence to this effect?" I ask, my heart pounding. Lady Marguerite often hears things around the palace that others want to keep from me.

"No one has said anything to me, ma'am," she says. Her pink face is earnest. "It's just intuition and possibly quite . . . quite untrue. But it struck me today as a distinct possibility, given all the other strange and terrible things happening here."

"And in Renovia," my mother says. She shivers, even though she sits close to the fire. Outside, snow has begun to fall, soft but fast. Flakes hit the panes of my window and dissolve. I hope it's just a passing cloud, not a real storm. Piled snow will confine us in this place even more. It will dull the sound of approaching horses and approaching armies. It will obscure unseen enemies creeping about Castle Mont, with their poisons and magic. Everything I see and hear makes me feel more paranoid, more tense. More afraid.

"Thank you, Lady Marguerite," I say, trying to sound calm. "You may leave us. We will serve ourselves."

My mother waits until she leaves the room, then stands, rubbing her hands.

"I like none of this," she says, pacing to the window. "Either that girl is impertinent, or she knows something she dare not confess."

"Perhaps she's just scared," I suggest. "She is generally very reliable and loyal."

"Well." My mother's face is a mask again. "I am here with you now, and I can admit that we may be vulnerable. For that reason, my dear, I would feel much better if I could sleep here with you. We could have double the guards outside these apartments rather than spreading them across two."

The light outside is fading, but my mother lingers at the window, peeking through a shutter so she can peer down at the courtyard.

"If you wish, of course," I say. She seems very interested in something below, so I walk over to the window to join her, gazing past the splotched flakes. It's almost time for the braziers to be lit, and for us to be closed in for the long wintry night.

In the courtyard, men from the Renovian guard mingle with the Montrician soldiers. Another party has arrived, it seems, and the stable hands have gone out to take their horses.

One man swings down from the saddle, and I know by the way he moves who he is, even before he strides over the cobbles in his mud-splattered boots and heavy cloak.

It's Cal.

Chapter Twenty-Four

Caledon

THE ATMOSPHERE IN CASTLE MONT is tense, as bleak as the weather. It's clear to Cal that the mood here is worse than it was when he rode out to Renovia. The city itself looks shuttered and unnaturally quiet, its narrow streets of terraced houses deserted. When he rode in, the only signs of life in its main square were three goats chewing some strewn hay, and crows huddled on the frozen-over fountain. Snow falls, but it doesn't stick, as though even the weather has the sense to move on from this troubled place.

In the castle stables, there is a cool welcome from the grooms. They seem to regard him—and Rhema and Jander—with suspicion, as outsiders or potential spies. That Rhema was born and bred in Montrice doesn't matter. They're associated with Caledon Holt, and Cal is associated with the queen. Lilac's reputation has hit a new low, it seems. He hears them talk in low voices about the bizarre attack during the Winter Races, and tries to piece the story together.

Lilac. Cal longs to see her, but Queen Lilianna has arrived, and Cal thinks it's best to keep a respectful distance. That's what he tells himself, anyway. The truth is more unpleasant. If he bounds up the stairs to the Queen's Secret tonight and knocks on the door, how will he feel if nobody answers? All it will be is confirmation that Lilac and Hansen are sleeping together in the king's apartments.

If that's the case, Cal really doesn't need to know.

Tomorrow he has to seek an audience with Queen Lilianna, because in returning to Mont, he's defying her order to investigate the attack on Violla Ruza. Cal needs to explain why he and his apprentices have hurried back here, and why he thinks it's essential that the two queens be separated before the Aphrasians mount another attack.

Martyn, the court physician, ambles over to tend to Rhema's injured leg, admiring Jander's healing work in the field. She lies on the ground with her bad leg propped on a hay bale, Cal holding a taper close to light the physician's work.

"It's good to have you back, Chief Assassin," Martyn says, reapplying a poultice to Rhema's wound. "As soon as you left, the castle seemed to fall into chaos. The queen's own priest was poisoned in a most unusual case that still confounds us."

"What?" Cal is aghast. "Has the culprit been found?"

Martyn shakes his head. "Perhaps you could visit the chapel sometime, to see if you can make sense of the scant evidence the guards have assembled?"

The court physician explains the manner in which Father Juniper's body was found, and the presence of a chalky obsidian-like substance around the priest's mouth.

"Have there been any more sightings of a dark monk?" Cal asks, and the physician shrugs.

"The scribe remains adamant, but there is no other testimony or evidence to support his claims."

"Apart from the priest's murder," Rhema points out, flinching every time the physician prods her leg. It's red and raw where the beast clawed her, and bruised from her calf to her thigh. A shape-shifter did that, Cal thinks, an Aphrasian monk transformed into a dangerous creature. Some of them can turn into animals; some of them can even turn *others* into animals. The same may have happened here in Mont. But that would mean there were Aphrasians inside the castle.

"The tower is well-guarded," Martyn says, clearly puzzled. "The mystery remains unsolved. And then, of course, there was the flagrant example of black magic at the Winter Races. Unsettling."

The physician is master of the understatement. Another shape-shifter? Cal wonders. But at the Winter Races it was a horse that was bewitched or possessed, a horse that transformed into a creature of destruction. The Aphrasians' dark magic seems to have grown in power and ferocity.

"We're back now," Rhema says, sounding confident. "We'll work out what's going on."

Jander moves quietly about the stable, tending to the horses and listening rather than speaking. Rhema, with her all feistiness and feral instincts, has reminded Cal over and over again of Lilac, when she was still Shadow. Rhema is no substitute for Lilac, but one thing she has over Lilac: She's in charge of her own destiny. Lilac lost that power the moment she accepted her royal role in life, and married Hansen. Cal has no idea if the two of them have slept together yet, but it seems more than likely.

In the morning, snow falls again, coating the castle yard in a fresh white sheen. Cal joins the captain of the guard in the queen's chapel, another calm white space, and just as cold as the yard outside.

"Glad you're back," the captain says, echoing the physician's sentiments. "I would have traveled north myself by now, but I can't leave the castle without a safe pair of hands in charge. There's no sense to anything that's happening now. I prefer an enemy you can see, not one that appears and then disappears into thin air."

In the chapel, any traces of the killer are gone by now: Too many people have picked through everything. There's no scent either, because the small high window has been opened to blow away the stench of death. All Cal can smell is the minerality of the stone and the wax of the tapers. The bench where the queen always sat, the captain tells him, has been removed. Lilac is a ghost here, just as much as the murdered Father Juniper.

The captain walks back with him toward the stable block. Cal prefers to sleep there, in a small room with a wooden pallet, rather than in some paneled apartment among the courtiers. He likes to be free to move, and ready to leave at any moment.

"We need an increased guard here at the castle," Cal tells the captain, voice lowered so the throng in the yard can't hear. "We cannot have a repeat of what happened in Serrone."

"Recruitment is an impossible task," the captain mutters, his head close to Cal's. "We've had numerous defections as well. Ever since the Winter Races and what people saw, or told other people they saw. Our country folk are a superstitious lot."

"Are there enough guards here to protect Their Majesties?" Cal asks.

The captain stops to cough, almost bending double with the effort of it. He's not a well man, Cal has heard, and he knows that Montrice has too small a fighting force, and too feeble a fighting spirit.

"Forgive me," he says. "It's this damp weather. We are too few here, in my opinion. Some of the apprentice assassins have traveled north with the guard, and the ones who remain—well, they've made little progress, I'm sorry to tell you. Without someone of your caliber here to drill them, and with all that's been going on . . ."

"I understand," Cal tells him. "Have Their Majesties come down to inspect the guards at all? That might be good for morale, especially for the recruits who've never seen them in person."

The captain coughs again, clutching his ribs. He grimaces at Cal.

"To be truthful, I haven't seen the king or queen at all since . . . since that day."

"The races?"

"Yes. It's my understanding that the king has barely left his chambers. He has no appetite for the hunt, even though it's prime season for hares and a number of boar have been spotted in the hills."

"Not like him," Cal says, trying to hide his contempt for Hansen. A time of crisis in his country, and the king is hiding.

"And the queen has been confined to her chambers," the captain continues.

"She has not been doing her usual training with a Guild member?" Cal tries not to sound too interested, or too alarmed.

"I understand that Their Majesties are hoping to, ah, begin a family. With such safety concerns at present, the Small Council wishes the queen to remain safe indoors. For health reasons."

"I see." Cal can barely trust himself to speak. Is Lilac already with child? Does everyone in the entire castle know the king and queen's personal business?

"From my point of view, they're both better where we can guard them, rather than roaming about. The portcullis is kept bolted at all hours, and we search all the people and wagons entering the castle. Most of the courtiers have been removed to their manor houses, to curtail the amount of coming and going. We have too many people in this castle with too little to do, and no ability to fight."

Jander materializes at Cal's elbow in his usual silent, startling way.

"You're wanted at the Small Council," he whispers to Cal. "It's just the fat duke and Lord Burley."

The chamber in which the Small Council meets feels blazing hot after the damp cold of the yard. Jander is right: Only the Duke of Auvigne and Lord Burley are present. The room smells of dog, though, so perhaps Hansen has already paid them a visit.

It's not until Cal draws up a seat to the table that he realizes how much he was hoping to see Lilac here, and how rotten with disappointment he feels when she isn't present.

"Their Majesties are well?" he asks, and the duke makes a face, as though the health of the monarchs is irrelevant.

"No doubt you've heard about our . . . unfortunate incidents," Lord Burley says, dabbing at his plump cheeks with a lavender-scented handkerchief. "A priest killed in the most puzzling way. And the business with the horse. I don't know. A terrible business."

"Trust you to have missed all this, Holt," grumbles the duke. "Gallivanting around the cesspits of Renovia while we're beset with terror!"

"You sent me there, sir." Cal bows his head.

"Be that as it may." The duke scowls at him. "You're back now, and you might as well make yourself useful. I don't suppose you found the Deian Scrolls or anything important?"

"No, sir. But we did engage with Aphrasians, we believe, at Baer

Abbey. There's no doubt they are present there. At the very least, their dark magic is in evidence."

"And the palace in Serrone, burned to the ground!" Lord Burley exclaims. "Could you not have stopped that?"

"We were at the abbey at the time."

"Always in the wrong place at the wrong time," says the duke. "Not a good thing for a Chief Assassin. Why seek black magic in a distant mine when we have more than enough here in Montrice? Half the guard are in the northern lands, dealing with whatever dark deeds are occurring there. Meanwhile, here in the capital we tremble for our lives. The incident at the races reveals that even our own royal family are not immune from these magical impertinences."

"Again, sir, I traveled to Renovia on your orders."

"Yes, well, it all looks quite suspicious."

"May I ask, sir, of the Chief Scribe? Is he well?"

"Poor Daffran," laments Lord Burley. "He is an invalid at present. He has not even the strength to feed his birds. They gather on the ledges of the tower, waiting for him, while he lies in his bed ranting about dark monks. He saw one just before the murder of the priest, you know."

"I don't care about that Father Jumper or whatever his name is." The duke is red in the face, blustering. "He's just another commoner and the castle's full of 'em. The bewitching of the horse, that's another matter. If a man can't trust his horse, he can't do a thing. Begin investigating that, and don't bother with training these idiots the captain has dragged in, who will never be anything but apple pickers and shepherds. And not very good apple pickers and shepherds at that. First sight of the enemy, they'll run, that's my prediction. If they need you in the north to kill a few things, you can head off there."

"Sir, I wish to suggest something." Cal doesn't have much faith in the wisdom of this Small Council, but he needs to share his theory with them. "I believe that the attack on the palace of Violla Ruza might have been intended to drive Her Majesty the Dowager Queen Lilianna here, to Mont. It's the natural place for her to seek sanctuary. But the result is that we have three monarchs in residence, and the castle has already proved itself vulnerable. We must reinforce this place and stop sending men north. In addition, I don't believe it's safe for the dowager queen to stay here. If something were to happen . . ."

The two men look at him, Lord Burley horrified, the duke bad-tempered.

"What?" Lord Burley asks in a whisper. "What might happen?"

"I don't know, sir. But we don't want to wake in our beds to find the entire castle on fire."

"Well," says the duke. "You must stop that, Holt. You must stop anything else from happening. Simple as that."

"Perhaps a banning of tapers," Lord Burley muses, but the doors to the chamber open before he can make further suggestions.

Queen Lilac stands in the door. Cal clambers to his feet and bows, while the duke and Lord Burley take their time following suit.

"I see you have returned, Chief Assassin," she says, her voice cool, walking to her accustomed seat near the fire. "I believe you arrived yesterday. But you have not presented yourself to me or the king or to the queen mother. A strange business, wouldn't you say?"

"Your Majesty," he says, bowing again. She's angry with him, he can tell. "I arrived too late yesterday to seek an audience."

"Not true." Lilac's voice has a tremor in it, and he knows that sound: She's hurt as well as angry. "My mother and I observed you arriving in the early evening. She was shocked to see you here, since you had been instructed to investigate the arson attack in Serrone."

Cal doesn't know what to say. Lilac looks pale and drawn, her hair pulled back in a severe way. Her gown is voluminous and more ornate than anything Cal remembers: She's drowning in it. Drowning in this place, he thinks, and he longs to hold her.

"Your Majesty," mumbles the duke. "We have kept the Chief Assassin busy this morning, I'm afraid."

This is odd, Cal thinks. The duke is never usually so deferential.

"We were just asking him to help sort out our problems here," explains Lord Burley, talking slowly as though Lilac were a child. "There are to be no more wild chases to Renovia."

"All is lost there," adds the duke, and Lilac blanches. "It's quite the waste of time."

"Sir, you and the king insisted that a mission to Renovia was the most important matter of state business," Lilac says, unsmiling, glaring at the duke. The logs in the fire snap and settle; the lights in the tapers flicker, as though a cool wind is passing through the room.

"Well, things have changed, as you know, ma'am." The duke is standing his ground. "Montrice needs the Chief Assassin now."

"Renovia needed him!" she snaps. "The palace there has burned to the ground!"

Cal feels intensely uncomfortable. Not only does Lilac not seem pleased to see him, but she's arguing that he should have stayed in Renovia.

"Let us not keep the Chief Assassin sitting here, shall we?" Lord Burley asks. "He has much to do here in Mont."

"Quite right," says the duke, scowling at Cal. "Away with you, Chief Assassin! You have hopeless assassins here to train. None of them were any use at all during the carry-on at the races. They should have thrown themselves in the way of danger. Instead they were too busy tying ribbons to things and simpering with the ladies. One of them should have been cut to shreds with those iron knives, not a fine horse. A travesty!"

Cal stands to take his leave. Lilac turns her head away and says nothing. She's out of sorts, clearly. Maybe she's ill, or looking wan because she's been cooped up. Worried about her mother too, and distressed because of Violla Ruza burning.

On the winding staircase down, a horrible thought hits him. Maybe the reason Lilac looks so pale and tired is that she's expecting a child. This perhaps is why she has visited the Small Council meeting in such a temper, simply to argue that Cal should be in Renovia still and not back in Mont.

Perhaps she doesn't want him here at all. He wasn't expected back for months, and turning up like this might be the last thing Lilac needs.

Not when she's carrying Hansen's child.

CHAPTER TWENTY-FIVE

Lilac

EVERYTHING RATTLES ME. MY MOTHER'S arrival. The return of Cal. *Seeing* Cal at the Small Council meeting yesterday. I didn't behave well, I know. Everything irritates me at present; I'm on edge all the time. I'm still shocked by the incident at the Winter Races, and in mourning for Father Juniper, and reeling from the loss of Violla Ruza and many of my family's most faithful friends and attendants.

My mother is safe, thank Deia, but my mother is also in my room, sleeping in my bed with me. This isn't like her. She only suggested it, I realized later, after we witnessed Cal's arrival.

She sees everything, and what she doesn't know, she suspects.

My mother's presence here reminds me of my duty, and of the political ramifications of everything I do—or that is done to me. It also reminds me that I'm not in charge of my own destiny.

Queen Lilianna leaves my chambers first thing in the morning, telling me she wishes to speak to Lord Burley, and there's no need for me to attend as well. When she returns, she sinks into a chair, ordering ginger tea and sitting there shivering while we wait for it to be delivered.

"This castle is such a cold place," she says. "When I think of our beautiful palace in Serrone . . ."

"I know," I say. There's no comparison between Violla Ruza and this place. It's horrifying to think that the jewel of Renovia lies in ruins.

"We shall be quite cozy here by the fire, I suppose." My mother draws an ermine-trimmed blanket over her knees. "We can both read and sew."

"Actually, I was thinking about a training session," I tell her, pacing up and down by the window like a caged beast. The snow has stopped, and the remains have been swept into icy drifts against the walls of the yard. Maybe if I request a training session, Cal will take it himself. At the very least, I may get to see him up close. This time I can smile at him rather than snap. I need to be close to him, before I explode.

"Out of the question," my mother says in her most serene voice, as though I were a small child who's asked for too much honey cake. "On a day like this, you must stay safely indoors, my dear, and study your Montrician history."

Daffran, the Chief Scribe, has sent some dusty volumes up for me to read. Lady Marguerite was summoned to collect them not long after my mother set out for her audience with Lord Burley, and she returned complaining about the weight of them, and about the impertinence of the guards outside the tower.

The books smell of must and taper wax. My mother wants me to learn more about my adopted home, so I can dazzle the courtiers here with my knowledge of its history and traditions. Most of the courtiers are gone, though, and the ones who remain are Hansen's greatest friends—in other words, the stupidest ones, who care more about the finer points of trout fishing than who begat whom hundreds of years ago.

"It's not that cold, and I can't stay inside for the rest of my life," I tell her, trying to stay calm. My request isn't unreasonable. I've slept in forests, scaled trees, been washed down rivers, and climbed cliffs; I've fought wild beasts and demons. Just because I pretended to be a delicate flower to the Small Council doesn't mean I really *am* one. My mother should know that.

"I'm not talking about the cold, Lilac. I know perfectly well that you are hardy and resourceful, and that you've coped with weather far worse than this. But there are other dangers more pressing. Both Lord Burley and the Chief Assassin were most clear on this point."

"The Chief Assassin?" I'm breathless with surprise.

"Yes," my mother says, rearranging the blanket and not meeting my gaze. "I asked him to attend the meeting this morning. He was supposed to be investigating the arson at the palace. I wanted to know why he'd abandoned his duties in Serrone and returned here so quickly."

I gulp back emotion, trying to match her calm tone. "And the reason he gave?"

"More than one reason, of course. It was a considered decision, I'm quite persuaded of that. His star apprentice was wounded in action at Baer Abbey, and he wished to bring her here to receive treatment. Nothing serious, it turns out, but he was anxious to consult with the Chief Physician."

"I see." So Cal is abandoning his post because Rhema Cartner has been hurt. *Nothing serious.* A tide of jealousy laps up and into my throat.

"And then there are his fears about the true reason Violla Ruza was burned. Holt believes that the Aphrasians are responsible, and wished to drive me into exile here. With you and me and King Hansen all present at Castle Mont, we provide a compelling target. So in seeking sanctuary here, I may simply have brought more danger."

Just as Lady Marguerite suggested, I think, but I don't remind my mother of this.

"But what can we do?" I ask her. "Should we all leave this place?"

"And go where? Nowhere is safe for us at present. The Aphrasians want to destroy the Dellafiores. We've always known that. And I have been informed of the sightings of gray monks here in the castle."

"That's only by one person, Daffran, the Chief Scribe," I tell her. "He's elderly and easily spooked. Nobody really believes him. Besides, they've searched every inch many times over, and found nothing."

My mother stares into the fire, a profound sadness settling over her beautiful face.

Neither of us speaks for a while. I look out the window and down into the yard, where the last of the recruits are marching. They're beginning to look more like an actual fighting force rather than an unruly rabble. That's something we can be grateful for, at least.

From the stable block on the far side of the yard, Cal emerges, the thin winter sunlight full on his face. I noticed earlier at the meeting of the Small Council that he has what may be a new scar on one cheek, but of course I couldn't ask him about it. His face is more sunken than usual, and his beard is long and untidy. But he's still my Cal, my own dear love.

He pauses, turning back to the stable door, speaking to someone. That's when I see her. Rhema Cartner. She walks out to join him, and while I can detect the slightest of limps, she does not seem injured or in urgent need of a physician's attention. Her auburn hair is tied in a high bundle on her head, and she smiles at the sight of the marching guards. She and Cal lean toward each other—she's talking, he's listening. He raises a hand to rest on her shoulder, and I flinch. If he was doing that to Jander, I would think it a companionable pat on the shoulder, a sign of their rapport, but Rhema Cartner is not Jander. She is an attractive young woman who has traveled to Baer Abbey with Cal and fought alongside him, suffering some kind of injury so negligible she can stroll around the castle yard, but so important to him that he must dash back to Montrice, defying the queen's orders, so his favorite may be tended to by the court physician.

Perhaps he's moved on, I think, fighting back tears. And why shouldn't he? Hansen said that a man like Cal would never be content to play the part of my lapdog, hanging around the castle rather than fighting and traveling, living the life he was born to live. While I live the life I was born to live, as a captive queen.

Even Hansen is right once in a while, I suppose. I may have been fooling myself all this time, imagining that I would never—could never—be replaced in Cal's affections. I didn't count on an extraordinary young woman like Rhema Cartner turning up, reminding him of what he loved about me when I was Shadow, and what he lost when I became the queen.

"Dear one, you should come away from the window," my mother calls from her fireside chair. "It's so cold there, and you are on display."

"Really, no one can see me," I tell her, but I obey. Cal hasn't raised his eyes to my window once. He has other things on his mind.

I sit down near her, and she pulls a hand from under the blanket to pat mine. She still feels cold, I think. This place doesn't agree with her at all.

"I forgot to mention," she says, "that His Majesty the King made a brief appearance at this morning's audience. He did not intend to join us, but he had mislaid a particular dog collar and was seeking it in Lord Burley's chamber."

With anyone else I would think that was a flimsy excuse, but knowing Hansen, it's quite possible.

"He suggested that you dine with him tonight. Just the two of you. What a lovely suggestion, don't you think?"

"Not particularly," I reply, aware I sound sulky. I doubt that this plan was Hansen's idea. From what I've heard, Lady Cecilia is there, day and night, recovering from the trauma of her slaughtered horse. She's one of the few ladies in his entourage who hasn't returned to her country manor.

"I insist," my mother says, in a voice that permits no disagreement. "You will dine together, husband and wife, and I will not expect you to return afterward."

"Mother!" I exclaim. This is too much. "You're welcome to stay with me here in my chambers, but you absolutely cannot exile me from my own bed! I am queen here too, in case you'd forgotten."

My mother gives me that I'm-disappointed-in-you look that I

used to see on my visits as a girl to Violla Ruza. "Sometimes I wonder," she says, "if *you* have forgotten that."

I grit my teeth, so furious I could shout. "I will dine with the king," I manage to say. "Though it will give neither Hansen nor me any pleasure, I can assure you. But afterward I will return to my own chambers. I have no intention of spending the night with my husband while he flaunts his mistress around the court."

"I thought she had been sent away," my mother says, frowning.

"She is still here. Apparently she says that His Majesty has promised to buy her another horse, and she is awaiting its arrival."

"He said nothing about this." My mother is still frowning.

"Strange. I wonder why?"

Queen Lilianna looks at me, stern rather than motherly.

"Sarcasm does not become you, Lilac. Dine with your husband tonight, and remind him of his dynastic duties."

I sigh—long and heavy, the way I did when I was an impatient girl. Dynastic duties—haven't we got more important things to think about? But there's no reasoning with my mother. Tonight I'll dine with Hansen, but I won't sleep with him. Lady Cecilia is an excuse, and I plan to use that excuse for as long as I can.

Chapter Twenty-Six

Caledon

THE DAYS FEEL SHORT IN the castle, and claustrophobic. After riding through the wilds of Renovia, Cal is reminded that he doesn't really belong in a place like this, with its high stone walls and narrow windows, its gray circle of sky.

Rhema is making an outstanding recovery, but all that means is she's bored and restless, following him around and chattering about her various theories. Jander is his quiet self, happiest with the horses. He spends much of his time with the Chief Physician, exploring his own theories—about the obsidian residue and its poison—and assisting in the investigation of Father Juniper's death.

The day's activities feel pointless—an audience with Lord Burley and the Dowager Queen Lilianna to explain why he left Renovia, and then another fruitless search of the castle's cellars, dungeons, kitchens, and barracks. For all the danger and discomfort of the Renovian swamps, at least there Cal was master of his own life, making his own decisions. There is nothing like being back in Mont to make him feel like a flunky.

The elderly scribe remains a bundle of nerves who interrupts his bird feeding in the yard to corner Cal and lament the attitudes of Lord Burley and the Duke of Auvigne. Cal abandons him with Rhema, so the two can talk at each other and leave him in peace.

Seeing Lilac is impossible. When Queen Lilianna summoned him, it was to Lord Burley's chambers, not Lilac's apartments. He knows that mother and daughter are sharing a bed there, so any nighttime visit via the Queen's Secret is out of the question. Lilac remains inside at all times, and Cal is afraid to ask if it's true she is already with child. Who would he ask? Rhema is a good conveyer of castle intrigue, but she hasn't mentioned the queen. Hansen appeared briefly at the audience in Lord Burley's chambers, but Cal had already been dismissed, and there was nothing in Hansen's blank, handsome face that indicated any happy tidings.

All that Cal heard Hansen say was "I say, you haven't seen a dog collar lying around here anywhere, have you?"

In the evening, the dowager queen asks to see him, the message delivered by a page to Cal's room off the stables. At last, he thinks. The chance to see Lilac. He doesn't count the Small Council meeting, which was brief and unsatisfactory. He needs to see Lilac in person and alone—or almost alone, at least—to gauge her state of mind and her state of health. He bounds across the yard, a bitter wind biting at his face and hands, and up the main stairs to the royal apartments. Guards are posted at every door and landing, and so many tapers are lit, the usually gloomy gallery of paintings is as bright as a party scene.

When the doors are opened for him, he hears Queen Lilianna's voice, talking to someone, and Cal's heart gallops: It has to be Lilac. But a few steps in he sees the gray hair of the woman in the other chair, and recognizes her rounded shoulders and soft laugh. It's Moriah, far from home, holding the dowager queen's hand. Lilac is nowhere to be seen.

Moriah isn't one for ceremony: She stands up to hug Cal and gives him a warm smile.

"How are you? How is Aunt Mesha?" he asks, and Queen Lilianna gestures for him to draw up a stool.

"She is well," Moriah responds. She looks tired, he thinks, after what must have been a long, cold journey.

"I had no idea you were coming," says Cal.

"Nobody did," Moriah says. "The Guild helped me get here, then spirited me into the castle."

"So much for Mont as a safe place," Queen Lilianna says, one eyebrow raised.

"It's good that you're here." Cal swallows his disappointment about Lilac's absence. She may return at any moment. "You read my mind."

"Actually, I read a letter, written in code—stitched, in fact—along the seam of a flour bag. It was sent to me by an old friend, a Guild member named Varya, who has visited Lilac here in the palace and was very concerned. Together they conjured up a vision in the fireplace—this fireplace, I believe. It was of a figure that Varya calls the Obsidian Monk, and she believes him to be present, in some form, here in the castle."

"As your scribe here has been saying," Queen Lilianna says, and Cal nods. It's not that he doesn't believe Daffran: He just can't find any monks of any kind, obsidian or otherwise.

"It took a long time to reach me," Moriah continues. "Varya was being careful. She suspected, perhaps, that an ordinary note would be intercepted. It arrived just after we had word of the palace burning in Serrone."

She pauses to pat the queen's hand and give her a sympathetic look.

"Mesha and I agreed that one of us should travel here right away. I have no idea if we can be of use."

"What can be done?" the queen asks no one in particular, raising her eyes to the ceiling. "How can anyone help us?"

"Actually," Cal says, drawing his stool closer to the two women. "Actually, I think this is the best possible thing that could have happened."

"The burning of the castle?" The queen looks horrified.

"Moriah's arrival," he says. "A secret arrival, yes?"

"I came in the place of the woman who usually drives the potato cart. She's another Guild member, and was able to summon up a spell that turned my eyes green like hers, just long enough to journey across the drawbridge and into the yard. Varya was waiting for me in the kitchen cellar, to take my place back on the cart. To the guards here, all older women are more or less interchangeable."

"Moriah brought up my supper tray," the queen tells him.

"The guards outside this door were about to change shifts," Moriah says, her eyes twinkling with glee. "The new shift will have no idea how long I've been here."

"How long can you stay?" the queen asks. Cal rarely sees this much emotion in Queen Lilianna; she's usually austere to the point of being aloof. Now it looks as though she might weep. "Or how long *should* you stay? I have no idea how safe or dangerous the world is right now, though I must admit everything seems dangerous. Even these chambers."

"You have been through far too much trauma, my dear," Moriah says. "It's no wonder you are on edge. But remember that we in the Guild are stronger than any guard or any army."

"That's true," Cal says, thinking aloud. The queen needs to leave Mont, and she needs to be protected. Moriah's arrival has provided the perfect solution. "Your Majesty, I believe it's best if you go home."

The queen looks at him as though he's deranged. "I have no home! At least here with Lilac I have a roof and walls. Even if this is an ugly place, and I can sense fear and death all around me. It's an animal pen of the most base emotions."

"I hear they have a very nice summer palace, these Montricians," Moriah observes. "But this castle! Built by ogres, in my opinion. And there's a stench here, you're quite right. An Aphrasian stench. I smelled it as soon as the cart entered the courtyard."

"This is why you must leave, ma'am," Cal insists. "It's quite possible the Aphrasians sought to drive you here by burning Violla Ruza."

"They will never forgive me for the way Esban suppressed them," she says, lifting her chin. She's a proud woman, Cal thinks, and doesn't like to show weakness. Just like her daughter. "The only Dellafiore they recognize is the one they worship, King Phras. If they wish to wipe out what remains of the Dellafiore family, then I am its figurehead, I suppose. But I'm more concerned about Lilac and Hansen, and the children they hope to have. The children they *must* have. We should worry less about me and more about them. I've had my day. Theirs is still to come."

Cal tries not to flinch at the mention of royal children. He can't trust himself to speak.

"Nonsense!" Moriah exclaims. "You have plenty of fight left in you. Cal can protect the king and queen here. You need to return with me, to the farm. You know that Mesha and I can create an enchanted field around the house and fields, to protect us all. With the three of us together, the powers of Deia will sing louder than our bees."

"I know how skilled you and Mesha are, both in combat and magic." Cal needs to pull himself together, and to interrogate Moriah's plan. "But can you be certain you can keep the dowager queen safe from potential assassins?"

"Please." Moriah's tone is kind but dismissive. "How do you think we kept Lilac safe while she was growing up? There's a powerful circle of enchantment around our home already. And it's never been compromised."

"You will need to be smuggled out, ma'am," Cal tells the queen. "Your carriage must remain here. It must seem that you are still in residence in these apartments."

"The potato cart," says Moriah. "Varya is returning for me at daybreak. I will drive you out of here myself. We can hide you among the sacks."

"An ignominious exit," the queen says, but she's not objecting to the plan.

"I will ensure you have safe passage," Cal tells them. "And we will work out a way to keep your departure secret as long as possible."

"Lilac's ladies should all be dismissed," the queen says, too quickly, as though this has been on her mind all along. "Even that Lady Marguerite. Though perhaps, on reflection, her intuition is sound. We can trust no one. They must all return home to their estates tomorrow. Queen Lilac and I do not require their services. We are quite content with our own company."

It's agreed that Queen Lilianna will visit the king—and Lilac—at their supper table to present the plan. Cal, she says, will not be required at that meeting. He bows his head, hoping his face gives nothing away. He still hasn't seen Lilac alone. He certainly doesn't want to see her with Hansen.

"Cal," Moriah says, her tone questioning. "Is there just one door out of her rooms? This main door with the guards?"

For a moment he can't answer. He's never lied to Moriah. But is the Queen's Secret his to divulge?

"Come now," she says, and he's conscious of the two women staring at him. "Do you know of another entrance?"

"I do," he says. Queen Lilianna's face blanches. She must have suspicions about his relationship with Lilac, he realizes. He won't be surprised if she orders the door barricaded.

He leads Moriah to the far end of the room and lifts the tapestry away from the paneled oak door. "The queen has the only key," he tells her. "The door leads to a small antechamber, and then stairs down three floors into a cellar. The access there is by a secret panel."

"Nothing is secret for long in a place like this," she mutters to him. "You must know that. Queen Lilianna can leave by this staircase, so the guards don't realize she's departing. But after that it must be secured. I can create a temporary enchantment in the cellar, though I'm not sure how that will hold if Aphrasians want to break it down."

"That will not be necessary." The sound of the dowager queen's voice makes Cal jump. Her step is so quiet he wasn't conscious of her approach. "After I leave tomorrow, Lilac will no longer sleep in this chamber. Officially, she and I will both be moving into the king's apartments, where there are many more rooms. This is a matter of both politics and security."

Cal takes care not to react, but inside, his mind is racing. Lilac still hasn't moved into the king's apartments? And once she does, she's moving in with her mother? Perhaps there is hope for him and Lilac yet.

"You should go to His Majesty now to secure the plan," Moriah tells her. "Be ready for me at daybreak. You can bring nothing with you, I'm afraid."

"I have nothing," says the queen. "The fire took all that was precious to me, apart from Lilac."

"May I escort you to the king's chambers, Your Majesty?" Cal asks. No more Queen's Secret. No more nights with Lilac. She'll be with Hansen from now on, under lock and key.

"The guards will take me," she says, and the look on her face tells him that he's dismissed. He leaves without even a farewell to Moriah. Outside, a breathless page is arguing with one of the guards.

"He said I wasn't to interrupt," the page tells Cal. "But Lord Burley wants to see you now, in the physician's quarters."

It's late in the day for a scientific breakthrough, but at least, Cal thinks, this might take his mind off losing Lilac. That's how it feels, even worse than if she was fleeing the castle herself tomorrow, smuggled out in a potato cart.

When they're halfway down the gallery, the page grabs Cal's arm.

"I didn't want to say this in front of the guards," he whispers, so close that Cal can smell the onions on his breath. "But there's been another death in the castle."

Chapter Twenty-Seven

Lilac

My intimate dinner with Hansen starts well enough, while servants are present. We speak in civil tones to each other, and I tell myself that this is how we could proceed as a married couple who are friends and allies. But I can barely summon up the appearance of interest in his conversation about which hunting dog is better: pointers or retrievers.

It doesn't take long for us to run out of safe things to say, and to turn to more dangerous topics.

"We should have dined together sooner," he says, pouring himself more wine. "We need to think more about how things are perceived by other people. Our lives are not our own."

"Alas," I say.

Hansen puts down his napkin. "If only Holt wasn't back in Mont. We can't have people thinking that you're having an affair."

"Excuse me?"

"Don't play the angel with me. It won't wash, Lilac. It really won't wash. If it weren't for your mother sleeping in your chambers with you, I would have to call for both your heads."

"Why haven't you?" I ask. Truly, I am curious.

Hansen takes a sip from his goblet. "Accuse the queen of adultery and start another war between our kingdoms? I hope you don't think I am as daft as all that. Or cruel." He turns up his fine, aristocratic nose at the thought. "All that useless bloodshed for what?"

So that's why. Hansen hides behind a façade of disinterest and yet he cares about his people, so much that he even cares about me, about my welfare. If I didn't have to love him, I could probably like him. We could have been friends. Maybe we still can.

"Well, you have nothing to worry about, I assure you," I tell him.

"I wish I could turf him out of here tonight. But that's probably not realistic. It's quite late. Tomorrow. I wish I could turf him out of here tomorrow."

"Holt is here to protect my mother."

"Is that all?" He stands up, throwing his lace napkin onto the table, and marches to the fireplace. The effect would be more dramatic if he didn't march back to pick up his goblet of wine.

"I can swear to you," I tell him, "that nothing has occurred between me and the Chief Assassin since his return to Mont. We've never been alone together, not for one instant. I've seen him at the Small Council, but that's it. My mother is with me at all times, as you've pointed out."

"Thank Deia," he says archly. "Maybe Holt is seeing sense now. That's what I hear, anyway."

I pour myself more wine, willing my hand not to shake.

"What do you mean, that's what you hear?"

"Do you really have no idea why Holt trusts this Rhema girl and no one else? Of all the fighters he could ask for, he chooses her. My darling, you'd have to be dense as well as stubborn not to realize that they're lovers."

I try not to gasp, and fail. But of course. Hansen is right; it's what I've suspected all along. Of course Cal and Rhema are together. Anyone can see it, even the king.

Still, I can't let Hansen win. "But, darling," I drawl. "You can't have it both ways. You can't accuse me of a relationship with Holt, and then tell me he's actually sleeping with his apprentice."

Hansen shrugs. "A man can have more than one relationship at a time." Hansen's pleased with himself now. "I know that better than anyone. You're not as clever as you think you are, Lilac. Holt is using you to consolidate his own power in the kingdom while he enjoys himself with another woman. He's more ambitious than you realize."

"I think it's time for me to retire to my chambers." I'm worn out by our conversation.

But before I go, Hansen reaches for my hand. "Lilac, I am not your enemy. Our fates are bound to each other. Think about it. Maybe your precious assassin was the one who burned down the palace in Renovia. Who else could have done it?"

"That's ridiculous," I snap.

"Who else has the skills to burn down a heavily guarded palace undetected?"

"He has no reason to do such a thing."

Hansen looks triumphant. "A very good reason, actually. He knew that the dowager queen would come straight to Montrice to find sanctuary. And that was all the excuse he needed to return here himself. To you."

The idea of Cal burning down Violla Ruza is ludicrous. The idea that he's having a relationship with Rhema Cartner . . . maybe not so ludicrous.

No. I can't let Hansen get inside my head.

"I really should go," I say, rising from my chair. "My mother is expecting me."

"No she isn't," Hansen replies, still smug. "She told me she hoped that you and I would spend the night together."

"That's not happening!" The fury in me is rising again. But before I can step away from the table, there's a knock at the door, and a page is there announcing the arrival of the dowager queen.

Chapter Twenty-Eight

Lilac

My mother has gone. I didn't even see Aunt Moriah, who slipped into the castle yesterday with no one's knowledge, and has left this morning driving some kind of cart, my mother hidden under its canvas. Their departure drew no attention from the guards. I watched from my window, shifting the shutters just enough to peep through. I mustn't draw any attention to myself, either, as my mother always reminded me. We need to maintain the secret of her departure as long as we can.

When my ladies arrive to dress me, I will tell them that the dowager queen is breakfasting with the king, and they must pack all our clothing without a moment's delay, to be transported by pages to the king's apartments. I have slept in this room for the last time.

Then I will dismiss them all and suffer their wailing and crying, their vows of loyalty to me. They are all to be sent to their manors and country homes, to their fathers and mothers and rich, disgruntled Montrician families. Not even Lady Marguerite is permitted to remain. But I will remain, in this interminable winter, in this ugly castle with its long, dark galleries and smoky fireplaces.

In Hansen's apartments. In Hansen's bedchamber.

Last night our argument at dinner ended only when my mother arrived: She was there to announce her dramatic plan, concocted with the Chief Assassin and my aunt. Hansen didn't protest. It sounded sensible, he said, and quite exciting. My mother's withering glare seemed to have no effect on his boyish enthusiasm for a secret escape. I knew, of course, that his enthusiasm had another cause: If my mother leaves Mont, it means Cal can be sent away as well.

The smile soon fell from his face when she laid down her various conditions, including an immediate move to his apartments and the dismissal of my ladies.

"And another lady," she said, in her most imperious tone. "Lady Cecilia, I believe she is called."

Hansen turned bright pink—or brighter pink, I should say, because he was already flushed from drinking quite a lot of wine.

"I would request that Your Majesty dismiss her from court, as well, in the morning."

He seemed to think for a moment, then nodded.

"A new start," my mother said, and took both our hands. I don't know who was more miserable—me or Hansen.

"We wish you a safe journey, ma'am, and the most protected of sanctuaries in Renovia," he says. He can make a pretty speech when required, I suppose. "And here in Mont we will do our best to live up to your expectations, and those of my late parents. You can be assured of that."

Lady Cecilia won't be happy, I thought, but why should any of us be happy in this miserable place? How will Cal and I ever be alone together again? How long will Cal be permitted to stay in Mont?

Now daylight is upon us, and this stupid day I've long dreaded is here. By tonight this will be my private space no longer. I know what I have to do. I can't betray the crown. I have to give up my happiness. After my mother left this morning, I locked the secret door and threw away the key. I had to. My heart broke when I did it, but I had to. What is love compared with the safety of our kingdom? Of our people?

Everything is over.

I don't wait for my ladies to arrive to wash my face in the basin near the chest or to pull a simple woolen gown over my linen shift. I pull back my hair into a short bun. There's no time today to fuss over appearances. They must effect my move to the king's chambers and then make their farewells.

There's a tap on the door, a little earlier than I expect, and Lady Marguerite's worried face pokes in.

"Your Majesty is already awake and about?" She looks surprised.

"Yes," I say, hanging my mother's ornate traveling cloak over the back of a chair. She left the room in nothing but her shift and a woolen robe, planning to take a servant's cloak downstairs for the journey. It's essential that her fine clothes and shoes remain here, so my ladies believe she's still in residence. "Queen Lilianna is breakfasting with the king. There is much to do today."

"And I bring news, ma'am," Lady Marguerite says, slithering into the room and closing the door behind her. "Terrible news, I'm afraid. There has been another murder. The Chief Physician has been found dead—quite dead, with the black marks around his mouth—in the same manner as your priest. His throat cut, too, with something sharp that also left a black residue."

"Obsidian," I say, my heart thumping. Varya's vision in the flames of my fireplace was not just a fanciful notion. It was a warning. The Obsidian Monk is here in the castle.

"He was found last night," Lady Marguerite continues. "By that apprentice of the Chief Assassin—the girl with the red hair. She was visiting him, she said, so he could examine her injured leg. But can we trust her, ma'am? Might she not be the killer, with her superior skills? I hear she knows the magic of the Guild, and is as strong as three or four men. And her leg does not seem particularly injured. I myself saw her striding about the yard yesterday, among all the guards, without any impediment."

"Let us not speculate, Lady Marguerite," I snap. Who knows if Rhema can be trusted? Who knows anything?

Martyn is dead. Why has he been killed? Why Father Juniper? Did they see something, or know something, that someone else wished to remain hidden?

At my desk I scribble a note to the Duke of Auvigne. The Small Council must meet without delay. This time, I'm not waiting to be invited. I'm demanding that we assemble and establish a plan.

"One other thing, ma'am." Lady Marguerite sounds meek now, scuttling about with my mother's cloak folded over one arm. "I observed an unexpected arrival in the castle when I was on my way here."

"Who arrived?" I'm still sharp with her. I hope she's not going to mention the potato cart. I'm getting tired of her eagle eyes.

"Ivanis, the ambassador of Stavin, I believe. In a grand carriage, ma'am, followed by twenty guards on horseback. The livery was red and silver."

"Stavin's colors," I say.

She nods. "Was his visit expected?"

Not by me, I think, and not by Hansen. Ivanis is no doubt coming with bossy instructions from his king and more complaints about our borders. Really, his timing could not be worse. The last thing we need in the castle now is interference.

Chapter Twenty-Nine

Caledon

Cal's in the worst possible mood. Another person has died mysteriously in the castle, and this time it's under his watch. A physician has been sent for from the town, to examine Martyn's body. And now, to complicate everything, the Stavinish ambassador has arrived, traveling from his great manor house outside the city for an unscheduled visit. When he descends from the carriage, the ambassador sniffs the air as though Castle Mont is an unsavory place and recoils from the crows that swoop too close, their mocking caws echoing around the courtyard.

With Jander and Rhema, Cal looks over the dozen apprentice assassins who report for training in the courtyard. Three of them show a little promise, he thinks, but the rest are just soldiers, eager to fight but without the cunning and swiftness he seeks in an assassin.

One of the most promising candidates smirks at Jander and calls him "stable boy" in a muttered aside. Cal has to resist hurling him across the flagstones and breaking his neck. Instead he assigns him to stable duty for a week, mucking out the horses' stalls.

Three practice hand-to-hand combat with Rhema: She can fight them all off without any assistance, relying on nothing but a snapped branch for a weapon.

"Will the new physician be here soon?" Jander asks Cal. His face is drawn. He's taking Martyn's death very hard. "I would like to be present for the examination of the body, if he permits it."

But before the physician arrives, Cal is summoned to an urgent and impromptu meeting of the Small Council. The meeting is already in session when Cal walks in. The king and queen are both there, at opposite ends of the table, with the ambassador from Stavin positioned between them. Lord Burley looks pained, his usual expression, and the Duke of Auvigne seems ready to erupt into a rage. Daffran is a glum presence, his chair pushed back from the table, his face puffy as though he's been weeping.

They glance at Cal but say nothing, and he takes a stool several feet from the table, in the shadows near the window.

"I cannot emphasize enough," the ambassador is saying, "that this is the message from His Majesty the King of Stavin, and it is of the utmost seriousness."

"Of course, of course," says Lord Burley, and the duke makes a low growling sound like a dog poised to attack.

Cal is listening, but he's also observing Lilac and Hansen. Lilac looks upset. No wonder, since her mother had to sneak out of the castle. Hansen looks more sulky than upset, perhaps because his day of indolence has been interrupted. From time to time he glances toward Cal, and Cal averts his gaze. Perhaps, he thinks, Hansen is just checking on his dogs, who are sprawled in front of one of the fires, the only content beings in the room.

The ambassador from Stavin is complaining that refugees from

Montrice are flooding into his country, creating a crisis at a time of year when supplies are short.

"I'm afraid they simply don't believe that Your Majesties can protect them," he says, in his whiny voice. "They feel that nothing has been done since that northern village was attacked. And, of course, the stories from the capital have reached them. Stories of the very unfortunate race in which the queen's horse turned into a cloud of knives and savaged another beast."

"An exaggeration," barks the duke, but the ambassador shakes his head.

"Eyewitness accounts attest otherwise."

"Really," says King Hansen, shifting in his chair. "I'm getting quite tired of all these threats from Stavin. Rather than point fingers at us, shouldn't you be investigating the actual cause of the trouble? It's probably in Argonia. I would put money on that."

"Your Majesty, I doubt that very much."

"I wonder," Lilac says, interjecting quickly, afraid Hansen will make more inflammatory statements, "if the truth lies elsewhere. I believe that the peace between our kingdoms is being disrupted by a common enemy, but I don't think it is Argonia. Our enemy, gentlemen, remains the Aphrasian rebels who want to seize control of the whole region. They possess not only the will, but the knowledge of dark magic that so besets our nations and spreads terror. Surely we have to work together to investigate and address this."

"We *are* working on it!" Hansen protests. He jabs a finger in Cal's direction and all heads turn to look. "We sent the Chief Assassin to rout any gray monks in Renovia. Unfortunately, he had to interrupt his mission when the palace in Serrone was burned to the ground."

"And now he is back in Mont," the ambassador observes with a sneer. "Has the destroyer of Violla Ruza been captured? Is mining safe again in the environs of Baer Abbey? Or have these missions simply been abandoned so he might return to the castle? My own sovereign wonders why your Chief Assassin has not been sent to the border with Stavin to investigate our own issues, when he is the most able man in the four kingdoms."

"You're quite right, Ambassador Ivanis," announces the Duke of Auvigne, and the others all look at him, surprised. "Caledon Holt should be sent to the border. There's no reason for any delay."

"But what about the deaths here?" Lilac demands. "My priest and the—"

"Yes, yes," interrupts Lord Burley, and Cal wonders whether the Chief Physician's murder is something he does not want discussed in front of the Stavinish ambassador. There are already too many lurid stories in circulation. "Unfortunate business. But small, in the scheme of things, when we have . . . incidents, shall we say, elsewhere."

Cal wonders if the deaths would be "unfortunate business" if someone more noble had been murdered, like Lord Burley himself or the duke.

"I must agree with the Duke of Auvigne," says Hansen, staring down Lilac. "The Chief Assassin should ride as soon as possible. Ambassador, please tell Grand Duke Goranic that we are acting in the firmest possible way to deal with the crisis."

"We've been training new soldiers." The duke pours himself a large goblet of wine, oblivious to the splashes on the table and his own rich robes. "New assassins too. Holt can lead a party of our best fighting men north. No time like the present."

"I would prefer castle business to be settled before all our assassins are permitted to depart," Lilac says, but Cal can tell she doesn't have any support around the table. If the king and the duke want Cal out of Mont, then there's no way he can stay. Lord Burley would rather the two murders in the castle were hushed up than resolved. And the ambassador from Stavin wants to make himself seem invaluable to his monarch, possibly so his next posting will be to Argonia, where the weather is better, the food is richer, and the manor houses are more sumptuous.

At least Lilac wants him to stay. That's something. But the door to the Queen's Secret is locked now, and she is moving today to the king's apartments, to live with him as his wife. His lover.

In his heart Cal knows his time here is up. If he's honest with himself, it was up a long time ago—the day Lilac married Hansen.

Chapter Thirty

Lilac

THIS FEELS LIKE THE MOST depressing day of my life. My mother has gone. Cal is to be sent away, even though we have two unsolved murders in the castle, both clearly related to the Obsidian Monk that Varya conjured up for me in the fire. Why does no one take this threat seriously?

Carriages have been summoned for my ladies so they can return to their homes. An angry energy boils inside me. My bad temper unsettles my ladies, who are trying to organize their own things as well as transport my belongings and my mother's to the king's apartments. The official story is that my mother, breakfasting with the king, felt unwell, and is lying in a darkened room there to recover.

I'm tense with anxiety about everything I know and everything I don't know. Even the crackle of the fire annoys me, and I consider throwing an entire pot of tea onto it. Varya saw a dangerous darkness in there, and I feel powerless to stop it.

Lady Daria, one of the youngest of my attendants, slips in with my boots.

"I have been re-stitching the lining, Your Majesty," she tells me, gaze lowered. "There was a tear in the rabbit fur and I was afraid it would admit water. I can't believe that we must leave you! Who will tend to you?"

"I have no idea," I say, bracing myself on one of the bedposts. I feel almost dizzy with the speed at which everything is happening. Tonight I will be sleeping in Hansen's chambers. "Please take my boots to the king's apartments."

Lady Daria scuttles out of the room, despondent. I wish she'd left the boots here, so I could kick them around the room.

Darkness falls in the late afternoon, and most of the ladies have already been driven away. Lady Marguerite has contrived to remain one more night in the castle.

"I have the farthest to go, ma'am," she tells me. "It's best for me to leave first thing in the morning rather than attempt the journey in darkness. There is still much that needs sorting and moving. I will undertake it all. I don't trust the maids here with their sausage fingers. They will break things or steal them."

"That's a relief," I tell her, but nothing is really a relief at the moment. Lady Marguerite kneels on the floor to pack my writing things, my ink and vellum, my royal seal, into a box lined with Argonian silk. In Hansen's apartments I will have my own morning room where I can read and write, and receive visitors. It's smaller than this chamber, and has no view of the yard. It looks out across the overgrown moat to the rooftops of the capital. On a clear day, I'm told, the mountains are visible in the distance. They're capped with snow all the year.

"Lady Cecilia is supposed to have left by now," Lady Marguerite tells me. "Her carriage was readied early this afternoon, but she sent it away. She has been weeping in her room and refuses to pack her trunk. Perhaps she thinks His Majesty will relent and allow her to stay."

"Perhaps he will." I stand at the window, gazing out at the twilight. The sky looks soft as velvet. Another carriage jerks into action and rattles away over the cobbles, taking another sobbing lady back to her dull country estate. They must be very dull indeed if courtiers are so reluctant to return to them.

Daffran, the Chief Scribe, wanders the yard in a daze, sprinkling his birdseed in the dirt and muttering to himself. Since the death of the court physician, he seems beside himself.

"Someone should take the scribe inside," I say, my breath fogging the glass. "It's too cold and too late for him to be out feeding birds. The poor old man."

"I shall do it myself," Lady Marguerite volunteers, clambering to her feet. "And when I return, I shall bring you some ginger tea."

Now I know what relief is—being alone. My bedchamber feels half empty, though the four-poster bed is still there, of course, stripped of its sheets and blankets and curtains, and my chairs and table will remain: Hansen has too much furniture, he says, and of a much better quality than mine. I keep peering down into the yard, hoping to see Cal. But the only assassin there is Rhema, talking to the guards outside the tower. She'll be leaving with Cal in the morning, I suppose.

Hansen can't be right, can he? He can't be right about Cal and Rhema.

She and the guards stop talking when Lady Marguerite approaches, steering Daffran toward the tower's door. The guards admit them both, and it's some time until Lady Marguerite emerges again.

When she returns, Lady Marguerite is bearing a tray of ginger tea, as promised, and I sit by the fire to drink it. She props my feet on a stool, and starts going through my trinket box, polishing each item with a soft cloth.

"Is he all right?" I ask her.

"Upset about the death of the physician," she says, "and confused about the time of day. He said he thought it was dawn, not twilight. I settled him in his chair and persuaded him to drink a little wine. He's probably dozing off now."

I feel dozy myself. Today has drained me. Too much worrying about things I can't control.

"I have heard," Lady Marguerite says in a low voice, as though the walls had ears and might be eavesdropping on our conversation, "that Lady Cecilia has been saying some rather . . . unhinged things, ma'am. Talking about the death of her horse and holding you, of all people, responsible. Saying that it is because of you that she is being exiled from Mont."

I sigh. I'm tired of this castle chatter.

"I had *nothing* to do with the incident at the horse races. My horse was a gift from His Majesty the King, and he had no idea it was enchanted. And as for the banishment—even my own ladies are being sent away, and all at the king's request. This is not my doing."

"Of course, ma'am. Your true friends and supporters will never doubt you."

I don't reply. It's warm by the fire, and I've lost the energy—fueled by rage and resentment—that kept me going for much of the day. I close my eyes and listen to Lady Marguerite's soft movements about the room, along with the whinnies and stamps from the yard where the carriages wait, and the call of one guard to another across the battlements.

When I hear a piercing shriek from outside—a woman's voice, I think; a woman screaming—I wake from my half doze and try to stand up. But I can't. I'm immobile. My hands and feet are numb. When I open my mouth to speak, no sounds emerge.

I stare at Lady Marguerite and see two of her, three of her, her face so many moons in the sky.

I've been drugged.

Chapter Thirty-One

Caledon

CAL IS IN HIS ROOM off the stables, piling sweet straw onto his wooden pallet, when he hears the scream. Then there's another scream, and then men shouting, and women crying out.

He grabs his sword and rushes to the door. It's dark but not late, and the yard is still busy. Braziers are lit and people are running in every direction—mostly guards, he realizes when his eyes adjust.

Jander materializes next to him, eyes wide.

"No idea," he responds to Cal's unspoken question. There's no more screaming, just wailing, coming from the far side of the yard. Rhema marches toward them, a lit taper in her hands.

"There's been an accident," she says. "Lady Cecilia."

Hansen's mistress. She was supposed to leave today, Cal knows, with the other ladies of the court.

"She was spotted by guards staggering along the ramparts," Rhema tells them while they hurry over. "When one tried to stop her, she tumbled to her death, over there."

Kitchen servants kneel in a heap, obscuring the body. The courtyard fills with more guards, with servants and courtiers, and lights blaze at every window. The castle is in an uproar.

"Smashed," says Rhema, in her usual unsentimental way. "Head split open. Nothing we can do."

Jander sprints away from them, in a hurry to reach the body. Cal's mood is grim. Another death in the castle, but a different kind. A discarded mistress, enraged and desperate.

"I don't know what good he can do," Rhema says, her hair bright as the flame she's holding. "It's a bit late for one of his poultices. He's getting quite ghoulish, our Jander. Nothing like a dead body to get him running about."

"Holt! Glad you're still here." The captain of the guard approaches, his jerkin unlaced. He lowers his voice. "My guard tells me the lady was talking about Her Majesty the Queen. Calling her—"

"What?" Cal demands.

"A, uh, witch." The captain can barely say the word. "She told the guard that the queen had bewitched her horse, and that now she had poisoned the lady herself."

"Poisoned?" says Rhema. "These people are crazy."

"The guard reports the lady was frothing at the mouth. The froth was black."

"All right," Cal tells the captain, leaning toward him to keep their conversation private. "The last thing we need is more talk of witchcraft. We need to clear the yard."

The captain starts shouting orders, and the onlookers—some curious, some alarmed, some wailing—are shepherded back toward the castle's buildings. Rhema uses her taper as a weapon, pushing back a crowd of servants toward the kitchen and cellars.

Cal walks over to the body. Guards are pulling the weeping servants away, and Cal gets glimpses of the prone form, dressed in black. A dark wetness pools beneath the fair head. Two guards stand up on the battlements, peering down: That must be the spot where she fell, or jumped.

Two kitchen maids pass, supporting each other.

"The queen," one says. "This is the queen's doing."

Jander is behind them, and he pulls Cal by the arm to move away from the throng.

"They think the queen wanted to harm Lady Cecilia because she was the king's mistress. I've been hearing it for days."

"Where?"

"Kitchen. Back stairs. The queen, people say, uses black magic to achieve her ends."

"Why didn't you tell me?" Cal demands. A guard jostles him, and another woman screams. But it's not a scream and not a woman, he realizes. It's a crow, disturbed from its sleep, flying low over the yard.

"I never bother you with gossip." Jander sounds indignant. "Every great house and castle I've ever known has been rife with it."

Gossip can be dangerous, Cal knows, especially for a queen from another country, living in a scared and hostile city. He surveys the hall keep, and the floors above it. Light comes from Lilac's apartments, though her ladies are all supposed to be gone and by now she would have moved to the king's chambers. Faces cluster in most windows facing the yard, but no one gazes out from Lilac's window. Why is it lit if no one is there?

Rhema walks up, still brandishing her taper.

"Have all the queen's ladies left the castle?" he asks her.

"I think so. Apart from the one with the cow face, Lady Marguerite. I saw her out in the yard about a half hour ago, bringing the old scribe indoors. She was in the tower for a while, then she went back to the hall keep. Up to the royal apartments, I assumed."

Cal has a bad feeling, a churning in his gut. An icy rain is falling now, each drop a sting on his skin.

The burning of Violla Ruza was a diversion. So is the public death of Lady Cecilia.

Cal takes off running, headed for the hall keep and its main stairs to the royal apartments. The secret staircase is sealed with an enchantment, and its door at the top, in the Queen's Secret, is locked. He has to enter through its main door.

Every taper along the gallery of portraits is extinguished. Outside Lilac's door, three guards slump on the ground, unconscious. Cal doesn't pause to check if they're dead or alive. He has to get inside.

The door is locked, and it's heavy. He kicks it four times before it begins to budge, then shoulder-slams it so hard he reels with the impact. He grabs an iron brazier from the passage and smashes the lock, over and over. Nothing is giving.

He's raised the brazier for another attempt when the door handle turns, and the door clicks open.

Someone is letting him in.

Chapter Thirty-Two

Caledon

THE FIRST THING HE SEES is Lilac, sitting on a chair by the fire, her feet on a stool. She's still, like a doll someone has propped there. Her eyes are open but her lids droop as though she were falling asleep. The only sounds are the crackle of the fire and muted cries from the courtyard below.

The door behind him closes and the lock clicks.

"Well, look who it is," says a woman's voice. He turns; it's Lady Marguerite. She's holding a dagger. Her eyes are wild. "The Chief Assassin! A little late, but that's all right. You didn't need to break in, you know. You might have just knocked. I was expecting you."

"Lay down the weapon, my lady," he says in a steady voice. "Let us leave the queen to sleep."

Lady Marguerite sidles around the back of Lilac's chair, the knife gripped in her hand.

"The queen!" she says in a mocking tone, her face twisting. "She is an outsider. A witch. She is not a suitable consort for the King of Montrice. Look what she did to those poor children! Drowned them all and didn't care one bit. She must be stopped before she bewitches the king and gives birth to some half-breed changeling."

Lilac's face and body remain immobile during this speech. She's been drugged, Cal thinks, with some kind of sleeping draft, perhaps.

"The queen is no witch," Cal says, calm but firm. "And she has always spoken highly of you, Lady Marguerite."

"If you think I am Lady Marguerite," the woman says, "then you are not as intelligent as I thought you to be."

"A shapeshifter?" Cal asks. From the corner of his eye he glimpses Lilac's hand flex, just a little. Perhaps she's shrugging off her stupor. Lady Marguerite—or whoever has assumed her form—is still too close to Lilac, the blade of her knife too close to Lilac.

"Once she's dead, you will get the blame," Lady Marguerite tells him. "The jealous lover, furious that the queen has locked her secret door and is about to move into her husband's bed. I am a lady of Montrice and devoted to Her Majesty. No one would believe me capable of such a thing. I am too soft and gentle, too good. You—you are a *Renovian*!"

Lady Marguerite leans over Lilac, knife poised, and in that split second Lilac's right hand shoots up, grabbing the woman's wrist. With a cry of surprise, Lady Marguerite tumbles forward, and they both roll to the floor. Cal leaps toward them and reaches for Marguerite. Although Lilac is still holding on, she clearly has little strength.

With an animalistic roar, Marguerite pushes Lilac off her. Lilac sails backward and hits the table, sliding onto the floor with a thud. In the blink of an eye, Marguerite is on her feet again. There's no way she has such strength, Cal knows, circling her so she backs toward the door. Shapeshifters are much stronger than ordinary mortals. Is this the demon they have been hunting? Whoever is possessing Lady Marguerite's form has an advantage over Cal. He wishes he still had the iron brazier he'd been using outside.

Lady Marguerite laughs and points the dagger at him. Cal has his sword, and in one fluid motion he grabs the poker from its resting place next to the fire. He lunges at her with the sword and swings the poker at her head, but even two weapons aren't enough. With her dagger she parries both, quick and true, and when he tries again, she knocks the poker from his hand with such force it flies straight across the bed to the other side of the room.

"You should know better, Assassin," she says. "You are no match for the power of the Aphrasian order. No Renovian is. You should never have refused me when I offered myself to you."

Cal blinks. Marguerite's face shifts—from a dull one to a wickedly flirtatious one—one that's all too familiar. Duchess Girt! She escaped during the chaos of the duke's unmasking, and returns now for revenge.

Cal takes aim with his sword, the clang of the weapons echoing through the room as they hit and dip. He reaches blindly for a taper stand and manages to swing it at her, gaining just enough time to leap over a chair and get a better position, away from the wall. But Lady Marguerite matches him at every turn, batting away the stand as though it were a twig. It hits Cal's leg, and for a moment he loses his balance, staggering a few steps sideways. It's all the shapeshifter needs to smash the sword from his hand. It crashes to the ground, and Lady Marguerite laughs with wild delight.

There's a crack like thunder, and the oak door blasts open. Lady Marguerite turns to see, and the distraction is all that Cal needs. Quicker than a snake, he slides down to the floor, retrieves his sword, and plunges it into the shapeshifter's chest.

Marguerite—once a witch who'd styled herself as Duchess Girt—slumps to the ground, blood pooling out of her.

"Good timing," he tells Rhema, who's standing at the door, her own sword drawn.

She grins. "I thought you might need some help."

He grunts. His heartbeat is thudding in his ears, and he realizes that the low groan he can hear is coming from Lilac, who is trying to pull herself up from the floor.

"I was aiming for the heart," he says. "But I'm not sure if it has one."

"Cal . . ." Lilac's voice sounds small and distant. "She . . . she drugged me. I only had enough energy for one attempt, and it failed miserably."

Cal reaches a hand out to a trembling Lilac. "You're all right."

Lilac's touch, so soft and familiar, makes Cal tremble as well. He wants to wrap her in his arms, but all he can do is prop her on the bed while Rhema pulls a blanket around her shoulders.

Cal is still holding Lilac's hand, too overwhelmed to speak, or to let go. Tonight he almost lost her. What he wants to say now is that he loves her and will do anything to protect her.

But Rhema is there, and footsteps are thundering down the gallery outside—guards, no doubt, too late to be useful.

"It was the duchess," he tells Lilac. "She'd found a new face."

"Duchess Girt!" says Lilac. "And the duke? He must be here if she is."

Cal nods grimly. The Duke of Girt was the latest face worn by the demon king Phras, but Phras had left the duke's body before they had burned it.

"Was she a demon?" asks Rhema.

"Maybe," says Cal thoughtfully. "There's only one way to find out."

The body lies supine, deflated, blue eyes staring upward.

"Thank you both," Lilac rasps again, smiling at Rhema this time.

And even though it hurts him to do it, with a pain so intense it's physical, Cal releases her hand and steps away from the queen. There is work to do.

To His Grace Grand Duke Goranic
from the
Ambassador to Montrice

Your Grace,

I feel the urgent need to report a strange and secret ritual that members of my household witnessed in the early hours of this morning, in the Montrician capital.

Intelligence from the castle had informed us that during the night, a lady of the court—indeed, a member of the queen's bedchamber—was intercepted in an attempt to murder Her Majesty Queen Lilac. This lady, I am told, was disarmed and put to the sword. It is all an upsetting business, and my informants ventured a number of conflicting theories. These Montricians, I fear, are not to be trusted as sensible witnesses, and I will endeavor to discover more before writing to Your Grace again.

What I feel able to tell you now is this: One of my castle informants arrived at the embassy today before dawn, and alerted my staff to a ceremony about to begin outside the city walls. Two members of my household went there in suitable disguise. The body, they report, was burned on a pyre while a group of elderly women cloaked in brown murmured and then chanted incantations. These women are, I understand, members of the fabled Hearthstone Guild, though they look quite different from our own Guild members in Stavin.

My staff was mystified by the procedure and said it was more like an exorcism than a funeral rite. The chanting continued long after the body had begun to turn to ash and only the bones were left and the sun had risen in the sky. Perhaps it might behoove Your Grace to consult with the members of the Guild in Stavin to discover what they know of this?

The death of this lady was not the only mysterious death at the castle in recent days, and the place seems both cursed and dangerous. The court of Renovia and Montrice is an unhappy place, and Your Grace may want to consider recalling this mission altogether. At least we understand now why so many of their subjects are fleeing to Stavin.

I remain your faithful servant,
Ivanis, Ambassador to Montrice

— III —

The Assassins

Chapter Thirty-Three

Caledon

THE SUN IS UP, AND Cal stands by the still-smoldering pyre. The winter field is bare, all dark furrows of tilled soil flecked with dirty snow. In the distance skeletal trees mark out the line of the horizon, the foothills that lead to Montrice's mountain range. What remains of the fire is black and ashy, easily covered by the next snowfall or blown away by the next strong wind. With this wintry weather, in a day or two there'll be no trace of the ritual that took place.

Most of the others are gone now, apart from two elderly Guild members surveying what's left of last night's fire. Rhema is pacing the boundary line, picking through some debris. There's nothing to find there, Cal suspects, but Rhema isn't one for sitting around. She's trying to make something of this stakeout in a field outside the capital, because otherwise they've wasted most of the night here, and accomplished nothing.

They'd brought Marguerite's body here in a white shroud, to burn in the fire of Deia as custom demands, supervised by Guild members who materialized from the streets of Mont and the nearby villages' houses without any summons. They all sensed the possibilities, he supposed, that Lady Marguerite's death offered. By burning her body before the sun rose, the Guild could force the demon's spirit free of her form and destroy it once and for all.

But after Lady Marguerite's dead body was set alight, nothing extraordinary happened. The Guild members kept up their chants for over an hour, circling the pyre again and again, till Rhema announced she was feeling dizzy. The incantations summoned nothing.

Lady Marguerite was Duchess Girt, but she was no demon. But she must have had help to have infiltrated the court so well and to have maintained her disguise. Daffran must be right. There must be at least one Aphrasian secreted in Castle Mont.

Once the sun is up, there's no reason to stay. Cal signals to Jander and Rhema to get the horses. Then Cal stares out at the bleak expanse of the wintry field, at the morning sky that already seems heavy with snow. These long vistas in Montrice are still foreign to him. For all their perils, he still prefers the swampy forests of Renovia. There's a blankness to this place; it's hard to feel at home.

"Come on." Cal stands over Jander, sounding more gruff than he intends. In all his relief about thwarting the threat to Lilac, he let his guard down. He should never have encouraged Jander to have so much hope that they would find the demon. When they return to Mont, they can go to the tower together to talk once again with the nervous scribe. Perhaps he saw or heard something last night when Lady Marguerite helped him back to his chambers.

They ride back to the too-quiet city, a subdued procession. Cal notices Rhema tending her injured leg, rubbing at it when she thinks no one is looking. She had been brave last night and leaping at the door may have jarred the leg, or even reopened the wound. She doesn't complain—aware, perhaps, of Jander's profound gloom and of their failure, once again, to destroy the threat to the kingdoms.

There's a feeling in the air of the pregnant stillness that precedes snow, and the citizens of Mont scuttle about, tending to animals or lugging provisions. Cal wonders whether news has spread of the events at the castle, and what people are saying. He doesn't wear livery, so nobody sees him as a castle denizen; in his drab cloak and dirty boots, he could be a groundskeeper for one of the aristocratic families, or a hunt leader. The name of Caledon Holt is famous in all the kingdoms of Avantine, but his face is quite unknown. That's the way he's always liked it, as long as he wasn't invisible to Lilac.

He's not sure that she sees him anymore. They've been kept apart so thoroughly since he returned to Mont. With every passing day he realizes that he and Lilac might never be intimate again. The pain of that thought wallops him in the gut, a harder punch than any Aphrasian could deliver.

After they dismount in the castle yard, a page approaches Rhema and mumbles something in her ear. Without another word she disappears into the main building. Perhaps Lilac has summoned her, Cal thinks, trying not to feel the sting of jealousy and disappointment. Rhema had certainly helped save the queen's life last night. Jander leads the horses away, and Cal pauses to observe the captain of the guard. He's trying to assemble the last batch of recruits for the march north: They're clearly jittery this morning, and there are fewer of them than Cal remembers from yesterday. He wonders how many of them have run away overnight, spooked by the body of Lady Cecilia smashed on the cobbles and the wild story of a would-be murderer in the queen's chambers.

The captain doesn't look like he's had much sleep. He barks orders to the young men shambling about in loose formation, their faces either scared or mutinous. If these are the men Cal's supposed to be riding north with, he doesn't fancy their chances against an Aphrasian enemy. The frights of last night at the castle are nothing compared with the dark magic he faced in the Renovian mine. They should have set off by now as well, because at this time of year there are too few hours of daylight.

He walks over to the captain, frowning at the ineptitude of the new soldiers. They're hopeless. Some of them will desert, he's sure, before they arrive at their destination.

"If we're moving out today," he says, "there's little time to waste."

The captain shakes his head.

"No one's going anywhere," he tells Cal. "Orders of the Small Council. They've changed their minds again, after what happened last night." He sounds exasperated and rubs his face, clearly exhausted.

"Makes sense, I suppose," Cal says, though he grasps the captain's frustration. A military campaign fraught with danger needs preparation and execution, not endless postponements. For all the duke's bluster, he's never fought in a military campaign, and Lord Burley doesn't look as though he's ever got his hands dirty with anything. The Chief Scribe has never lived anywhere but this castle.

"I fear we've lost control of this place that should be our stronghold," the captain tells Cal. He lowers his voice, glancing around to make sure no one stands too close. "We need to scare out the rats here. I've got a good mind to dismiss this lot altogether."

He gestures at the young soldiers, who march in a wide, ragged circle, half of them out of step. Two crows swoop overhead, their piercing caws mocking the pretense of a fighting force.

"They're no use and never will be. If you lose the heart of the people, then you're not going to persuade any of them to fight for you."

"That's what you think has happened?"

The captain looks away. Maybe, Cal thinks, he's afraid that he's said too much.

"Not my place to say," he replies, and walks back toward the bumbling circle of fighting men.

Cal walks to the place where Lady Cecilia's broken body lay last night, the stone still rosy with bloodstains, despite the best efforts of three maids to scrub it away. Her case is perplexing, and since Martyn's death there's no physician now to investigate or advise. The new physician left soon after examining Martyn's body, as he was needed elsewhere. But some think he left in fear.

Lady Cecilia had a blackened mouth and was frothing black foam, as though she'd been poisoned. But unlike Father Juniper, she still had the strength to walk and talk, and to be overheard blaming the queen for her misfortunes. Who would be the next one discovered with ashy blackness on their faces—or, as in the case of Martyn, their throat slit with a sharp piece of obsidian? Everything points to an Aphrasian infiltration, but how has a gray monk been able to operate in such a guarded place, and evade every search of the castle? Why has Daffran seen one of them, but still lived to tell the tale?

He's deep in thought when Rhema rejoins him.

"You can still see the blood," she says, and he frowns at her.

"Keep your voice down. Assassins don't shout their business."

"Oh—yes. Sorry." Rhema doesn't sound sorry, but she does lower her voice. "I just thought you'd want to know where I was. Why I was summoned."

"No doubt the queen wished to thank you for your work last night." Cal tries to sound disinterested.

"I wasn't summoned by the queen. The king wanted to see me."

"Hansen?" Cal blurts, and Rhema looks bemused.

"Didn't realize you were on first-name terms."

"Of course not." Cal has to get a grip. "I'm tired. What did he want? Why did he want to see *you*?"

"He wanted to thank us, actually, but only I was around," Rhema says. "The queen has moved into his apartments, so they can be together at all times. He wants her to be safe and thinks it'll be easier to protect them if they're in the same place. You know, day and night."

Cal doesn't trust himself to speak. So it's finally happened. The king and queen will share private quarters at last. They'll have a real marriage now, with all that implies. Cal may as well be riding off today.

"He's asked me to serve as a special bodyguard and lead the night watch outside their apartments."

"What?" Cal is incredulous. The king should have spoken to Cal directly. He is in charge of Rhema. Whatever she did last night, she is Cal's apprentice, not his equal.

Rhema is pretending to examine the stones at her feet, poking at a loose spot with one foot. "He said that he and the queen trust me and want me to stay close. For the time being. You're not angry, are you?"

"Of course not," Cal says too quickly.

"I couldn't say no to the king," Rhema admits. "I know I'm your apprentice, but—"

"I understand," says Cal. He does, of course. Rhema must follow the commands of the king. The assassins of Renovia-Montrice serve at his pleasure. "Was the queen not present during this conversation?"

"She was sleeping in another room," Rhema tells him. "Recovering from last night and whatever she was given by Lady Marguerite. A woman from the Guild was summoned to tend to her."

"Varya," Cal says, and Rhema looks surprised that he knows.

"Where's Jander?" she asks.

Cal shrugs. "In the stables, probably."

"It's just that yesterday he told me the Chief Physician was getting very close to identifying that black stuff around the mouths of the dead. Jander was helping him, using some knowledge from those Guild aunts we visited in Renovia. I'm wondering if Jander should go back to the physician's chambers and continue the work alone. Nobody else here knows as much as he does."

They walk to the stables to talk to Jander. The captain of the guard is dismissing the soldiers, telling them to return to their camp outside the city walls. There'll be no more training today, and their expedition has been postponed. A half-hearted cheer greets this news, and the lower officers lead the men out of the castle through the city to their makeshift encampment.

"As soon as they're all out, we're locking the portcullis again," he tells Cal. "No one is to leave or be admitted without my permission. You must be able to do your work, sir, without this infernal din and all these comings and goings. A woman died here in this yard last night and these oafs are tramping all over it."

"Thank you," Cal tells him. "We will need to search the castle again, I believe—every corner, every cellar."

"As soon as this is complete," the captain promises, and bows.

In the far stable Jander's horse stands in its stall, chewing on hay, a blanket warming its back. Cal's and Rhema's horses are also there, also at rest. But Jander is nowhere to be seen. The stable hands say they saw him pack a small bag, perhaps to go somewhere. Running away? they joke.

Cal frowns. It's not funny. Jander is part of his team; he's one of them. He belongs here.

"See if you can find him," he tells Rhema, and she nods, walking away quickly to look for their friend.

Chapter Thirty-Four

Caledon

ALTHOUGH THE GUARDS SAY THEY haven't seen Jander leave the castle, Cal isn't convinced that he's still there. Rhema organizes the other Guild-sanctioned apprentices into a search party, starting with the physician's chambers, but Jander remains elusive.

Jander is an observer, a keen student of human behavior. He isn't strong enough for hand-to-hand conflict, and a stocky soldier could easily take him down. But he's wily and would have been weighing his chances to leave undetected. Maybe, Cal thinks, Jander's been waiting for this opportunity. He has little interest in the long trip north if their only work there is to break up skirmishes and keep order. There's a mystery to be solved here in Mont, and after last night's failure, he may have decided to try his luck alone.

Jander has his own mission, of course, that transcends the threat from Stavin. The boy wants to break the curse of King Phras that has plagued him so long. So where is he headed, exactly? Somewhere his sharp wits will count for more than skill with weapons and sheer physical strength? Jander is smart, but that won't save him from the claws of a possessed wild animal—or from a shape-shifting demon, its hands sprouting poisonous knives with obsidian blades.

Or from the Obsidian Monk, whoever that might be.

Rhema is back, and she bites her lip in worry.

"No luck yet," she tells Cal. "I'll go upstairs to the royal residences, but—"

"I know." Jander's not a person to seek out the powerful and the public. Cal takes his own search below stairs, through the hall keep's vast and bustling kitchens, through the frigid cellars where wine and dried meats are stored. Another apprentice is ordering the cooks to open every cupboard and pantry, as though Jander might be hiding in one.

Cal follows the cellar passageway that leads to a hidden door, beyond which lie the stairs to the Queen's Secret. Moriah's holding spell is still working: The panel disguising the door won't budge. Cal circles back to another long passageway, the castle dungeon in one direction, and its catacombs in another. He has less-than-pleasant memories of this dungeon—his dank cell; the sounds of men moaning or screaming; the clank of heavy keys and thick doors; the rustle of rats in the damp straw. He spent time in a cell waiting—expecting—to be put to death. Instead he was released, after Lilac accepted a punishment on his behalf, marrying Hansen and uniting their two kingdoms.

The door to the catacombs is solid, the iron handle cold to the touch. When Cal pulls on it, he's surprised that it creaks open. These subterranean chambers are Jander's kind of place, Cal thinks, but before he can go down there to investigate, he needs a lit taper. The catacombs are dark as a winter night, and colder than one, as well, the damp of the season settling in the long staircase and caverns.

With a flame lighting the way, Cal quickens his pace down the stone stairs. He should have come here first, and the fact that the door was unlocked—and so easily opened—suggests that Cal isn't the first person to seek this place out today. At the base of the stairs, he pauses, swooping the torch from left to right.

Down each side stand tall tombstones, engraved with the names of the dead, looming over carved urns that contain their ashes. The statues of the dead stand in a silent row. The flagstones are worn from centuries of royal mourners. There's the faint scent of lavender, but that doesn't mean anything in particular, Cal knows: It's often laid here in the summer, next to the tombs, and left to dry. He scuffs some of the once-purple debris with one boot, musing, as each stem disintegrates, on how much the flowers look like insect husks.

No Jander. Cal walks past the tombs, pointing the quivering flame into the shadows, but he's the only one down here. If Jander was here earlier, he's gone now. What would he be looking for, down here? What would he hope to find? The lavender would tell him nothing. The tombs can't talk.

Near the tomb of King Phras, Cal pauses. It's the oldest one here, because when Phras took power, all those centuries ago, he ordered the destruction of the Dellafiore dynasty's tombs. He wanted to be seen as the first ruler, not the usurper that he was, the last ruler to preside over a united Avantine. His three-hundred-year reign of terror and sorcery destroyed it, and after his mortal death the region splintered into four kingdoms. The cult followers of Phras, the Aphrasians, withdrew to their Baer Abbey stronghold with the Deian Scrolls. Only Deia herself knows where those scrolls are now. Maybe in the north Cal would find them at last—though he doubts that. In his heart, he still believes that the supernatural beasts guarding the depths of the abbey have been conjured to protect something far more valuable than obsidian.

The tombstone of King Phras is taller than all the others. Even in death he looms over his descendants, the kings of Montrice who tried to salvage something from the wreckage of the great land of Avantine. Cal lights up its deep-cut letters with his taper, wondering if Jander made this same futile pilgrimage earlier.

Cal hadn't considered the significance of Phras's tomb until now—that is, he hadn't connected the tomb of the dead tyrant with the castle's dark magic and all its unexplained deaths. The tomb is just a tomb, surely—a piece of stone, an urn of ashes. That Jander might seek it out today is unsurprising: Phras is the one who cursed him, all those centuries ago.

Another failure on his part, Cal thinks. The king's most recent reincarnation, Duke Girt, was killed, but he wasn't burned in the fire of Deia in time. The demon lives on. Not in the form of the bewitched Lady Marguerite—that is clear now. But somehow he is here in Castle Mont, creating terror and bringing death. The mission to the north might be postponed right now, but sooner or later Cal will be forced to ride there on the orders of the Small Council. Doing this without discovering how King Phras and his demon power have found a way back into Mont would be the most calamitous failure of his career as an assassin. Lilac would still be at risk. Jander would still be trapped.

His father would be deeply ashamed of him.

Jander must know something, Cal thinks. What did Mesha give him when they were conferring in the cottage's cramped cellar? Why were they so careful to keep Rhema out that day? What did Martyn discuss with him? They were "getting close," according to Rhema. That's what Jander told her. And now the physician has been murdered, and Jander has disappeared.

His instinct tells him that Jander hasn't left the castle. The darkness they seek to destroy is here, within these high stone walls. Mont is rotting from within. This morning Jander didn't know that the mission to the north was postponed; he was in the stables when Cal had the conversation with the captain of the guard. Looking at this from Jander's point of view, there's no way he was going to set off for the north and leave the demon at large here.

The torch in Cal's hand flickers, and light darts to the dusty ground around the tomb. Something dark catches Cal's eye and he drops to examine it. At first he thinks it's an obsidian blade, flat but shaped like a spear tip. But when he holds the torch closer, he sees the object is less surprising.

A single black feather lies on the ground by the tomb, pristine and fresh. It looks like a crow feather, Cal thinks, reluctant to touch it or pick it up. How could a crow enter the catacombs? There are no windows, and there are many passageways and staircases between this place and the outdoor spaces of the castle. Someone must have brought the feather here—or brought a bird down here. But why would they do that?

The feather reminds Cal of something he heard people say about the bewitched dark tornado that killed Lady Cecilia's horse at the Winter Races. It was "all claws," they said, a monstrous thing unknown in nature.

And the other thing people said about that creature: It was black, darker than the darkest cloud on a thundery day. Black, they said, as a crow's feathers.

Magic made a horse turn into a beast. What if it could turn a crow into an Obsidian Monk?

⚜

Chapter Thirty-Five

Caledon

CAL RACES UP THE STAIRS from the crypt, not sure where he's going. Jander must still be in the castle, a step ahead of Cal, a step ahead of everyone else, he hopes.

When Cal pushes through the heavy door, he hears shouts from the courtyard, the clamor of many voices. In the courtyard he's faced with a crowd, not just guards and stable hands, but a gaggle of the remaining courtiers, servants, and a man carrying a crate of onions and standing with his mouth open, perfectly still. Cal darts past them, irritated by the obstruction. They're looking at something, jockeying for position, and Cal needs to see.

It's Jander. Cal would have been relieved to find him, but there's something strange going on. Jander stands in the middle of the courtyard, away from the pressing huddles of onlookers. He is still, his arms extended, his face tense with concentration. No one approaches him, and it takes just an instant for Cal to see why. Arrayed around Jander is a circle of black—not feathers, Cal realizes, but something that looks like shards of obsidian—fragments in the shape of arrowheads. Dotted between each piece is a small heap of seeds. Cal steps forward, his eyes drawn to the sky where crows circle.

A hand grabs his arm and Rhema is there, red hair filling Cal's peripheral vision.

"It's not safe," she mutters, still grasping his forearm. "We should stay back. He has the protection of the talismans."

She means the obsidian arrowheads, he realizes. It's a Guild charm, part of a ring of enchantment that Jander has created around himself.

"Will it be enough?" Cal asks her. The crows above squawk and loop, getting closer to Jander. He remains immobile. "I think the crows might be enchanted. Or they might be Aphrasians in disguise."

"What?" Rhema looks aghast.

"This is their way into the castle. They enter and leave as crows. That's why we haven't been able to find them. He may be in terrible danger."

"We're all in danger here," Rhema says. She's gripping her sword, Cal sees, and his right hand moves instinctively to his own. If Jander needs them, they're ready, like the members of the guard poised with spears.

A crow lands on the ground within the circle and peers at Jander. Its head swivels toward the seeds.

"My birds!" Daffran pushes his way through the crowd. "What are you doing to my birds?"

"Stand back!" Rhema grabs his arm and he tries to shrug her off, his face petulant.

"I won't have him hurt my birds," Daffran complains, but he doesn't attempt to get closer. He stands trembling while another bird lands, then another. No one violates the obsidian circle. The crows are black magic made visible.

Jander stands there, arms open, ready to receive something, or someone. The crows peck around his feet, cautious at first, until one makes its way to a pile of seed. Daffran is muttering a prayer under his breath.

Jander raises his face to the sky, a heavy gray by now, and closes his eyes. There's no sound but the cawing of birds, the beating of wings, and the gasps of onlookers as a murder of crows fill the sky, turning it black. Dozens of crows become hundreds, swirling overhead and swooping lower and lower. The yard echoes with their racket, incessant and menacing. There have always been crows around the castle, haunting its battlements, perched on its stones, but Cal has never seen this many crows in his life. His grip tightens on his sword, ready to strike—though who he will need to strike, he has no idea. Will he have to lash out at birds? There are so many of them now—hundreds and hundreds.

Something even stranger is happening. The birds on the ground haven't touched the seed yet. They seem suspicious of it, circling Jander, mimicking the shape of the obsidian circle. The birds in the air dip and cluster, so low that some birds brush Jander's head with their wings. All are agitated, feathers ruffled in the wind, claws extended. Cal steps forward again, but there's still nothing he can do.

"Hold," Rhema tells him in a low voice, and he does what she says, even if it goes against every instinct. "We can't cross."

Daffran's head is lowered and tears dribble down his miserable face. His eyes are squeezed shut. He's still murmuring his fervent prayer, trying to save his beloved birds.

If he looked up, Cal thinks, he wouldn't be so worried. A crow dives at Jander's head, smashing into his skull with its sharp beak. The crowd gasps again; someone near Cal and Rhema cries out in surprise. Another crow dives and then another, but Jander stands his ground, flinching with each hit, but refusing to move. Blood seeps from his scalp onto his pale face, but the thin boy remains steady, arms extended, feet planted on the icy cobbles. He stares straight ahead and his lips are moving in a whispered incantation. Cal can't get close enough to hear what he's saying.

The crows whirl above, a darting cloud of blackness, attacking again and again—Jander's face is red with blood—then they drop to the ground around him, now within the obsidian circle. Some fly up against his legs, wings flapping, their caws angry and urgent. With sharp beaks and claws they rip at his leather leggings, but he stands firm. The strength that Cal has always known Jander possesses, his inner greatness, his true heart: This is what's keeping him upright, in the absence of physical power. The longer he stands, the more crows he lures into the obsidian circle, Cal realizes. The ground is already covered with their blackness, and some are pushed close to the heaps of brown seeds.

Poor Jander is beset by birds. Cal wants to leap in and swipe those birds off his slight frame. He could kill half a dozen with one blow of his sword. But that wouldn't be enough; there are too many. And as Rhema told him, they can't cross the obsidian line. What was it Moriah said—that the Guild's magic is more powerful than any army's?

He glances at Rhema and sees she's closed her eyes. Her head is tilted back and she's sniffing.

"Can you smell it?" she says, as though she could sense that he's looking at her. "Something like a nut. Linseed. And something rotten."

"Aphrasians," Cal says, so low it's almost a whisper.

"He's poisoned the linseed." Rhema opens her eyes. "You might be right about this one, Chief."

Whatever Jander is chanting seems to be working, because the attacking crows begin to fall around him like a shedding pelt.

Rhema flinches as though she were the one being attacked. What if Jander's plan doesn't work? Cal thinks. What if they don't take the poison? But now that the crows have tired of hurling themselves at Jander's slender, bleeding form, some are drawn to the nutty heaps of linseed. Once a few of them start jabbing at the miniature piles, others push forward to shove them out of the way.

The crows who eat the poisoned seed stagger beyond the obsidian circle and drop to the ground. This doesn't seem to deter the ones behind them, who push to reach the food. The first crow who ate the seed begins to convulse, and the crowd instinctively backs farther away.

"My birds!" Daffran cries again, his voice quivering. The crow is on its back, bucking and twitching, while others who've eaten the seed start dropping around it.

Thunder rumbles above the courtyard, and black lightning splinters the sky. People in the yard cower, some running to hide in the stables. The first crow twitches again. Its yellow eyes are bright, a livid blotch of color on its ink-black body. When its beak opens, an unearthly caw erupts. The sound is something between a roar and a scream, a rage-filled battle cry. In an instant, the bird explodes before everyone's eyes, its body morphing from creature to man in an instant.

A man in a gray cape, his features hidden with a black mask. Flat on his back in the yard, staring up at the sky.

"Aphrasians!" someone shouts, and more of the crowd scatters. But Cal doesn't move and neither does Rhema. The Aphrasian monk is dead, poisoned by Jander's linseed.

One after another, the crows that have eaten the poison lie convulsing in the dirt. Every single one of them caws with rage or pain, their eyes glowing like a ball of flame, and then explodes into the form of a cloaked man. Black feathers shoot through the air, smacking people in the face. Cal raises an arm to keep them away, but he is soon pasted with damp feathers that he has to scrape off. They stink of sulfur.

The whole yard has the rotten smell of death, and people cover their mouths, recoiling from the sights and smells before them. The still-living birds clamber over the dead monks until their own moments of explosive transformation, until the bodies lie heaped around Jander's obsidian circle, so high that Jander himself is half obscured. He's still standing, the blood on his forehead and cheeks drying into a caked mud.

Another flash of black lightning cracks the sky. Wails of fear ripple through the crowd, and the guards seem agitated, some of them pointing their spears upward, as though they're waiting for more evil to descend from the sky. But no more crows circle or descend. The ones left alive on the ground peck at the poisoned seeds and follow in the steps of their predecessors.

Daffran turns to Cal, his face no longer pink and swollen with tears. The scribe looks furious. He opens his mouth to speak and an almighty caw erupts, so loud that it echoes around the courtyard. Cal watches the scribe rise from the ground, as though the black lightning crackling above is pulling him into the sky. He's a whirling tornado now, towering above Jander, turning and turning, changing color. His face is huge and enraged, and his limbs are a flashing mass of black claws, glinting and razor-sharp. The wind whips up small stones and dust, and Cal blinks and squints, hand on his sword, trying to focus on Daffran's new form.

"You will not defeat me!" Daffran roars, more giant crow than man now, whirling until he touches down on the cobbles of the yard. Black lightning splinters the sky. Daffran reaches out an arm that has become something between a huge wing and a vicious claw, pointing straight at Cal.

"Cal!" It's Rhema, by his side, her sword also poised. "I can't move!"

Cal tries to lift his sword but his arm is heavy, and his legs won't move. Everyone around him is still, as though time has stopped. Daffran has cast a spell on them all. Like Rhema, Cal feels his body freezing into position, as though he's been turned into stone.

Chapter Thirty-Six

Lilac

When the noise erupts outside, Hansen and I are in my old apartments, where the windows face the yard. Maids have been working here today, clearing the last of my belongings, and we walked over together earlier to ensure everything is moved. A fire is burning in the grate. The only things left to remove are a small miniature of my mother, propped on the mantel, and my bow and quiver of arrows, hanging on the wall.

Loud cawing and thumping draws Hansen to the window, and he unlatches the shutters.

He looks outside and gasps, backing away from the window. "Crows! A whole lot of them—hundreds, maybe—flying in the courtyard!"

I look up from the fireplace. "You're jesting. Why would there be hundreds of crows in the courtyard?"

"I'm telling you, there are!" Hansen shrieks. "Come see!"

Hansen is given to hysterics. I poke at the fire so an ashy log rolls over.

He walks back to the window and looks out. "They've surrounded that strange, skinny boy—the mute."

"He's not a mute," I say. "If you're talking about Jander."

"Yes," Hansen says, increasingly agitated. "One of the Chief Assassin's gang. In the name of Deia! What is going on?"

Our guards are with us, standing poised at the door with their weapons out, but what we see will defy any spear or staff. I nudge Hansen out of the way so I can see, though it's freezing by the window and Hansen has turned the glass frosty with his breath.

The first thing I see in the courtyard is Jander surrounded by crows—covered in them, in fact. Hundreds, just as Hansen said.

I try not to scream. He's bleeding, but standing his ground. I know what he's doing; my aunts taught me about something like this years ago.

"They call it a drawing-in," I say, shaking, and only when Hansen asks me what I'm talking about do I realize I'm speaking aloud rather than thinking. "You create a circle of enchantment to trap your prey. But the danger is that you have to stand within it, as well, and it's likely you'll be attacked before the magic works. If the magic works."

"Ridiculous." Hansen drums his fingers on the glass. "If he wants to kill crows, he should just use an arrow or a slingshot, like a normal person."

"There are too many crows for arrows," I tell him, standing on my tiptoes to look for Cal, my heart racing. I spot Rhema first, with her blaze of hair, and then Cal next to her, both poised to spring forward, by the looks of it. They know enough to stand back from the circle. Crossing it mid-enchantment would be too dangerous. There's nothing they can do for Jander.

"Look—they're all falling to the ground," Hansen says. "Whatever he's feeding them mustn't be the right kind of thing for birds. It's like that time I gave my hound honey-covered sweetmeat, and he vomited it up all over my shoes."

"He's poisoning them." One by one, the crows are gobbling the poison laid around the circle and staggering beyond it. Why he's doing this, I don't know.

"In the name of Deia!" Hansen shouts again, clutching at my arm. "An Aphrasian!"

Neither of us can believe our eyes. Each dying crow erupts, feathers flying, into the form of a hooded man.

"So this is how they've been getting into the castle!" I say, my breath tight in my chest.

Black lightning slices through the clouds, and feathers paper the courtyard like black snow. I'm sick, nausea surging through me. Not again. Not this again. A demon creature of claws and whirling blackness, cutting through something living. It whirls up above the pile of bodies, its face human. Not Jander—please, not Jander. I know that face, but it's so hard to make it out in this black fog of feathers.

"Why is nobody *doing* anything?" Hansen demands. I don't understand either. Why are Cal and Rhema just standing there, holding their swords but not moving? What are they waiting for? The creature to slash everyone to pieces?

They're completely still and unmoving. Their poses are unnatural, I realize, as though they've been frozen in place by a dark spell.

"By Deia, it's Daffran," says Hansen, "the Chief Scribe. That's him—with the claws!"

Hansen's right. Daffran's face is giant, spitting with anger. All those times we saw him feeding the birds.

"This is how they got into the tower," I say, face pressed to the glass. "In through the high windows. Inside, he could transform them."

"But he told us about them!" Hansen protests.

"So we would never suspect him," I say, and then we both recoil. Daffran's form grows until it almost reaches the windows, a towering man, two or three times as tall as anyone in the courtyard. His body is cut from blackest obsidian, his face ugly with rage. I know that face. It's in a painting that I used to see every time I visited Violla Ruza, a portrait that hung in the grand entranceway.

King Phras. The old demon himself.

Hansen jumps back from the window. "This is not happening," he says. "Tell me, please, that I'm seeing things."

"Everyone around him is frozen," I say, pointing at the guards below, their spears still. "Everyone who was touched by the falling feathers."

"We must send more guards!"

"There's no time. The demon will kill Jander. It will kill Cal and Rhema. It'll kill everyone."

"Rhema," Hansen repeats. Now this means something to him. The crack assassin, the only one he trusts. The demon picks up the nearest guard by his frozen spear and flings him against a wall.

I want to scream Cal's name. I want to save him. The demon is laughing now, a demented caw that cuts through the wintry day. His eyes are yellow, like a beast's.

"Here," Hansen says, hitting me with something. "Here!"

I glance at him, mouth open, my heart skipping with fear. He holds my bow and the quiver of arrows that he tore from the wall. He thrusts the bow at me and pulls out an arrow.

"You have one shot," he tells me. "I've seen you train. I know you can do it."

"Light the arrow tip," I say. "There, in the fire. Go!"

I fumble with the bow, moving it to my left hand. I need the demon's attention. I need for him to look up here. When I shove the window, it swings open with a crack.

"King Phras!" I shout down to the courtyard. "It's me—the queen!"

The demon stretches his giant neck and glares up at me, his yellow eyes glowing.

"I'm a Dellafiore!" I shout. "The last and greatest of my line! You killed my father, but you can't kill me!"

The towering demon opens his mouth, his face contorted with rage.

"We're back in power!" I bellow. "We're uniting the kingdoms again! Your legacy will be defeated and destroyed!"

Hansen passes me the flaming arrow, and I swing the bow up and out the window.

"Now," he says. "Now."

I take aim, and the arrow springs from my bow. It arcs toward the demon like a shooting star, sizzling with light. King Phras reaches out a hand veined with obsidian, trying to grab it, but a cloud of black feathers drifts past his face, obscuring his vision. The arrow soars into him, striking him in the heart with its burning tip.

With a mighty roar, he buckles, then shatters into a heap of obsidian, the sound as loud as the ice on a lake giving way. The pieces clatter onto the stones of the yard, and I can hear people shouting and scattering. Charcoal dust billows into the air, shooting high into the sky.

"Not a bad shot," Hansen tells me, relief in his voice. "It was my idea, of course."

"Of course," I say, my heart still pounding. I bend over, trying to catch my breath. "Can you see anything?"

"Too much dust. Come on!" Hansen bolts toward the door, the guards scuttling to catch up. We have to get down there to make sure everyone has survived the shattered black glass.

I have to find Cal.

Chapter Thirty-Seven

Lilac

THIS TIME WE CAN'T MAKE a mistake. Tonight, the members of the Guild were called to cleanse the place of black magic. When the mess of black feathers are cleared in the courtyard and they picked through the shattered obsidian, they found a body, wizened and elderly, but completely unmarked. Daffran. The last body that Tyrant King Phras would occupy. Something for us to burn in the fire of Deia, at last, after all these centuries.

The urn of ashes in front of his tomb down in the catacombs was empty, as it turned out. The Guild knew that his dark spirit moved from body to body, possessing them and extending his demonic stranglehold on Avantine.

Outside the walls of the city we gather to burn Daffran's body, and local Guild members encircle the pyre with a ring of incantation. In their brown robes—the color of the earth, from which we're all born—they resemble the piles of linseed that Jander laid out in the courtyard. And the linseed that Daffran fed the crows every day. His linseed, too, had contained powerful magic, enough to keep the

Aphrasian monks disguised as birds, loose in the castle just long enough to slash or poison.

Jander replaced the magic with a poison that forced the evil out of each dying bird. He told me he'd concocted this potion with Aunt Mesha's help, when he and Cal and Rhema last visited the cottage. He'd had a hunch about the crows even then, but kept it to himself in case it was just another false hope.

The demon's destruction when my burning arrow pierced his heart sent a billowing cloud of ashy dust high into the sky. This message summoned Guild members from far afield in Montrice. While we ready the fire and lay the shroud on the logs, more and more elders in their earthy robes pour into the field. We've all been waiting for this moment for so long. With Phras finally dispatched, we have hit the Aphrasians in their gut. Without a spiritual leader, without a future, they no longer have a cause.

The Small Council has permitted me to attend this fire of Deia, possibly because they're all scared of me now. If I can kill a demon with one arrow, what could I do to them? They'd forgotten, I think, that I'm a Dellafiore, with a heritage longer and more storied than anyone in Montrice. They'd forgotten that before I was a queen, I was an assassin.

I asked Hansen if he wanted to see this ritual fire as well, to witness history, and for a moment I thought he was tempted. But as night fell and cold air swarmed the castle with its bone-chilling damp, he decided it was too much of a risk for him to be outside for all those hours. Even the promise of Rhema to guard us both with her life wasn't enough.

For those important moments in my apartments, Hansen and I

were on the same side. He was the one who thrust the bow into my hands. He was the one who lit the arrow in the fire. But he can't really change. None of us can. We are who we are.

Pieces of the puzzle are starting to click into place. Father Juniper was killed, we think, because a crow entered the high chapel window and he witnessed it transforming into an Aphrasian monk. Varya told me that the method of killing was probably an obsidian poison, force-fed to a victim, which is why we saw the black chalkiness around my poor priest's mouth.

Martyn, the Chief Physician, had worked this out—in consultation with Varya and Jander. He'd also detected traces of a seed, Varya told me, and now we realize that was linseed. He must have shared this information with Jander, but Daffran didn't know that. So Martyn was killed to keep him quiet. No one could be permitted to suspect Daffran of acting as a portal for the Aphrasians.

Lady Cecilia, we think, was poisoned in order to point the finger of blame at me, and encourage a Montrician rebellion against me, perhaps even an assassination attempt. And poor Lady Marguerite—when she ran down to the yard to help Daffran back to his chamber, she was possessed by Duchess Girt, who'd been smuggled into the castle as one of the crows, of course. The duchess, now Lady Marguerite, was given the enchanted draft of tea for me to drink. The real Lady Marguerite was no Aphrasian sympathizer, I know. She was simply in the wrong place at the wrong time, used by Duchess Girt and Daffran—in his possessed form, at least—to further the Aphrasian cause.

Ridding our world of the Dellafiores.

At midnight the chants begin, and the Guild members prepare to light the fire. Jander is among them: He's been embraced, it seems, since he has proven himself so accomplished. He was the one who forced the demon to reveal himself in the castle; he was the one who solved the puzzle, and destroyed dozens upon dozens of Aphrasian killers. All by using his mind rather than wielding a sword.

Now his slight form moves with the others, pacing around the pyre. He's the one handed the torch to light the fire. My aunts would be proud, I think, if they were here. They taught him well.

I stand outside the circle, but close enough to feel the heat of the rising flames on my cold face. Rhema stands to my left, a step behind me. To my right is Cal. We've said very little to each other tonight, but that's all right. We're all nervous, I suppose, about the fire of Deia working this time, of ridding Avantine of centuries of evil and conflict.

Just knowing Cal is there gives me a feeling of peace. I could reach out for his hand if I wanted to. I really want to. Things will have to change now in the castle, in the joint kingdoms, in our lives. I can't go on living half a life, separated from Cal. I can't go on being some kind of captive.

The flames lick the sky, darting and shooting into the darkness. It's hot now, stinging my eyes, but I don't back away, and neither does the Guild. They move in measured paces in their circle of incantation. Jander, such a slight figure, a waif, walks with them. The fire lights his pale face so it looks as bright as the moon. He's the real captive, of course—held captive for centuries by the king's curse.

When the fire leaps high, burning bright and hot, Jander lets out an oh! as though he'd felt some pain or a sharp discomfort. He stumbles, clutching his stomach, and instinctively I step forward to help him. But there's a hand on my left arm—Rhema's—and a hand on my right.

Cal's.

"Leave him," Cal says in a low voice, his breath warm against my neck. "It's time."

Of course. The body burns in the fire of Deia, and the curse on Jander is lifted. He straightens and glances toward us with the most serene smile I've ever seen. Cal is right: It's time. Before our eyes, Jander's form melts away into the darkness. The circle of Guild members keeps moving, keeps chanting, but Jander is gone.

The curse is broken. Tears prick my eyes, and it's not just the smoke causing them. Jander's disappearance into thin air confirms what we knew, or what we hoped. The demon who has been orchestrating terror throughout the four kingdoms is gone forever.

I'm sad, naturally, to be losing Jander. But I'm profoundly grateful to him, for ridding us of evil. He deserves to rest in peace. He deserves his freedom. Isn't that what we all deserve?

Then something else happens when the smoke clears.

In the ashes of the demon's body, a small golden box appears.

My eyes meet Cal's. I know that, like me, he is thinking of the key we found in the duke's study. "Go on," I tell Cal, and give his hand a squeeze.

"What's going on?" whispers the crowd.

Cal moves toward the golden box and turns the obsidian key in the lock. His hands are shaking. He opens the lid, and a brilliant flash of light bursts from its depths.

"Is it?" I ask.

His voice is barely a whisper. "The Deian Scrolls."

Chapter Thirty-Eight

Lilac

Cal has found the scrolls. The king bound his life to the scrolls, and when the sacred fire consumed his demon spirit, the scrolls appeared. Cal's oath is completed. He is free. He will return them to my mother, as he promised. The scrolls will be in the safekeeping of the Hearthstone Guild, and magic returned and shared with all the people of the kingdoms. The Aphrasians have lost their leader and many of their ranks. If they rise once more, they will be matched by magic as powerful as theirs. When we return to the castle just before first light, I am so dizzy from everything that has happened that I walk without thinking down the gallery to my own chambers, trailed by Rhema and Cal, and a small contingent of guards.

"Your Majesty," Rhema says in a pointed tone, gesturing in the opposite direction. That's right: I'm supposed to be going to Hansen's apartments. That is my home now, with him, my husband. At least Hansen has given me my own room for now, where Varya has been caring for me after the attack by Lady Marguerite. That feels like weeks ago. Was it really just two nights ago?

"Yes, of course," I say, uncertain, wanting to play for time. Once I return to the king's apartments, that's it. I won't be able to see Cal. I won't be able to speak to him again—not unless Hansen is present, or the Small Council. Jander is gone, and I don't want to lose anyone else tonight.

"Actually," Cal says, "I need to speak to Her Majesty in private for a moment. There's no need for us to disturb the king at this late hour. We could just step inside her former chambers here, if the guards can stand at the door, keeping watch."

"A good idea," I say, trying to sound brisk and regal, in charge of my own destiny.

Cal looks at me, his eyes meeting mine. I have to look away. Not yet. Not with all these guards around us; not here in a public part of the gallery. There's something vulnerable in his expression. The sight of his face, rugged and angular, with his dark, anxious eyes, melts my heart. But I can't do any melting until I close a door on everyone here.

"I'll tell His Majesty that you've been delayed for . . . for a moment," says Rhema. "In fact, he's probably asleep right now. I won't disturb him."

"Thank you," I say, so grateful I could kiss her. When we turned to leave the pyre earlier, her face was streaked with tears. She'll miss Jander as well, I realized. I can't believe I wasted so much energy and time being jealous of Rhema, mistrusting her. She's proven herself again and again. No wonder Cal values her so highly.

And he is free now, to do whatever he pleases. To love whomever he pleases.

But even if he doesn't love me anymore, even if he doesn't care that I'm about to become Hansen's wife in more than name, I want to tell him how I feel. This might be my last chance.

Rhema marches off with two of the guards to Hansen's apartments. The other two station themselves outside my doors, and I lead Cal in. The Queen's Secret is locked, forbidden to us forever, but here we are, together and alone. At last. We've walked into my almost-empty chambers through its main doors. Perhaps for the last time—I don't know. I don't know anything anymore. Everything has to change, but I don't know how to make it possible.

When the doors close behind Cal, I walk to the fireplace, though it's cold and dark, ash from earlier in the day lying in subdued drifts. Cal lights two braziers with the taper he's carrying, so we can see each other.

"You're free," I say, but before I can say any more, Cal steps toward me and pulls me into his arms. In an instant we're kissing each other, his mouth soft and warm against mine. I wrap my arms around him, feeling the tight muscles of his back, the firm, slim shape of him. When we press against each other, I want to swoon, though I've never been the fainting type. I've missed him so much. I've missed *us* so much.

With this kiss, this embrace, it feels as though all these weeks of frustration and jealousy, of our being kept apart, are melting away. But I have to say something. It needs to be said aloud.

"Cal," I say, pulling back, still close enough to feel his breath. "I love you. I've never stopped loving you."

"I've never stopped loving *you*," he says, and we fall together again. It's late and I'm tired, or at least my body is tired. Inside I'm exhilarated, tingling. I want to stay like this forever, my face pressed against Cal's.

The doors fly open with a crash loud as thunder. We spring away from each other. Though the room is cold, I can feel my face burn.

It's Hansen, his face grim, staring at me with ice-blue eyes.

"Out," Hansen says to Cal, his voice tight. And in an instant, just like that, Cal leaves the room. He says nothing. I say nothing. It all happens so quickly, I can't think. And Cal, I know, cannot disobey the king.

Chapter Thirty-Nine

Caledon

Cal spends the next several days and nights journeying to Renovia to present the scrolls to Queen Lilianna. Now he has returned to Montrice for a sleepless night. For a long time he lies awake on his pallet topped with straw, listening to the quiet night noises of the castle—a hooting owl, horses snuffling in their stalls, a guard calling to another when the shift up on the battlements changed. Soon the rude calls of early roosters warn him of the coming sunrise. It should be the most peaceful place in the four kingdoms now that King Phras has been vanquished and the scrolls found. Cal has finished his task, has been released from the blood oath. His life is finally his own, but there is no joy in him. For Cal there's nothing but turbulence and fear. He's made things bad for Lilac. Very bad. He can only hope that Hansen hasn't been malicious toward her, and so far Cal hasn't heard that the king has taken vengeance for finding her in Cal's arms.

There's his own fate, of course, but Cal is resigned to whatever is flung his way. He's been imprisoned before and survived. Or with the Aphrasians conquered at last, he might need to oversee a new beginning for operations in the obsidian mines of Renovia, checking all the passages and tunnels to reassure miners they're safe. Strange to think of doing this alone, without Jander, and maybe without Rhema, since the king has asked for her to be part of his personal guard.

Cal doesn't care. As long as Lilac is protected and respected, he can be sent anywhere and ordered to do anything. Their vision of a secret life together was always just a dream, a fantasy. They were lucky to have a few months together. As she told him last night, and he told her, they never stopped loving each other and never will. But the affairs of state—and the rules of this royal game—had to interfere at some point, and bring an end to their dream.

In his fantasy, Lilac would ride away with him and turn her back on all the insanity and hypocrisy here. With the Aphrasian threat gone, they could escape into the Renovian swamps and live by their wits in the endless forest. But he knows, deep down, that that won't happen. Queens can't run away. And the Chief Assassins sworn to serve and protect them can't run away either.

He has his entire life ahead of him, unencumbered by the blood oath that hung over him since he was a child, and yet he does not feel free.

When the sun rises, Cal's eyes feel dry and itchy. He hasn't slept this little for a long time, even when he and Jander and Rhema were camping out in Renovia in the freezing rain.

Someone bangs on the door and Cal springs to his feet: He lay down before dawn fully dressed, not even bothering to take off his boots, knowing they could come for him anytime.

"Chief!" It's Rhema's voice. He opens the door and squints at her. She looks tired as well.

"I don't think I'm going to be Chief Assassin much longer," he tells her, and she shrugs.

"You know, when we went on the road, I thought we got up early. But these castle courtiers—what is wrong with them? A moment after dawn the king gets a visit from that old duke, the one with the gravy stains on his tunic."

"The Duke of Auvigne."

"That's the one. He's on his way."

"To see me?"

"He wants you to rally the apprentices. We have an outing today, apparently—all of us."

"But—but—" Cal stammers. He has no idea how much Rhema knows, or doesn't know, about Hansen bursting in on him and Lilac that fateful night.

"Just play along, won't you?" Rhema says, a wariness in her eyes. "Who knows what's going on. We'll work it out."

Cal doesn't understand what Rhema means, but there's no time. He can hear the Duke of Auvigne making his way across the yard, barking orders at guards. He pulls on a jacket and steps into the stables. Rhema ducks behind a stall and disappears. She clearly has no desire to listen to the duke anymore.

"There you are, Holt," says the duke, sniffing as though the stables are too foul-smelling for his delicate nose. "Glad to see you're up and ready."

"Ready for what, may I ask, sir?" Cal hopes he sounds polite and obedient. He's antagonized enough people already.

"You won't know this, as you're from wherever it is," the duke says, hands on hips, legs astride. "Renovia, yes? Of course. But today is a special day in the Montrician calendar. On this day every winter the monarch rides out to a small village called Chana in the foothills. There's a ceremony about breaking ice in a well—all a nonsense, you see—but it's symbolic, about the coming of spring, and so on."

"I see," Cal says, stifling a yawn.

"Well, it wasn't going to happen. Not with that business with the king and queen being disparaged in public, and the stories going around about the queen and black magic. But now it can. We sent out town criers to announce the news about destroying the Aphrasians and winning the war and whatnot. All about the queen firing the fateful flaming arrow into the heart of the beast. Excellent stuff."

Cal bows his head in agreement.

"So a midwinter ritual today is timely. Get Their Majesties out there to receive the accolades and gratitude of their people. Break a bit of ceremonial ice. Herald a new year and bold new era, and so on. Good for public morale. Good for the king and queen."

"The assassins will be ready."

"Glad to hear it. We need full security detail and everyone looking sharp. No reason for any trouble today, but best be wary. We'll set off as soon as Their Majesties are ready."

The duke stomps off, and Cal stands watching him. He's always wary, he wants to say. Wary of what might happen. Today he'll protect the king and queen, and worry about his own fate later. *We'll work it out*—that's what Rhema said. It's an odd turn of phrase. Assassins are asked to work things out, to unpick mysteries, and to hunt down people who don't want to be found. But working out their own fate has never been possible.

Get through today, Cal tells himself, and worry about tomorrow afterward.

Chapter Forty

Lilac

I CAN'T HELP BUT BE nervous about this first trip out of Mont. Our last attempt to visit a village was disastrous. Things have changed now—we know that. But do the people of Montrice know? The duke sent out dozens of messengers not long after the Tyrant King's defeat, but I'm not sure if they'll believe all that they're told.

The village of Chana isn't a long ride from Mont, but it feels like it's taking hours to get there. The road is slippery with ice, and the mountains in the distance are heaped with snow. There's sun out for the journey—a good omen, I suppose—but the cold is bitter. I was offered a closed carriage, but both Hansen and I agreed that we should make the journey on horseback. People need to see us, me and Hansen, not feel as though we're still too scared to show our faces. As the royal caravan passes farms and small settlements, people emerge to watch us—a child herding goats, a man hauling a sack of potatoes, women with willow brooms in their hands or babies on their hips.

Smile, I tell myself, even if they're not smiling or waving. At least they're not booing or running for cover. No one is muttering "witch" at me and hurrying their children indoors. Our job today is to look serene and confident, pleased that the Aphrasian threat has been destroyed at last and the scrolls returned to the Guild.

I ride alongside Hansen, with mounted guards surrounding us. Cal's apprentice, Rhema, rides behind me. Hansen has asked her to remain close to us at all times—mainly, I think, so Cal doesn't have to be anywhere nearby. I have yet to see him since he returned. He is somewhere here, observing and managing, alert to any perceived threats. I can't see him, and haven't seen him, in fact, since we set off from the castle. But that's the way it should be, I suppose, with a Chief Assassin. He is everywhere at once, and nowhere. I know he's riding with us because the Duke of Auvigne insisted on it. The duke must be nervous about this excursion as well, even though it was his idea. A Montrician tradition, he announced, in his pompous way, that we should observe now that the threat is gone.

He wants the people to love us again, and that means they need to see us putting on a united front.

As for Hansen—he's barely spoken to me today. When he came to my chambers several days ago to drag me back to his, and found me in Cal's arms, he seemed furious. But after he marched me back to the royal apartments, he let me go to bed in my own room, the one where I'd slept after being drugged. For the next few days he left me alone. I was starting to think I might keep my head on after all. This morning Varya woke me early to tell me the duke was eager to speak to both Hansen and me, and after that we had to make haste to embark on this journey. We had no time for conversation, and it is just as well.

Now we ride, side by side, swaddled in wool and fur like well-fed woodland creatures, smiling at everyone but each other.

Soon we'll arrive in the village of Chana and dismount just long enough to be served a mug of ale in the tavern, and preside over the breaking of ice covering the community well. The duke described it in general terms, but Rhema knew more about it: Even in the mountains, she said, they talk about it, and long to see it. Children wearing wreaths of thorny heather will sing, and we'll be presented with something made from mulberries, a local specialty. All around us, the guards will stand with spears poised, ready to skewer anyone who tries to get too close or makes any sudden movement. I'm not sure this is quite the effect intended by the duke, but we're all still on edge.

Things have to change. Things *can* change, now that the Aphrasians have been flushed out and defeated. Now that the scrolls have been found at last. I have to change as well. I'm the Queen of Montrice as well as Renovia, and I must accept this country, and grow to love it as my adopted home. Beautiful and impressive as it was, Violla Ruza was always my mother's palace, not my home. My home in Renovia was at the farm, with my aunts.

So how can I make this new life work for me, rather than against me?

It's midmorning when we ride into Chana. It's a pretty sort of place in the summer, I'm told, but in winter its lanes are thick with mud and the village smells of pig manure and smoke. The crowd is small, and I don't know if that means locals have chosen to stay away or if the guards have insisted on a small and compliant group, to minimize any risk to us.

Hansen usually loathes this kind of thing, but today he almost bounces off his horse, a hard thing to do with all those layers of robe, and pulls off his leather gloves to make his tankard of ale easier to manage. My job today is to stand close to him and play the part of a dutiful wife.

The local lord is there, in a rustic cape made from hare skins, to bow and usher us to the well. His name is Fordan, and his plump wife, Taryn, is red in the face, clearly overwhelmed with her task of accompanying me. She curtsies for so long I wonder if she needs help getting up. But she's a kind person, I realize, and eager to make me feel welcome.

"We are so honored to have Your Majesties here," she whispers as we pick our way along a narrow path made of straw tamping down the worst of the mud. "We have all heard the news of the glorious defeat of the Aphrasians in Mont. We are in awe of Your Majesty's skill with a bow and arrow. You yourself dealt the fatal blow!"

"It was my idea," Hansen calls back over his shoulder. "I handed the queen her bow and lit the arrow in the fire."

"My husband and I are always in perfect harmony," I tell Lady Taryn, and she beams at me so warmly I feel like crying. Perhaps it's really true: The people of Montrice will accept me and grow to love me.

"We are lucky to have you here," she says. "Not just in Chana, ma'am, but in Montrice. You are most welcome—*most* welcome. I always hoped that the Dellafiores would return, but I dared not say it. We have lived so long with darkness and threats. Now perhaps we will have the chance of a peaceful future, all united again as we were in the old days, all those years ago."

Tears are prickling my eyes. My mother would be delighted to hear this. My father—the man I never knew—died trying to secure such a united future.

"May Deia bless you," I say, squeezing Lady Taryn's hand, and she blushes. My mother would be aghast at me touching a member of the local gentry: Her idea of physical contact with nonfamily members is to permit them to kiss her hand, a gloved hand. But I don't care. The last time Hansen and I rode out of Mont, people were against us. Against me, most of all. Now someone—one person, true, but it's better than no one—is being kind.

Around the well a motley crowd of children are arrayed—girls in their thorny wreaths and boys wearing dried pigs' ears, a Montrician custom that I'll never quite understand. Hansen thumps the boys on their shoulders and pinches one girl's cheek so hard she cries out. One of the boys gives Hansen his own pig ears to wear and Hansen gamely puts them on with a smile. A girl hands me a heather crown that I place upon my brow.

The children's song is short and discordant, but it's quite charming, really. The words are some confusing ode to the forthcoming spring, and quite a few people in the crowd mouth along. They may have sung it themselves when they were children and Hansen's parents were the ones visiting the village. I clap and smile when they're finished, but the duke—who already seems impatient to be back before his fireplace in Mont—hustles them away.

Hansen is handed a rustic ice pick, which he brandishes in such a wild way, the watching locals shuffle a few steps back, clutching at one another's hands. He beckons me over and I fix a smile on my face. It's time for my speech. I had to practice it this morning with Varya, over my rushed breakfast.

"In the depths of the winter," I say, my voice sounding more calm than I feel, if a little strangled and high-pitched, "we look to Deia's sky. We look to Deia's earth. We look to the water she gives us, the source of all life. Beneath its seal of ice, fresh water bubbles from the depths. The year turns, and here, on its darkest day, we know that spring will return to Montrice."

Now it's the turn of the locals to smile and clap, delighted that the new queen has managed to get the words of the ancient speech right.

Hansen smashes the well's skin of ice, and it shatters, shards flying into the air. A few of the dignitaries around us flinch, as though they might expect knives rather than ice. When nothing terrible happens, everyone around us begins to cheer, and the noise ripples through the crowd.

"Long live the king! Long live the queen!"

Hansen is beaming and nodding at everyone, still clinging to the ice pick until it's pried from his hands. I see he's still wearing the child's pig ears and I motion discreetly for him to remove them. He catches my gesture and does so.

"An excellent tradition," he says to nobody in particular. "So happy to share it this year with my wife! After we have defeated the Aphrasians together!"

Everyone within earshot cheers wildly at this announcement, and the enthusiasm spreads throughout the crowd until the noise is deafening.

We head back to our horses, Lady Taryn holding my train, though my hem is already saturated with mud from the ride here. I wish I'd worn boots, much more sensible for this weather and these conditions, because my leather shoes, laced around thick stockings, do nothing to keep the damp from seeping into my bones.

Hansen is evidently pleased with himself, particularly as he's managed to wrangle a second tankard of ale to drink before he mounts his horse again.

"That was quite a success," he tells me as we turn our horses to face the road home, the mounted guards closing ranks on us again. "Everyone seems to love us again."

"Yes," I say, unable to suppress a shiver. The sun's power is weak today. We may be heralding the spring with songs and speeches, but it's still the depths of winter.

"This was a good idea of mine," he says, waving at some locals leaning over a fence. There seem to be more people out now, word of the royal procession having spread.

I choose not to point out that this outing was the Duke of Auvigne's idea. Yes, Hansen does it every year, but he had no intention of leaving the castle today until the duke's early-morning visit.

"Maintain the annual ritual to test the waters, as it were." Hansen is still talking. "None of that unpleasantness of the Winter Races now, is there?"

"None," I say, and that's true. Something has turned, not just the weight of the season. But still, I'm anxious. I wish I could see Cal. Where is he? I wish I could ask Hansen how he intends to punish Cal, or make him pay. I can't believe that Hansen will just let what he witnessed go without further comment or further action. The fact that he's said nothing to me so far means little. I don't know how to read Hansen yet—not today, anyway. But I need to think quickly and be ready to counter whatever he throws at me, or at Cal. I can outwit Hansen, as well as outfight him.

"Look at them waving at us—they're so happy we slaughtered the demon," Hansen says, sounding smug. I can't let this pass without comment.

"Jander was the one who realized what was going on," I tell him. "He worked it out, not us. He was the one who drew the crows back into the castle to poison them and flush out the Aphrasians."

"Yes, I suppose so," muses Hansen. He sniffs, then wipes his nose with the back of a glove. "Funny that, isn't it? The apprentice was the one who solved the mystery. The Chief Assassin wasn't able to."

I brace myself. Is Hansen going to reveal something here? Is he going to tell me that Cal is demoted or fired or exiled or . . . worse? I won't have it. Time for a counterattack.

"Jander had hundreds of years of Guild knowledge," I say, staring at my husband. "Cal's still young. Young like you and me and . . . Rhema Cartner."

Hansen's eyes dart to Rhema's slim form, just ahead of us, riding her bay. She's light in her seat, and her auburn hair, tied up high on her head, bounces with each of the horse's steps.

"I don't know what that's got to do with anything," he grumbles. "We may be young, but we have responsibilities. Jobs to do. Roles to play. *Official* roles."

I don't reply right away. Instead I wave to some local people gathered by a stone wall, staring at the royal procession. When we reach a stretch of field populated only by grubby sheep huddled around a trough, I turn back to him, pulling my horse closer to his.

"I was thinking of what a good team you and I made when we killed King Phras," I say. Flattery usually works with Hansen.

"As we should." Hansen's sounding smug again.

"Of course. The King of Montrice and the Queen of Renovia. We may never be as popular as this again. This moment, after the vanquishing of the Aphrasians without a single battle."

"I was popular before, you know," Hansen says, in that familiar sulky tone. "Before I married you."

"And now I'm popular as well," I tell him. "Our people love us here, and in Renovia as well, I'm sure. So we should think about taking advantage of it."

"How?"

"I don't know," I say. My acting skills are improving. I can't shout my proposal at Hansen here as we ride along the lanes of Montrice, not least because we're in public. I need him to come to the same conclusions himself, believing them to be his idea. "But I wonder . . . oh, maybe not."

"What?" Hansen reins his horse in so sharply it bucks. We're almost touching feet, riding close, side by side.

"Just a foolish notion, I suppose," I say, pausing to wave at a group of women hauling pails of water from a well. "About our palaces. Violla Ruza needs to be rebuilt, of course. But that's Renovia. We live here in Montrice. I was wondering if we could perhaps beautify Castle Mont as well, so it's even more impressive than the old Violla Ruza."

"It's a palace, you know," Hansen tells me. "I don't know why you persist in calling it a castle."

"We could make it look more like a palace. Or more comfortable and useful, like your summer palace. I know we could never match its huge lake—"

"Best trout fishing in the four kingdoms," says Hansen, puffing up with pride.

"Yes—or the forests around it, and the mountains—I know. But if we brought all three residences up to the highest standards, using the profits from the obsidian mines at the old Baer Abbey, well . . . we could move the court as we saw fit. Or even maintain two courts, if we choose. What a show of our power it would be! What a show of our wealth! Which other kingdom has such riches?"

"Not Stavin, certainly." Hansen makes a face. "They have all the airs and graces, but the king's palace there is poky, I think. Gloomy sort of place, with stables for only a hundred horses, and the smallest kennel you've ever seen. The king can't keep more than twenty hounds, I'd say."

"I don't believe that Argonia would be able to match us either."

"Argonia!" Hansen scoffs. "Everyone goes on about it having the sea and good weather and so on, but it's a sweaty kind of place, in my opinion, and that sand gets everywhere."

"Indeed," I agree. "Rhema Cartner—she's from the mountains—and she told me that she thinks nowhere in Montrice is finer. Of course, she's biased."

"Actually, she's quite right." Hansen sounds indignant. "The mountains are the glory of Montrice. Forests bulging with wild boar, hares, foxes. Wolves higher up, but I would never hunt wolves, of course. A man has principles."

"Of course," I agree. The real reason, I think, is that wolves look too much like Hansen's dogs, and he's afraid of shooting at the wrong creature. "It's a shame that the Small Council won't let us spend more time there."

"It's not up to the Small Council!" Hansen barks. "We're the king and queen. Without us, they're nothing."

We enter another muddy hamlet, all its small but loud populace gathered outside to cheer us. Time to wave and smile, and leave

Hansen alone for a while. Hopefully I've planted some ideas in his head. They need time to brew and shape themselves into something he sees as his own schemes and plans.

I look for Cal and spy him in the distance, near the vanguard of our procession. He's doubling back on his horse, saying something to a guard. I would know his dark head, the strong curve of his jaw, anywhere. Instinctively I close my eyes, trying to imprint his face on my memory. I've gotten used to this, taking every glimpse of Cal and fixing it in my mind. That night, when we could be close again, albeit briefly, was like a dream. I could inhale him and touch him and feel the strength of his body next to mine. The taste of his kisses makes me almost delirious.

Maybe this is all I'll have of Cal from now on: the dream of him, the memory of those ardent kisses, the grip of his hand, the scent of his face. I'll have stored enough memories to keep me going night after night by myself, or in my husband's bed. Being a queen means I'm confined by many things—expectations and protocol, courtiers and guards—but nobody can control my dreams, memories, hopes, or my thoughts. Those are all my own.

Chapter Forty-One

Caledon

Back at the castle, Cal hands his horse over to one of the stable hands. It's afternoon and the sun has already set. Cal can't help but think about Jander. Jander's own horse is in its stall, covered in a blanket, chewing on straw. It was not a week ago when Jander placed the blanket there, Cal thinks, and now he's gone—gone forever.

The horse is a fine mare and should have a worthy new owner. Cal can't think of anyone at the court here in Mont who deserves her. Perhaps, when Hansen exiles him from the castle, Cal will be permitted to deliver the horse to Lilac's mother in Renovia. She and aunts Moriah and Mesha will cherish the mare the way Jander did. When the palace of Violla Ruza is rebuilt and Queen Lilianna returns there, she can take Jander's horse with her, to ride through the steep streets of Serrone. It can be a reminder of Jander's loyalty, and of his service to the crowns.

Cal loads fresh straw into the feed box and pats the mare on her sleek neck. She snorts, and he reaches up to scratch behind her ears. If Hansen decides to send him away now, as he certainly will, Cal thinks, at least he shared a last kiss with Lilac. At least they had the chance to talk to each other—properly, honestly—and speak the truth out loud. That they loved each other, a love that hadn't dimmed despite everything that's happened and everything that's kept them apart. And now Lilac is safe from Aphrasian assassins and their dark magic. If he has to leave her, Cal can at least be sure that she'll come to no harm. Anyway, Rhema will be here, and she can be trusted to take care of Lilac.

Not that Lilac can't take care of herself. She proved that with her bow and arrow.

In his room Cal packs his things. He doesn't have much; he's never had much. Just a couple changes of clothes, a compass, his sword and filleting knife, and the lilac-colored handkerchief that's his most treasured possession. He has to be ready to leave as soon as the summons comes.

In the kitchen he seeks out some supper—a hunk of nutty bread and some roasted fowl, with a bowl of dark, oniony gravy for dipping. It's noisy in the kitchen and too warm, with three roaring fires, but Cal sits at the long scrubbed table right there rather than taking his food to the main hall, where he's entitled to eat. He's not sure he's entitled to anything anymore.

Someone behind him coughs. Cal turns, hoping it's one of the kitchen maids with some wine or mead. But it's not. Standing behind him is a page, in the king's green livery.

"They want to see you, sir. The Small Council. In their chamber."

So they can't wait until the morning. Cal shouldn't be surprised, he tells himself. Today he was needed on the procession outside Mont, to add heft to the band of assassins. Now the trip is over, and there was no booing, no threat of attacks, no sign of an incipient rebellion. It was a success. Montrician feeling toward the queen has changed. Nothing has changed for Cal, though; nothing has changed about Hansen's rage at catching him alone with Lilac.

The king must have informed the duke and Lord Burley, or told them enough to persuade them that Cal must be punished or exiled. It's time to learn his fate.

Cal strides across the courtyard, the page scampering ahead, as though Cal might not know the way. In the hall keep that houses the royal apartments, the light from tapers glows yellow in its windows. Cal wonders if Hansen will even be present at this meeting, or if he'll let the duke and Lord Burley do the dirty work. That would be better. Cal's not sure he could take Hansen's sulky face right now, or see him self-righteous and enraged—and quite possibly vengeful—at the end of the long table. Not that Hansen is wrong to be upset about this. It was one thing—in the past—for Cal and Lilac to meet in secret, but Hansen had never been confronted with the reality of their relationship, their intimacy, until now.

He isn't scared for himself. If they'd wanted to arrest him, the guards would have come for him, not a page. But he *is* scared for Lilac. What will Hansen and his Small Council toadies do to her? Now that the threat of King Phras and his demonic magic is gone, they may feel more complacent. The worst threat is over. Let a normal reign—and a normal marriage—begin.

Or her fate may be worse than that. Will this discovery result in public disgrace, or even imprisonment? Lilac may be queen of the two kingdoms in name, but here in Castle Mont she's outnumbered. Hansen and his courtiers have the power to punish her. She's in their castle, in their country. Lilac has no family other than the dowager queen, and there's no longer a family stronghold in Renovia. Black magic burned that to the ground.

Yes, Lilac's burning arrow put an end to the terror of dark magic in Avantine, but that was last week. Today she's back to being a queen, on show to the people of Montrice, riding out at her husband's side and making pretty speeches. Her greatest threat now, Cal fears, isn't crows that can transform into Aphrasian monks or a possessed scribe, but the people around her in the court.

The page leaves Cal outside the Small Council's chamber, and one of the guards opens the door for him. There are more guards than usual—six, Cal counts—so that must mean the king is present. He walks in, expecting to see the usual faces set in disapproval. But there's no Lord Burley. No Duke of Auvigne.

Just King Hansen, sitting by himself in the chair closest to the fire, surrounded by his dogs.

The king is dressed more simply than he was earlier in the day, in his green hunting clothes. It's an odd choice for an evening in the castle, Cal thinks, bowing low. It's also odd to encounter Hansen here alone. King Hansen has never liked ruling alone. He's never seemed to like ruling at all.

Hansen nods a greeting and gestures at a chair at the opposite end of the table. One of his dogs, asleep by the hearth, twitches and whimpers with a bad dream.

The king says nothing for a while. They sit facing each other, the fire popping and crackling. Outside, down in the courtyard, the voices of the household going about its business floats up, disembodied. Something is different, and it takes Cal a moment to realize what the absence is: the sound of the castle crows. Horses clatter in and out—messengers, maybe, taking the news of the demon's conquest to the manor houses farther out in the Montrice countryside, and to the other capital cities.

Hammering begins, and Cal stifles a gulp. It sounds as though scaffolding is going up. Maybe this is the place he'll be arrested. Maybe the courtyard is the place he'll die.

Hansen starts, as though he'd been dreaming, like his dog.

"There's going to be some, uh, you know, celebration." He waves a hand at the window. "Since the queen killed the demon king. We have to let the people in and dance around the evergreen tree. A letter was delivered by the city's guilds while we were on our procession today. Do you know what else they want? The flaming arrow incorporated in the Montrician coat of arms, or some such thing. The duke's against it, of course, but I say—why not? They love the queen now. All good, all good. Of course, I was the one who gave her the bow and arrow, and lit the flame. What do you think of that?"

"It was very prescient of Your Majesty," Cal murmurs. This isn't at all what he was expecting from the king. Why has he been summoned here? What is Hansen planning to do with him?

He can't speak again unless the king invites him to do so. So they sit in silence again, while the dogs snuffle and scratch, and the hammering continues outside. Hansen taps his own cheek, waking himself up.

"The thing is," he says, "I've been thinking. Thinking and talking.

To the queen, of course, and I had a word when we got back with your apprentice. Rhema Cartner. She has good sense, you know. So spirited and courageous! Helpful as there have been so many attacks! Night after night. Hard to get sleep around here."

Cal nods, but doesn't dare venture a smile. He still has no idea where Hansen is going with this. Hansen sighs, rubbing his eyes like a sleepy child.

"After all this thinking and talking, I've come to a decision," he announces in an overly loud voice that wakes one of the dogs. "I'm the king. I don't have to be told what to do by this and that person. It's true that I have no particular interest in the dull bits of governing. That's what the Small Council is for—to take care of the dull things, like taxes and laws, and so on. And Lilac—the queen, I mean—she's quite good at that sort of thing. The Dellafiores always were. She's also quite good at shooting demons in the heart, as we've discovered."

Cal decides a small smile is permitted, though Hansen doesn't smile back. He's frowning now and rubbing his temples.

"Your problem," he says, jabbing a finger toward Cal, "is that you've forgotten the thing *you're* good at. What you were trained to do."

Be an assassin, Cal thinks, mystified. There's not a day in his life when he forgets this. And he's found the scrolls. For an assassin, he's a rather successful one, he would argue.

"You were trained," the king continues, "to be unseen. To remain in the shadows . . . not in the spotlight . . . next to the queen."

Here it comes. Cal braces himself. He's to be exiled from Mont, from the queen permanently. He has won his life and lost it at the same moment.

"The people only believe what they see, Holt, and they shall see their king and queen united, in marriage and fealty. A happy royal family, as it were," continues Hansen.

"Of course, Your Majesty," says Cal.

"But what happens in the shadows . . . what happens there, what they cannot see . . . that is none of their business, don't you agree? And as long as we keep everything in the shadows, well, then, everyone can go on believing the story." Hansen coughs.

Cal leans forward. He's starting to understand what Hansen is saying. He's starting to see that perhaps happiness is within reach.

"And we can control the story, can't we? I hope we understand each other, because things are going to change. Changes that suit everyone rather than the duke and Lord Burley."

"Certainly, sir." Cal thinks it's best to agree. "You have the power here. Everyone else serves at your discretion. From the highest to the lowest in the land."

"Quite." Hansen shrugs. "And something else that your apprentice pointed out, which I hadn't even considered. The duke and Lord Burley were the ones who appointed Daffran to the Small Council! Not me—them! And there he was, sitting right here, among us, at all our meetings, while he was possessed with the evil spirit of the demon king! I could have them executed, you know. For negligence, at the very least. But I won't."

"That is magnanimous, Your Majesty."

"Never been a fan of bloodshed," says Hansen. "My hope in marrying was to gain peace for both our kingdoms, and peace we will have. In the spotlight and in the shadows."

Cal shifts in his seat, feeling his cheeks flush with the heat of the tapers. A thought occurs to him, and he wonders whether he could be so bold as to suggest it. "Perhaps, Your Majesty, things can be even more peaceful than you had hoped. You and the queen are both rulers in your own rights. You should be able to live in splendor and comfort, as you choose."

Hansen sits up. "You have a solution you have devised?"

"Hear me out, Your Majesty. Castle Mont is not fit for you at the present. It's been stained by the Aphrasian rot."

"Indeed," says Hansen.

"And you, sir, have always preferred the summer palace, up in the mountains. The one with the lake and the forests that can meet all your hunting and fishing needs. It would make sense for you to move the capital there, don't you think?"

"Move the capital there?" says Hansen.

"And Renovia must not be neglected. The queen must oversee the reconstruction of Violla Ruza."

"Of course she must."

"Two courts," says Cal. "Renovia and Montrice. Two rulers. Aligned. A royal family, happy in the spotlight."

Hansen thinks it over.

"I shall, of course, have to assign one of my assassins to guard the king," says Cal. "I was thinking Rhema Cartner would suit you."

The king raises his eyebrows.

"Assassins, after all, remain in the shadows and keep ourselves scarce," says Cal.

"Two courts," says Hansen, mulling it over. "It could work."

"Your combined kingdom is very large, Your Majesty. It only makes sense that you are each needed in a different place." Cal is trying to keep his emotions in check, but if Hansen agrees, this could change everything.

Hansen looks intently at Cal. "I am told the queen will have some happy news to share with the kingdom soon."

"Happy news?"

"She carries my heir. She is several months along. Long before she shared my apartments," Hansen says meaningfully. "Not that anyone knows that."

Cal feels dizzy. If she is several months along . . . it means . . . the king is telling him . . .

"We shall be a happy family," says the king. "And none will be the wiser."

Cal's child will be Hansen's heir.

A royal child in the spotlight, but his child in the shadows.

Even after finding the scrolls, Caledon Holt is still bound to the crown. No one will ever know the child is truly his, perhaps not even the child. He will never be free of the shadows, of the secrets. But he will have this. His love. His child.

"Yes, Your Majesty," says Cal, bowing, his face unnaturally red.

"Send Rhema as soon as you can, will you?" asks Hansen. "She's quite different from the other ladies I've known. She seems to be interested in what I have to say." One of the king's dogs pads over to nuzzle his master's hand. Hansen flashes the beast a tender smile. "Even as she chats away about all sorts of things."

Cal knows all about Rhema's chatter. He isn't surprised that she doesn't modify her behavior, even with the king.

"I'm pleased to hear that, Your Majesty," Cal says, and bows again.

"Good luck, Holt," says Hansen, waving away the bow and offering his hand.

They shake like equals.

Cal realizes he never had reason to be jealous of the king. They were each trapped in their duties. But they have forged a path in the shadows.

And they will all keep the Queen's Secret.

Chapter Forty-Two

Lilac

On May Day I ride back into Mont from Violla Ruza in a carriage, greeted by a blue sky and window boxes bright with flowers, as well as streets thronged with cheering citizens. "Long live the queen!" they shout, and I wave and smile. The news has been announced: I am soon expecting a child. On the journey here I was greeted with happy crowds in every hamlet, farm, and village, lilac ribbons tied to window latches and tree branches. Small girls with lilac blossoms in their hair curtsied and blew me kisses.

I blew them kisses right back. While Renovia is my home once more, Montrice is my home too. We have agreed to go back and forth between the kingdoms.

Hansen, my husband, is happy as well. As far as everyone is concerned, the dynasty is secured. I'm going to bear the heir to the combined Kingdoms of Montrice and Renovia. My well-being is of the utmost importance, Hansen says, which is why I'm riding back here now while the new castle is under construction.

The king remains at the summer palace, near his beloved lake where the trout are fat and juicy, and the fields and forests bristle with quail and other game. We agreed that I should return to Mont now, before travel is too difficult for me. Varya is waiting for me and will care for me right through my confinement. My mother and aunts will arrive within the month, so I'll be well-attended *and* have the best possible care, as well as the best possible company.

We're all taking up residence here for a few months. Now that the Aphrasian threat is over, the obsidian mine at the abbey is in constant production, no longer stalked by deadly magical beasts, the miners no longer tormented by tortured sounds and mysterious winds and whispers.

The Hearthstone Guild is working hard at deciphering the lost magic of the scrolls, and plans are underway to open schools to train magic users from all over the four kingdoms.

We ride past the main square of the town, where lilac trees have been planted in my honor. And now the castle looms—still gray stone, but cleaner, I imagine, and less depressing in the sunshine. The moat has been cleared and is now filled with water, so swans can swim among the water lilies, and its banks are speckled with wildflowers. Next winter, I'm told, those banks will sprout snowdrops; in the spring, they'll be awash in bright daffodils.

The shield that hangs above the castle portcullis bears Mont's new emblem, the flaming arrow. This is what the city's guilds requested, and Hansen and I were happy to oblige. Even the Duke of Auvigne has conceded that it looks very bold and is sure to annoy the King of Stavin, reminding him exactly who saved the four kingdoms from the demon's dark magic.

I will take up residence in new chambers, an airy group of rooms that look out over the moat. I'll be able to lean out my window and watch the swans gliding across the water, or flowers springing to life on the grassy banks. Cal has his own chamber just off mine, linked to my apartments with a secret door. I had a new key forged.

He is my love, as Rhema is Hansen's love now. They seem as devoted as Cal and I are to each other.

Of course, the people of Montrice don't know that Cal is the father of the child I'm carrying. When the child is born, Hansen will return from the summer palace for a long visit, so we can undertake the public rituals together and the child can be proclaimed heir in the customary ceremony.

But there's something I haven't told Cal or Hansen. The day I realized I was with child, I was sitting by my fireplace at the summer palace, thinking about the time Varya conjured up the obsidian figure in my hearth. Not a monk, as she thought, but something close to it, a hooded bird that disguised a demon.

In the flames a small figure began to dance, and then split into two. They were sparkling with light, dancing in tandem, both wearing glittering crowns. One slightly larger than the other. In that vision I saw two children, not one.

One will be a prince and one a princess.

There will be two children. For Hansen will have a child of his own as well. Hansen and Rhema's child will live with them at the summer palace. The other will live in Renovia with me and Cal.

Both royal households will have a child. They will grow up apart but from the same family. For we are all family. My mother was wrong. There is a way to have love and duty. Perhaps when the children are old enough to run, we will visit them in the summers, when the fields are lush with golden grain, the hedgerows are alive with flowers, birds, and bees, and the children can play in the sun.

At the height of summer, when the days are long, and everything seems possible.

The shadows don't have to be a place of darkness, I've learned. They can be a place of peace, a place of escape. We can still feel the warmth of the sun. Cal and I can still love each other, Queen and Assassin, in secret, in the shadows, always.

Acknowledgments

So many thanks to the royal court at Penguin, first and foremost her majesty, my editor, Ari Lewin, and her noble assistant, Elise LeMassena; my queens Jen Klonsky and Jen Loja; PR princess Elyse Marshall; and copyedit czar Anne Heausler.

Thank you to my team at 3Arts, Richard Abate and Martha Stevens, and to Ellen Goldsmith-Vein and everyone at Gotham Group. Thank you to all my friends and family for all the support over the years. Thank you to my loyal readers.